MW00512727

KRANTOR'S MATE

M.M. Wakeford

Copyright © 2023 M.M. Wakeford

The characters and events portrayed in this book are fictitious. Any similarity to real persons, living or dead, is coincidental and not intended by the author.

No part of this book may be reproduced, or stored in a retrieval system, or transmitted in any form or by any means, electronic, mechanical, photocopying, recording, or otherwise, without express written permission of the publisher.

It is illegal to copy this book, post it to a website, or distribute it by any means without permission, except for the use of brief quotations in a book review.

First edition.
ISBN-978-1-3999-5236-1

Cover designed by GetCovers.
www.mw-author.com

TABLE OF CONTENTS

CHAPTER 1

Martha

I walk into the crowded café and cast a quick glance around, searching for my good friend Lulu. No sign of her. With a resigned sigh, I look around again, this time trying to locate a place to sit. In a far corner of the room, a loved-up couple stand, readying to leave. With an agility belied by my six feet height, I scurry towards their table and grab it before anyone else can call dibs on it.

Sliding into the plush seat, I quickly set about clearing away the dirty cups and dishes from the previous occupants, pushing them to the center of the table and then pressing the button for the clean-up chute. In seconds, it's all gone, and I swipe through the menu on the tablet display, ordering myself a coffee—my usual double expresso with a shot of cream, layered with frothy milk and a sprinkling of cocoa. I hold out my wrist to pay, and grimace as I see the balance on my bank account. Sooner rather than later, I'm going to need to find myself a new job.

In retrospect, maybe it was a mistake to have handed in my resignation before finding a new position. So what if my new boss was my ex-partner of three years, the man who had ditched me the minute he got offered the job. So what if I was the one made to leave the luxury housing unit we had waited years to get. There was no way Trent was giving that up! Others might have stuck it out, sucked it up and waited until they had a new prospect on the horizon. Not me though. With a toss of my long, chestnut-colored hair, I had walked out of the school—and my cherished job as an educator—head held high.

It felt cathartic and good at the time, but there was a price to my impetuous decision. Now I'm broke.

A bot arrives with my order, deftly sliding my coffee over towards me. I lift the cup to my lips and take a sip of the creamy, frothy and overpriced concoction. Ah, so good. This might be my last extravagance for a while until I get my finances in order. Better enjoy it.

"You look semi-orgasmic. Is the coffee here that good?" Lulu drops into the seat opposite me, grinning.

"It is!" I grin back.

Lulu gives the tablet a few swipes to order her own drink, then turns her attention to me. "So, what's up? Any news on a job?"

I shrug. "Mid-semester is not the best time to be moving schools."

"Have you thought about perhaps doing something else until the next school year starts?"

"Like what? All my training and skills are in educating. What else I could do?"

Lulu eyes me quietly for a moment, considering. "I have an idea, but I don't want you to reject it out of hand. Keep an open mind."

"What? You want me to sign up to be a sex slave or something?"

Lulu giggles. "Now that, I would pay money to see!"

A bot arrives with her coffee, and she takes a first sip of the hot beverage. "Mmm, you're right. This is good!" she drawls.

I wait with barely masked impatience for her to share what she thinks I could do to tide me over financially. I don't say anything though, as I know from experience that she'll only speak when she's good and ready. She takes another sip of her coffee, inhaling the fragrant aroma and sighing with pleasure once again.

2

Finally, she decides to put me out my misery. Taking out her communicator, she swipes to find what she's looking for, then hands it to me. I glance at the screen, splutter and hand it back to her. "No way!"

She gives me a stern look. "I said keep an open mind."

"Travelling to a far-off galaxy to live with aliens for six months? Are you kidding me?"

She wrinkles her nose. "Honey, we don't call them aliens."

I give an exaggerated sigh. "Fine, the Venorians."

"Ok, let's get things straight." She starts enumerating on her fingers. "First, you need to get as far away from the shit show that is Trent as possible. Get him out of your system. Second, for six months you'll get double your annual pay as an educator. Third, and this is the most salient point, you tick all their boxes. You're the right age range, in good health, unattached, with a background in linguistics. They want quick thinkers with strong powers of observation. That's you, Martha. I know you'll ace their tests."

"That's beside the point. This is a risky mission, Lulu. We hardly know anything about the Venorians. Once I'm on their planet, they could take advantage. Rape, torture, brainwash me, you name it, and there wouldn't be anyone to help me. I'd be stranded, light years away from my people and friends. I can't even!"

I finish my coffee irritably, no longer appreciating it as before. My friend extends her hand to mine, squeezing lightly.

"Martha, think rationally please for just one minute and don't let your hot head take over. What could the Venorians possibly gain from raping or torturing you? This is an exchange program, remember? A Venorian female will be coming to Earth and living in your unit, learning about us just as you'll be learning about them. Everything we've seen from these people is that they're rational and empathetic humanoids. If anything, they seem to be more evolved than us! Why assume they'll be barbaric?"

"But we just don't know. You think I'd be willing to take that risk?"

"Yes, I do, once you've cooled down and thought about it a little more. Honey, this could be the opportunity of a lifetime! And you need to do something to break out of this miserable life you've been living these past five years. Let's be honest. There's nothing really keeping you here, apart from me that is," she adds with a fake flutter of her eyelashes.

I can't help but smile even as I feel a little shard of pain at the mention of five years ago—when that fatal drone accident took Mom and Dad. Grief is a strange thing. Most of the times I think I'm doing just fine. Then it hits me right in the gut.

Truthfully, I am a little intrigued by this job. I've devoured every media post about the planet Ven and its inhabitants, the Venorians, ever since first contact was made last year. Calling them aliens conjures up an image of blue skinned creatures with fangs and horns, as imagined by many fantasy books of the last century. In reality, they don't look too different from us—taller and broader, their eyes and mouths a little larger than ours— but nothing so different that they couldn't pass off as humans. I would love to meet these people in real life and get to know more about them.

I shake my head. "You may be right. It's just …"

"The space flight," says Lulu, completing my sentence.

I nod unhappily. I've been in space once before, on a family vacation to Mars when I was a kid. I hated everything about it— the G-force as we were propelled out of our atmosphere, followed by a nasty bout of space sickness. To top it all, Mars was arid and boring as fuck. I'd much rather have spent that vacation at Grandma's ranch in Colorado. After that tragedy of a trip, I'd sworn never to go into space again.

4

"I hear the technology has improved greatly since you last went into space," says Lulu with a sympathetic smile. "I can't guarantee you'll have a pleasant and uneventful journey, but just think to what end—the opportunity to explore Ven and get to know its inhabitants, to come back here and have people hang on your every word, wanting to find out what it was like. You'd be a minor celebrity, and wouldn't that be a great way to stick it to Trent!"

My friend has unfailingly been on Team Martha ever since the split with my ex. Although he had been one of her college friends, and she'd introduced us to each other, she'd been quick to side with me when things went down. I love my friend. And her advice is usually sound. Still… going to live on an alien planet for six months is a mighty big step I'm not sure I'm ready for.

Lulu sees me hesitate and squeezes my hand. "Think about it," she says.

"Ok," I concede, "I will."

◆◆◆

Three weeks later

I regret to inform you that on this occasion, your application for the position of educator in linguistics has not been successful. May I take this opportunity to wish you every possible success in your future endeavors.

I delete the latest rejection letter and take a bite of my flaky custard Danish. It's been a month of searching, and nothing to show for it. Getting multiple job rejections is a guaranteed recipe to make one feel worthless and unwanted. Compound that with having been dumped by your partner, and is it any wonder I'm seeking solace in fattening sugary snacks?

I finish my pastry and grab my communicator again, opening it to a video clip of three Venorians meeting with our ambassador on Mars. I've watched this footage countless times.

I don't know why I keep coming back to it again and again. Something niggles at the corners of my mind, but I'm not sure what it is I'm looking for each time I watch the clip.

Our ambassador, Melinda Garcia, greets the three Venorians—two males and a female—with a formal handshake. They look at her outstretched hand curiously, then mimic her actions.

"Welcome to Mars," says Melinda.

They listen to the translator in their ears repeating her words in their language. Then they nod and one of them, a male who looks to be their leader, responds in his language, while a disembodied voice from his communicator translates what he says to English.

"It is our honor and pleasure to meet with a representative from the planet called Earth. May we show you how it is customary to greet people on our world?"

Melinda smiles nervously but answers, "Of course, we would love to learn about your customs just as we hope to share ours with you."

The Venorian steps forward, his eyes carefully scrutinizing Melinda. He places his right hand on her cheek, looking deeply into her eyes, then touches his forehead to hers. A moment later, he's stepping back. The other two Venorians follow suit, greeting Melinda in the same way, then turning to greet our other delegates in the room. The clip ends there, the general public not being privy to the conversations that ensued.

I'm fascinated by this Venorian ritual, though I'm not sure why. I've seen plenty of examples of different customs right here on Earth when it comes to greeting people. The Maori greet each other by pressing their noses and foreheads together. The traditional Tibetan greeting is to stick your tongue out at each other. The Inuits sniff each other's faces. Viewed from this perspective, the Venorian form of saying hello isn't that outlandish. And yet, something tells me it is very different to what we are used to on Earth.

I play the clip again, watching as the female Venorian looks deeply into the eyes of one of Melinda's aides, placing a hand on his cheek then touching her forehead to his. As she steps away from him, a troubled expression comes over her face for a split second, before it's swiftly masked. I replay the clip, focusing on that moment. What did that brief emotion on her face mean? What was it that she found troubling in that simple greeting?

I play the clip over and over again, my mind going around in circles, trying to make sense of what I'm seeing. After a while, I give up and stand to stretch my legs. I decide to go for a run, and burn these extra calories I've been eating.

I pull on some leggings, brace my generous breasts in a sports bra, and slip my feet into running shoes. Once outside, I tap my wrist to activate my training program. After a quick warm-up, I start my jog, aiming to maintain my heart rate at 125 bpm. While I run, I listen to a mixture of music and motivational mantras to keep me going. Whenever my heart rate is outside the target range, my device pings in my ear, telling me either to slow down, or more often, telling me to speed up.

Eventually, I manage to maintain an even keel, and I allow my mind to drift off. Without realizing it, I think back to that video clip and the troubled expression on the Venorian female's face. She steps forward, puts her hand to the man's face, looks him in the eye and touches her forehead to his. And in that short moment, something happens to make her worry. But what?

Then all at once it hits me.

Of course, that must be it. Why hadn't I made the connection before? It's so obvious now I think about it. The Venorians must be a telepathic race. The greeting—looking deeply into each other's eyes then bringing foreheads together—must be their way of reading the other person's mind. What a useful ability that must be, being able to suss out if the person in front of you is friend or foe, simply through a quick greeting.

That female Velorian must have probed the mind of Melinda's aide, and something of what she saw in his thoughts troubled her. Excited at my discovery, I stop and find myself a park bench to sit on, ignoring the scolding voice in my ear telling me to keep running. I turn off my training program and scour the media posts for any mention of the Venorians being telepathic but find none. Could I be wrong? Could it be nobody else has yet noticed this? It piques my curiosity.

Sitting on a park bench, drenched in sweat and still a little out of breath, I finally decide. I open the application form for the Venorian exchange program, and I apply. Then I do something I've been putting off for far too long. I book a transport to take me to Grandma's ranch in Colorado.

CHAPTER 2

Krantorven

I come awake slowly to the comforting sound of Prilor's even breathing in my ear. One of his arms is wrapped possessively around me, tucking my body to his. I stroke it gently, enjoying the feel of the soft hair on his forearms.

Prilor emits a low growl, tightening his hold on me as he too comes awake. His teeth nip my neck gently, sending a shiver down my body and making my cock stiffen. Seconds later, his hand slips down to my aching member, taking it in a firm grip and jerking it while he continues to nip at my neck and earlobe.

I love waking up next to Prilor. He knows my body as well as his own, and how to make it sing. Only Prilor, my oldest friend and lover, ever shares my bed. I often fuck my other somars, as is only right and fitting, but I never sleep with them afterwards. Even when I fuck a female—something I greatly enjoy doing—I end up wrapped in Prilor's warm embrace at the end of the night. I can only sleep well with the rumble of his breathing in my ear, the comforting feel of his body wrapped around mine and his unmistakable musk drifting into my nostrils.

Now, like many mornings before, I moan in pleasure as his hand worships my cock, feeling my climax approaching. "Drink me!" I manage to grunt out. In an instant, Prilor swivels around to bring his mouth down to my cock, taking it to the back of his throat, just the way I like. "Ahh!" I shout and spurt my climax into my lover's mouth. He drinks me down, not wasting a drop of my precious nectar. A kran's cum is sweeter than a mother's milk and more potent than the most powerful liquor. I watch the ecstasy come over Prilor's face as he tastes me and feels the effect of my cum. It makes me smile. I love making my Prilor happy.

I lean over to take hold of his cock. It only takes a few tugs for him to explode into my fist, his orgasm intensified by the magic of my cum inside him. His groan is loud enough to wake up the dead. It serves as the wake-up call for my other somars, who sleep in the rooms next door. I hear them stir, as I lean over and lick Prilor's sticky cum. It might not be as sweet or strong as mine, but I love it all the same.

The door opens and Fionbal walks in, absently scratching his balls and yawning. His beautiful long cock swings from side to side as he approaches my bed. "Good morning my kran," he says sleepily.

I kiss his lips. "Good morning, Fionbal mine."

Dovtar and Shanbri appear behind him, and we give each other our customary morning kiss. As Fionbal starts our communal bath, Dovtar goes into the closet to fetch my clothes and Prilor's for the day; Shanbri makes his way to the food preparation area to get our morning repast ready. Over the years, each of my somars have taken on separate roles and duties.

Foremost of all, they are my companions and protectors, but in addition to that, they each have carved out their own set of responsibilities. Nobody would dare touch the clothes in the closet without Dovtar's permission, just as the food preparation is Shanbri's domain. Fionbal bathes and grooms us. He also maintains my busy diary, arranging all my appointments and fielding any enquiries that come my way. As for Prilor? His special duty is to pleasure me each morning and to be by my side all through the day, sparring with me, listening in on meetings, giving me advice, and acting as my second in command.

I lean over and poke him in the shoulder, shaking him out of the post-orgasmic daze he's in. "Come on lover mine, time to bathe," I croon into his ear. He grunts, but remains immobile.

Fionbal re-enters the room and sees me trying to wake the sleeping giant beside me. He laughs, coming to my aid.

"This should make him stir," he says with a grin.

He bends down to smack a kiss on Prilor's mouth and run his fingers along his side, finding all his ticklish spots. It does the trick. Prilor rouses with a loud hiss.

"Fucking stop that!" he roars, but Fionbal's already slipping away before Prilor can punish him. I hear a splash as he jumps into our bathing pool.

"Come on grumpy," I soothe my rumpled lover. "Let us get in the bath."

A short while later, all five of us are in the bathing pool, enjoying the warmth of the water lapping around our bodies. Fionbal runs a washcloth over every part of me, ensuring I am clean from head to toe. Then he carefully washes my hair with a fragrant soap he makes especially for us. As his clever fingers massage my scalp, I silently say my daily prayer of gratitude for these four wonderful males who agreed to become my somars, even with the sacrifice that this entails. As my somars, they are not allowed to mate, but must devote their entire lives to me. I can never forget or take that for granted. I love them all, though Prilor best of all.

I observe him now and smile, remembering our first meeting at the military academy ten sun rotations ago. It was immediate attraction and instant love. I took one look at his massive, brawny frame and the sweet gaze in his molten honey eyes, and I melted like wax under a flame. We have been inseparable ever since. It was never in any doubt that he would become my somar when the time came for me to choose four good males to be my companions and protectors for life.

It is normal for somars and their kran to love one another, but perhaps not in the possessive way Prilor feels about me — and I feel about him. My mother worries my feelings are too

11

strong. Her concern is not misplaced. One day, I will surely find my fated mate and bond with her. Where will that leave Prilor? I try to push the disturbing thought aside. I have communed with countless females in my life so far and have had many delicious encounters. Never yet have I felt the stir of my senses, telling me I have met my mate. It could be many more sun rotations before this happens, so there is no point worrying about it. Why am I even thinking of it now?

Prilor senses my mind is perturbed. He does not have the ability to read my exact thoughts, but he can tune in to my moods. As Fionbal washes his body, he looks worriedly across at me. I shake my head and smile. "It is nothing," I mouth. To distract myself, I lean across the bath and grab hold of Dovtar's cock. It is long, but not as thick as the others' cocks. That is why he is my preferred person when I want a good fucking in the ass.

I kiss him, all the while stroking his stiffening shaft. "You ready to fuck me?" I ask.

"Always," he moans huskily. Fionbal lathers Dovtar's cock with a waterproof lubricant gel, then I am straddling him, easing my ass down slowly over it. I love that tight feeling as I am filled. Finally, my body closes around the entirety of Dovtar's shaft. I bite his mouth, licking across the seam of his lips. Then I start bouncing gently up and down on his lovely long cock. Shanbri leans down to take my own stiffening member in his lubricated hands, jerking them up and down my length. Under Prilor's watchful gaze, I fuck Dovtar and pleasure myself on Shanbri's hands.

It is not long before I feel my release approaching. In one swift move, I bring myself up to standing and grab hold of Shanbri's golden locks, pulling him towards my cock. Needing no further invitation, he encloses me in the hot, wet heat of his mouth and sucks me hard. With a groan, I come, pumping my sweet goodness into Shanbri's welcoming mouth. Full of my

12

cum, he sits up and locks lips with Dovtar, sharing the bounty with him. I smile at Shanbri affectionately. That boy does not have a selfish bone in his body, always sharing, never keeping anything to himself. They both sigh in ecstasy, feeling the effects of my cum. Fionbal transfers his attention to my two languid somars, massaging their bodies clean while they recline in the bath.

Once we are out of the water, we follow our regular grooming routine. I sit on the drying bench in the bathing room while Fionbal shaves my face with the automatic razor. My other somars also have a shave, except for Prilor who prefers to keep a well maintained beard — which I love running my fingers through.

Fionbal then turns his attention to my hair, putting it through the blower to ensure it is dry. After that, he carefully runs a comb through my long, silky tresses and braids my hair for me, while Dovtar massages cream into my body, starting at my feet and making his way up to the top of my arms. He even rubs some into my cheeks, ensuring my skin is soft and smooth all over, just the way I like it.

Prilor keeps me company, checking my communicator for messages and keeping me up to date on what is happening on our planet. Once the grooming is done, we get ourselves dressed and go to the dining room, where Shanbri lays out a delicious morning repast. Sitting around the circular table, we eat and joke playfully. I love spending the mornings with my somars.

And then, it is time to get to work.

"Absolutely not!" Prilor says, his voice rising in anger.

"I am afraid it is not up to you," my father tells him gently.

Prilor stands and starts pacing, watched by the people in the room with expressions ranging from amusement to alarm. My friend and lover can be quite intimidating when his ire is roused.

We are in the council room, where my father has his regular meetings with the senior members of our government. To his right sits Rivtas, the commander of our planet chosen by the people. She has been commander for two sun rotations, and I have great respect for her wisdom. Next sun rotation, our people will decide again whether she stays on or is replaced by a new commander. I hope they decide to let her continue in the role, but there is a good deal of competition for this position of power.

Beside Rivtas sit the chiefs of the five sectors of our planet. They too are chosen by the inhabitants of each sector. And then there is my father, the Kran, head of the Tor dynasty— my family—and the Holy Father of Ven. This will be my role one day, when he is gone.

To my father's left sits Dranlar, one of his somars. I have known Dranlar all my life. He is as dear and familiar to me as my father—perhaps more so.

Everyone's attention is focused on Prilor. It is highly unusual for him to utter a single word at a council meeting, let alone raise his voice, but the news just imparted has made him forget himself.

"Why cannot someone else go? We are a planet of two billion people; surely there are plenty of others to choose from?"

"But we have chosen Treylor. She was selected after a very rigorous process and is the best person for the job. Prilor, you know she does not need your permission to go."

"Anything could happen to her on this Earth planet. She could be raped, tortured, killed! That backward race would do anything for our technology."

Rivtas now speaks up. "Prilor, calm yourself. We have assessed the risks and they are minimal. All five of our people

14

selected for the exchange program will have untraceable communicators implanted in their bodies. We will be able to track her movements and listen in to her at all times. Just remember, our cloaked ship will be in their orbit throughout those six moon rotations, and can send reinforcements at a moment's notice."

That helps ease my mind, as Treylor's safety was my first concern too when I heard she had been chosen to go on the Earth exchange program. I rise and take a step towards Prilor, placing a comforting hand on his shoulder. "If it were not for the fact that she is your sister," I say, "you would be the first to suggest Treylor for a mission such as this. We both know how capable she is."

I rub his back soothingly, willing him to calm down. He takes a ragged breath, fighting to control his fear. If we were alone, I would enfold him in my arms, kiss him and whisper words of reassurance to him, but we are not.

I feel my father's piercing eyes on us. Being a kran himself, he understands more than anyone the complex and strong attachment that can develop between a kran and his somar. Many a time have I seen father embrace Dranlar lovingly, almost as often as he embraces my mother.

But that is not all. As a mated kran who has come into his full telepathic abilities, my father sees and understands far more than anyone else. I never need to tell father what I am feeling or thinking—he just knows. It is this capability that marks us as a family, and why we are entrusted with this most sacred position on Ven. As Holy Father, the Kran is both the spiritual leader of our people as well as the ultimate defender of our planet, ensuring our safety from the incursions of rival races.

"Not only is she extremely capable," my father now adds, "but she will be with a team of some of our best people on this exchange program. Had you waited to let me finish speaking,

Prilor, you would have heard that Pravol will going on this mission too."

Ah, that changes things. Pravol is one of our finest operatives—a tough fighter and a savvy negotiator. He was our representative in that fateful first contact meeting with the people of Earth. It is also no secret that Pravol is passionately in love with Treylor and plans to mate with her one day. He would lay down his life to keep her safe. As the news sinks in, I feel Prilor begin to relax.

"When do they leave?" he asks.

"At the next full red moon," my father replies.

Prilor nods, still frowning, but falls silent. The meeting continues as we discuss the aims of the mission and contingency plans before going on to discuss our other pressing issue—the Saraxians. We made a peace treaty with them six sun rotations ago, but there is fresh evidence of their presence inside the Utar belt, a neutral zone between our worlds. We are not a militaristic race. Our preference is always to live in peace and harmony with our neighbors, but unfortunately that is not always possible when it comes to the Saraxians. Something will need to be done to deter them, hopefully without starting an all-out war.

My mother appears on the screen. She is on the Onar, the spaceship she and father jointly command, which is currently navigating the Utar belt.

"Greetings," she says briskly. "We have picked up some debris in sector 8, which on analysis has a Saraxian signature, clear evidence that they are violating the treaty. Our data suggests the debris is recent, only a few rotations old."

"Have you scanned the area for any sign of their ships?" asks Rivtas.

"We have. Unless they have developed new cloaking technology that withstands our scans, there are no Saraxian ships in the sector currently."

"Any idea what they could have been doing there?"

Mother shakes her head. "There is nothing here that could be of interest to them. As you know, the sector is barren, with no planets that can sustain life and no minerals to mine."

Father speaks. "We need to find out what they are up to. There must be a reason for their presence there. Send anything you can find to Krantorven. He will make this his top priority." He looks to me, and I nod.

Mother's cool gaze briefly turns towards me. "Understood." Without another word, she disconnects, and the screen goes blank. My mother, unlike father, is not one for big displays of affection. Those who do not know her well think her cold and unfeeling, but that is far from the truth. Beneath her cool exterior beats a heart that is loyal and loves unreservedly. I feel that love with all my latent telepathy. Even if she does not express it overtly, I have no doubts of her devotion to me or father. I also have no doubts of her devotion to public duty and service. She makes an admirable mate for father, sharing the burden of being the Kran. I have hopes destiny will grant me a fated mate equally strong and admirable. I do not require affection from her when I have that aplenty with Prilor.

The meeting ends, and Prilor follows me out. He has already got his communicator out to speak to Treylor. She comes on the screen, takes one look at his face and sighs. "You know."

"When were you going to tell me? A moment before take-off?"

"Of course not! I am sorry. It is hard to find the right time, especially knowing how you will react."

"You can still change your mind you know."

"I will not." Prilor looks pained, but does not argue the point further.

"Come over tonight. Shanbri is making roast prot."

"If you want me over just so you can convince me not to go, then no."

"For fuck's sake Treylor! Just come. I want to see you."

She hesitates. "Fine. But one word from you trying to stop me from going and I am out."

"Understood."

She disconnects and we make our way to my quarters, where my other somars are at work. Quickly, I fill them in on the latest happenings. Shanbri, once again showing his empathetic side, takes Prilor in his arms before I get a chance to, kissing him sweetly. "I am sure she will be fine, especially with Pravol's protection. And honey, I will light a candle for her each morning. Our mighty god Lir will keep her safe."

Prilor nuzzles Shanbri's neck in thanks. Then I am on him, wrapping my arms around his bulky waist. "Come to bed," I grunt, pulling at his shirt and guiding him to my room. I know I cannot erase his worries, but I can surely ease them.

Once we reach the bed, I say in my commanding voice, "Strip." Prilor complies, the habit deeply ingrained. I divest myself of my own clothing until finally, the both of us stand naked, face to face. As ever, the beauty of his bare form leaves me breathless. He is large, even for a Venorian, with muscles perfectly carved, golden-brown hair swirling on his chest, two firm brown nipples peeking through the curls. I push him back on to the bed. "Lie still. Let me worship you."

I climb over him and kiss his surprisingly soft, plump lips. They part, allowing me to plunge my tongue into the heaven of his mouth and taste his precious flavor. I lick and suck him, feasting on his deliciousness. Then I start a journey down his body, paying homage to every part of him. I mark his neck with a glorious pattern of bites. Down his arm I lick, then back up I nip, burying my face in his musky armpit. He is ticklish there, but I hold him down, licking his essence and making him quiver. I do the same on the other arm, sucking each of his fingers once I have licked my way down, before biting a path up to his armpit. I am feral with need for him, burying myself in the forest of his chest, stroking and tugging at his hair, biting his gorgeous nipples and suckling them like a hungry babe.

Down, down I go, dipping my tongue in his navel, then down some more until I am rubbing my face in the fragrant nest of his pubic hair. His thickly engorged cock knocks against my brow, already dripping with precum, but I bypass it, journeying down his leg, kissing and licking each sweet spot. I reach his massive feet and slather them with kisses, ignoring his desperate writhing. I sample each of his hairy toes, their nails perfectly trimmed thanks to Fionbal's expert grooming. I suck them into my mouth, while Prilor groans his pleasure and his agony. Only when I am well and done do I lick and kiss my way up his other leg, towards my ultimate destination. I part his legs, baring the brown rosebud of his ass to my hungry eyes. I lick him in that most intimate place, eliciting a desperate moan. I lick again, and again, loving the taste and feel of him.

Finally, I lift my head up, noting Prilor's pleading gaze. He does not need to speak the words. I know. Swiftly, I anoint my cock with some lubricant from the bedside table and kneel before my lover. With much care, I push into his tight, hot heat, taking it slow until I am buried all the way inside. Our eyes lock, need answering need. And then I am rocking in and out, filling him with my girth, finding the sensual spot that sends him into ecstasy. On and on I grind myself on him, delighting in the firm, hot grip of him on my cock. My eyes instruct him to take his own cock in hand, and he obeys, our minds and senses in tune with one another. I thrust into him, and he jerks himself off, both of us readying to reach that precipice together.

I pull out of him just as I am about to climax. Then, we both groan at the exact same time, spilling our essence on to his belly. My cum and his mingle, a symbol of our entangled lives. I stare at it, as I catch my breath. Of their own volition, two of my fingers swirl the sticky emissions together, then I am lifting them up to Prilor's mouth. He sucks greedily, sighing in pleasure. Keeping his eyes on mine, he brings his fingers down to scoop up the creamy goodness and lifts them to my mouth. I suck them in, glorying in the taste of us combined. We feed each other some more, my potent cum beginning to have its effect on Prilor. His eyes droop as I rest my lips on his and kiss him gently. "Sleep, my love," I murmur. In no time at all, his body relaxes, and he falls into a deep slumber.

I watch him sleep, my heart aching with love. After a while, I scramble off the bed and make my way to the bathing pool which Fionbal has readied for me. I give him a gentle kiss of thanks before immersing myself in its soothing warmth. My helpful somar wrings a washcloth and takes it through to wipe clean my sleeping lover while I luxuriate in the steaming fragrant water.

I do not linger in the bath though. There is work to be done. As soon as I am clean, I dry myself and dress, leaving Prilor asleep on our bed. I join Dovtar, Shanbri and Fionbal in our workspace and check my communicator. Mother has already transmitted the data on the Saraxians. Soon, my somars and I get to work, trying to figure out what our pesky neighbors are getting up to in sector 8 of the Utar belt.

CHAPTER 3

Martha

As my transport lands in front of Grandma's house, I see the door open and her tall, upright figure emerge on to the front porch. A moment later, Grandpa appears behind her, placing an arm around her shoulders as they both watch me descend from the drone and make my way up the front steps.

Grandma eyes me sternly when at last I'm standing before her. "What time do you call this for a visit?" she barks.

I don't look away. "Much too late."

She snorts. "Where's that spineless fella you've been shacking up with?"

"We broke up."

At this, it's Grandpa's turn to huff. "About time!"

They make no move towards me. I guess they're going to make me work for it. I haven't been back here in over a year, the last time being an uncomfortable overnight stay with Trent. They hadn't liked him, and the shadow cast by Mom and Dad's death had made me wish I was anywhere but here. There were too many memories here. Too much pain.

I'm not sure what has prompted me to come back this time. Maybe it's the thought that I might never see them again if I'm accepted on the Venorian exchange program. Or maybe because it's time to let go of the grip grief has had on me, and to start a new chapter in my life.

"I'm sorry," I say.

"What for?" Grandpa demands.

"For staying away so long. For blaming you for what happened, even though I know it wasn't your fault. I'm sorry."

We stand still, the air around us thrumming with long repressed emotions.

"You think I didn't blame myself? I never should have suggested they take that new drone."

My lips tremble. "I knew it was a bad idea." My voice breaks. "But I didn't say anything. I wish I'd said something."

Grandpa opens his arms and I rush into them. He holds me tight as I sob into his chest. My voice is muffled by his sodden shirt. "I missed you, Gramps."

He strokes my hair with one hand, the other still holding me tightly to him. "Oh, dear girl. I missed you too."

Eventually I step back, eyes glistening, and turn to Grandma. She's a much tougher nut to crack than Gramps, so it's no surprise she continues to stare me down for a long silent moment. Then her mouth softens imperceptibly, and I walk straight into her arms. She holds me close, not speaking. I sigh in relief, only now realizing just how much of a burden my estrangement from them has put on me. All at once, my load feels lighter.

I come out of the embrace, letting Grandma examine me critically from head to toe. "City life don't seem to agree with you, Martha. You'd better come in and eat some proper food."

My face transforms into a grin. "Real steak and fries?"

"Only ever the real thing in this house."

I follow her inside, Grandpa shuffling behind me. The house is like a time capsule, standing unchanged for decades. We walk into the large living room I used to play in, and my gaze lands on the comfy couch I used to snuggle up in to read a book. I imagine this place was much the same when Mom played here as a child. Coming to Grandma's ranch feels like stepping back in time. Very little of the technological innovations of the last century seem to have touched this place. The only concession to modern life is the communicator sitting on a side table.

Grandpa settles down in his armchair, while Grandma goes into the kitchen to brew us some tea. I smell the sweet scent of baking in the air. "Cookies?" I enquire.

"Chocolate chip," responds Grandpa.

I sink into the couch with a smile. It's good to be home.

Sometime later, I sit back replete, having scarfed down the most mouth-watering, juicy steak in the universe, along with crispy French fries and a green salad—all the fresh ingredients sourced right here on this ranch. The synthetic meat I eat in the city is a good approximation, but it's never going to taste quite like the real thing.

I'm sipping on some iced tea, satisfied and content, when Grandma asks the burning question. "So, missy, why are you really here?"

"I wanted to see you."

She snorts. "Fine, you've seen us. What else?"

Nothing gets past Grandma. It's like she has a sixth sense or something.

"I walked out on my job when they appointed Trent as my new boss, and he decided to dump me that very same day. I've been at a loose end ever since."

Grandpa growls. "The rat!"

Grandma sighs loudly. "That impetuous streak of yours! I honest to God don't know where you get it from. Must be from your dad's side of the family."

"I know it probably wasn't my wisest move. But you should have seen the bastard, cold-shouldering me days after he'd said he loved me. He even had the nerve to demand that I submit to an 'evaluation' seeing as my teaching stats were a little on the low side."

Grandpa makes another grunting sound of disapproval, but Grandma gets straight to the point. "So, what now?"

"I've applied for a few jobs, but nothing's come through so far."

"If you need to stay here a while to save money, you know you're always welcome," Grandpa says gruffly.

I feel my eyes well up again. I take a deep breath and try to hold the tears at bay. "Thanks, Gramps. I'm ok for now, but it's good to have a safety net." I hesitate before I go on. "There's a job I applied for today. It's something different, not in education. If it comes through, I won't have any more money worries."

"What kind of job?" asks Grandma sharply.

"It's to go on the Venorian exchange program. I'd be swapping places with someone from Ven for six months."

The room goes silent. I rush to fill in the void. "It's a great opportunity to learn about them. All indications are that they're a civilized people, and I'd be part of a team from Earth to go there, so I wouldn't be without friends. In any case, it's a long shot. Thousands are bound to apply, so my chances of getting on the program are low."

"You'll get it. They'd be mad not to snap you up," says Grandpa.

I smile. "Thanks for the vote of confidence, Gramps."

Grandma is silent, but I can hear her short choppy breaths. I lean across to gently squeeze her hand. "I'm sure it'll be fine. A great adventure. Nothing to worry about. But I will be gone for a while. That's why I came to see you." The subtext is clear to everyone—in case I don't make it back.

Grandma turns her hand to enfold mine, gripping it tightly. Eventually, she says, "I'm sure it will be a great adventure. Of course, you must go if you get the chance."

Grandpa stands and wraps his arms around her. "She will be just fine," he affirms.

"Yes," Grandma murmurs, getting her emotions back under control. She smiles at me. "Ready for some pie?"

The rest of my stay is uneventful, but charmingly peaceful. I spend time out with Gramps in the stables; we go riding while Gramps oversees the work of his ranch hands; I help Grandma care for her vegetable patch in the back yard. I even get a chance to go skinny dipping in my favorite place—the rock pool on the edge of our land that has a small waterfall. After a week, I get news that they have invited me to interview for the Venorian exchange program. It's time to leave my idyll and get back to the city.

Early the next morning, my transport arrives to take me to my job interview. My grandparents walk with me to the small drone waiting in their front yard. Grandpa hugs me tight and kisses my cheeks. Then it's Grandma's turn. She holds out to me a little box.

"What's this?" I ask.

"Just a little keepsake my father gave me. It's yours now. You can attach it to a pin and wear it as a brooch or put it on a chain. Think of it as a good luck charm."

I take the box and open it. Inside is a beautifully crafted pendant made from twinkling gemstones that are shades of pink and purple, arranged in a swirling pattern. "It's beautiful," I whisper.

Grandma's voice is hoarse as she says, "Yes, it is. I know you were very young when your great grandpa died, so you probably don't remember him. He used to love to rock you to sleep and sing you lullabies. He wanted me to give you this when you were grown, so, it's yours now."

I snap the box shut and slip it into my purse. "Thanks, Grandma." Then we're hugging one last time before I turn and climb up into the cabin of the waiting drone.

CHAPTER 4

Krantorven

Treylor arrives in the evening, accompanied by Pravol and by my sister Sonlar. I beam in delight when I see Sonlar, for I do not see her as often as I would like. She is not a Tor, but the product of a union between my mother and Dranlar, father's somar. It is the right of every somar to have a child with his kran's mate after she has successfully begotten the kran's heir. It is only fair to allow our somars the chance to continue their line when they have vowed to live unmated as our companions for life.

Fortunately for my mother, who is not the most maternal of beings, Dranlar was the only one of father's somars that wished for a child. Which means I only have one true sibling in this world—Sonlar. She is three sun rotations younger than me, and the same age as Treylor. Over time, they have become great friends.

Sonlar has forged her own path in life, not following in the footsteps of her mother or father. She is an artist that designs clothes and jewelry, and in great demand for she is extremely talented. Her work takes her all around the major cities of our world, which means I do not often get to see her.

She steps towards me now, and I look searchingly into her eyes as I place my hand on her cheek. We touch foreheads, and I probe her mind to check on her wellbeing. I cannot as yet read the fine details of what someone is thinking—that will occur after I am mated—but I can detect moods, emotions and intent. I step back, relieved to have sensed only positive emotions from my sister. She is happy.

Unfortunately, her probe into my mind was not as joyful as mine. I am plagued with worries about the Saraxians, and some of this worry must have leaked out. All Venorians have a basic ability to read the emotions of others upon touching, although my family, the Tors, have a much more finetuned telepathic talent which allows us to read minds across a distance. Even with her lesser ability, Sonlar has sensed something is up and she gazes at me in concern. "What is troubling you, my love?"

I try to allay her worry. "It is nothing for you to be concerned about, just a few issues that have cropped up with the Saraxians. I am sorry to have bothered you with this, my dearest."

I am not sure I have convinced her, but she lets it pass. I turn to Treylor and offer her my greeting. In her, I sense nervousness, excitement and joy. Fortunately for me, her heightened emotions have dampened her ability to read mine, so I do not give anything away this time. Pravol is next. I sense his intense focus on Treylor, and his protector feelings out in full force. I have no doubt he will keep her safe on this visit to the planet Earth. As I step back from him, he raises a brow at me. I quickly say, "A little bit of trouble with the Saraxians, but nothing to set your mind to worry." I am not sure I convince him either, but he too lets it go.

Then Shanbri is summoning us all to the dining room, where a large roasted prot takes pride of place on the table, enticing us with its delicious aroma. Beside the meat is an assortment of delicacies, all cooked with Shanbri's masterful touch. He watches us eagerly as we partake of the meal, taking pleasure in our pleasure. If anyone were born to serve, it is Shanbri. He finds such joy in helping others, in giving of himself. I smile at him lovingly and summon him over to me. Once he is by my side, I pull him to me and kiss him lingeringly. "Shanbri mine, you have outdone yourself. The prot was meltingly tender and wonderfully spiced. Thank you, my love." His handsome face flushes, and I cannot resist kissing him one more time.

Prilor, sitting beside me, pulls Shanbri to him, nipping him gently on the neck. "It tasted fucking great," he says gruffly.

Treylor goes off into peals of laughter on hearing her brother's not so eloquent praise. Smilingly, she echoes his words. "It did taste fucking great! Thanks, Shanbri."

We enjoy a convivial evening together, catching up on news and discussing the forthcoming mission to Earth. By the end of the evening, I sense that Prilor has let go of the intense fear he was feeling, even if he remains a little fretful. We bid our guests goodbye and make our way to the bedroom, where Dovtar awaits to take away our soiled clothing. Once naked, we wash in the ablution room, drink our night-time tonic, then walk to bed hand in hand.

Prilor pulls up the soft covers and waits for me to get in before joining me. We tangle limbs and kiss for a long, long time. Finally, I draw back and say, "I love you, Prilor mine."

"I love you too, my kran," he responds.

Then I turn around and settle on my pillow, Prilor's thick, hairy arms wrapped tight around me. With his comforting warmth infusing my body, and his wonderful musk wafting over me, I drift off to sleep. My last sentient thought before I succumb to slumber is a vision of my future mate bearing Prilor's child. I imagine Prilor rocking an infant in his brawny arms—a child with auburn locks and honey-colored eyes—while I sit beside him and croon a lullaby.

Early the next morning, we slip on our sparring gear and make our way to the outdoor space where we work out, just beyond my quarters. It is our daily routine to train our bodies, keeping ourselves in top physical shape. Prilor is my usual sparring partner, though on some days I also like to practise my skills with Dovtar. He is quick and nimble, requiring me to use different sparring tactics than with Prilor.

On this occasion, I plan to spar with Dovtar, as I fear I have lost some of my agility and speed of late. I need to sharpen these up. "Prilor," I say. "Why don't you spar with Shanbri today, and I will take on Dovtar."

"As you wish, my kran."

We take our positions in the adjacent sparring rings, while Fionbal practises some Drekon poses on a mat he places nearby. Dovtar and I bow to each other. "Ready my kran?" he asks.

"Ready."

We begin. I pour all my concentration into the task, my eyes following every movement Dovtar makes and adjusting my stance accordingly. It is not easy, but I am pleased to see some improvement in my agility. Sweat is dripping down my brow as I battle to keep up with my quick and wily somar. Suddenly, I hear a sharp cry.

Instantly, we put down our weapons and rush over to where Shanbri is clutching his arm, a torrent of blood seeping into his gray tunic.

Prilor, looking upset, cries out. "I am so sorry Shanbri. I did not mean—"

"It is fine," grits out Shanbri, in obvious pain.

I crouch beside him and examine the wound. The gash is long, but not too deep. Fionbal is already by my side, handing me a wet cloth to clean it up. When the worst of the blood is wiped away, I kneel beside my somar and prepare to lick the open wound. I am born with a body different to ordinary Venorians. Along with my enhanced telepathic skills and my sweet, potent cum, both my saliva and my blood have the power to heal. I can only give of my blood to my mate—for to do so starts the process of our minds melding—but I can use the healing properties of my saliva whenever required.

Swiftly now, I lick Shanbri's wound, wetting it as much as possible with my essence. Already, it has stopped oozing blood and is beginning to pucker into a scab. Once done, I let Fionbal wrap a bandage around it.

"How do you feel now, Shanbri mine?" I ask solicitously.

He smiles his charming grin. "Better, thank you my kran."

"Let me kiss you to make it even better." I put my lips to his and let him plunge his tongue into my mouth. We kiss for a long time, my tongue dancing with his, allowing him to lap and suck mine, taking in more of my healing essence. Finally, we pull apart, breathless and aroused. In a thick voice, I say, "Let us return to our quarters for some loving and a wash, then we must begin our work."

He sighs in pleasure. "Yes, my kran."

One moon rotation later

We have been patrolling sector 8 of the Utar belt for half a moon rotation now, looking for any more traces of a Saraxian presence. In the meantime, mother returned to Ven and spent some time there with father, before he took the Onar on a diplomatic mission to some of our allies in neighboring galaxies, such as the Driskians and the Krovatians. Using his unique telepathic abilities, he is engaging in meetings with representatives from these races to try to gather more information on the possible threat from the Saraxians.

It is also an opportunity to negotiate some new trade deals. Our planet produces vlor, a precious stone that comes in shades of pink and purple, which is widely valued not just for its beauty but also for its healing properties. The most valuable is the purple vlor stone, as it has a powerful regenerative effect on the body. It can cut healing time for wounds in half simply by placing the stone on the affected area. It is also used to combat the effects of aging. Clients at beauty parlors all over the galaxy are willing to pay a high price for a purple vlor treatment to regenerate their skin and muscle tone. It is not something I myself do—at twenty-eight sun rotations old, I have no need yet for such things.

We trade shipments of vlor in exchange for other precious commodities that are hard to find on our planet, such as dorenium, a mineral we use to help power our spaceships. There is a dorenium mine on one of our colonies in sector 3 of the Utar belt, which is our main supply, but we also like to augment our reserves through trade with our allies.

In father's absence, mother is taking on his responsibilities as the Kran of Ven. It is a seamless transition for them to make thanks to their special connection. Through their unique bond as fated mates, my father and mother's minds connect as one. She knows all that he knows, and vice versa. They have no need to regale each other with their news when they reunite, because they already know it all. Every night as they sleep, even light years apart, their minds meld, sharing all information and knowledge each of them has gathered that day. This makes it easy for mother to take over father's affairs as the Kran when he is away from Ven.

One day I too will have such a connection with my mate. I am both curious and repulsed by the idea. It is a privilege granted to the males in our family to have a fated mate with whom we can meld our minds, and I am suitably respectful of that honor. I am also aware of just how useful that can be, especially when having to fulfil my future duties as the Kran after father is gone. But I am also wary of the prospect of having another being invade all my thoughts, especially when it comes to Prilor. What he and I share is intimate, our emotions powerful. How will it feel to have someone intrude on that relationship, to know all those secret words of love we exchange when we are alone? What will happen to Prilor when my mate inevitably shares my bed? Will he be relegated to a room next door with my other somars? The thought makes my heart clench in pain.

I have often wondered how my father manages his relationship with mother and his somars. It all seems to be harmonious, but I suspect it took time to get there. Dredging my memories of childhood, I can recall occasions when Dranlar slept in the same bed as both my mother and father. He also had his own private quarters, which my mother occasionally shared with him. On those nights, my father had the companionship of his other somars. What they have seems to work well for them, but I do not believe father's feelings for Dranlar are as intense as mine are for Prilor. Having fallen asleep to Prilor's breaths in my ear every night this past decade, could I relegate him to his own quarters, even for part of the time? I sense there will be trouble ahead, but I am powerless to do anything about it. I suppose I shall just have to deal with it when the time comes, and find the right accommodation between myself, Prilor and my mate. I am hopeful she will be someone sensible and wedded to duty, just like my mother.

My somars and I are aboard the Phtar right now, a small ship I command. It is more agile than the Onar and has superior cloaking technology, making it ideal for silent patrol of this neutral territory. Under cover of our cloak, we have been whizzing in and out of the barren planets, moons and meteorites of sector 8 of the Utar belt. We have not seen any further sign of the Saraxians. Our analyses have not come up with any rational explanation for why they were here in the first place. My instinct tells me they are playing games with us, using this as a distraction from their main objective. Could it be that they want to divert our ships here, so that they can take offensive action elsewhere? But where?

We do not have a massive fleet of spaceships. Including the Onar and the Phtar, we have a total of five ships. Two of them are mainly cargo ships, transporting commodities to and from our planet. We are using these cargo ships to transport our people on their mission to Earth. One of them will remain there for the duration of their stay, staying cloaked so as not to alarm the people of Earth; the other will return to Ven with the five Earth people on the exchange program. It is due to arrive back any rotation now.

We station the only other remaining ship we have in sector 3, its main function being to keep guard over our dorenium colony. It is commanded by Rivvol, a cousin of Pravol. She is highly experienced, and I have great respect for her abilities.

I turn to Prilor, sitting next to me at the main console of my ship. "Let us open a channel with Rivvol."

Moments later, Rivvol's face appears on the screen. "It is good to hear from you, Krantorven. How may I be of help?"

"Rivvol, it is a pleasure to see your dear face. I hope you are keeping well?"

"Indeed I am, my thanks to you for asking."

"Let me get straight to the matter, Rivvol. We have not found any more signs of a Saraxian presence here in sector 8. My theory is that this was a decoy operation to distract us from their real objective. Could it be they have set their sights on our dorenium?"

Rivvol frowns. "I have not noticed anything out of the usual here, but I shall increase my patrols. We will also send some probes to scan the space around the sector."

"Good. We will make our way over to you in our cloaked state, checking along sectors 4 and 5 along the way. Let us aim to meet in three rotations and discuss our findings."

"Understood."

Rivvol ends the connection, and I turn to Fionbal, sitting at his workstation further behind me. "Fionbal, send a message to mother briefing her on our proposed movements. Ask her to also increase vigilance on Ven, particularly on our Vlor mines, the warehouses and the ports."

"Will do, my kran."

Beside me, Prilor is already setting a course for sector 3, using a circuitous route so we can have a good look around the surrounding areas for anything untoward. As our ship changes its course, I sit in silence, my mind going over all the facts again to see if I have missed anything that could be important. The sinking feeling in my gut is telling me that something is wrong. But am I making the right decisions? What would father do if he were here?

Prilor's hand snakes its way to the back of my neck, massaging it gently. "Do not second guess yourself, Krantor. You are taking the most sensible course of action. Whatever it is that is brewing, we will face it together. I am right by your side, always."

I place my hand over his and squeeze it. I am so blessed to have this wonderful man by my side, sharing the burden of being a kran with me.

Later, as we get into bed, my communicator bleeps with a message from mother.

Mother: Your father is cutting his trip short and returning to Ven. Keep to your plans and report back to us anything unusual that you notice on your route to sector 3. We will talk with you and Rivvol when you meet up in three rotations.

Me: Understood.

CHAPTER 5

Martha

I've made it through the first stages of recruitment for the Venorian exchange program, scoring highly on the aptitude tests we were given. Now we come to the part I've been dreading—going into space. The remaining candidates and I are all being taken to Mars, where we shall undergo a final series of trials before being informed whether or not we have made it through to selection as one of the five humans to go to Ven.

All morning I've felt queasy at the prospect of the impending ride on the space rocket and the G-force as we break through our planet's atmosphere to reach space. We're all kitted up in our space suits minus the helmets which we'll pull on last, and sitting in a side room, waiting to board the rocket. In all there are ten of us left. It doesn't take a genius to work out that only half of us are going to make the grade.

Next to me is Eliza, a pretty blonde with cornflower blue eyes and a butter-wouldn't-melt look on her face. I'm not buying into her act though. Beneath the sweetness, I suspect lies an extremely competitive person willing to do whatever it takes to get selected.

I take a fortifying sip of water from my bottle and breathe deeply in and out, willing my stomach to cooperate. Throwing up during our space flight is not a good look. Eliza gazes at me sympathetically. "Have you tried motion sickness tablets?" she asks, not for the first time. It doesn't escape my notice that she says this just as Professor Norton, one of our assessors, walks past.

"I have taken some," I say quietly. "It will be fine." "

Are you sure?" Eliza frowns. "You do look a bit green."

Professor Norton pauses to cast a severe glance at me. I smile weakly and give a nervous wave. He nods his head in acknowledgement and moves on. Having scored her hit, Eliza gives me one last faux sympathetic smile and turns to speak to the person on her other side.

I will myself to stay calm, but my churning stomach isn't listening. Acidic bile makes its way to the back of my throat. All at once, I stand and rush to a nearby restroom, locking the door behind me. I get there just in time to retch violently into the toilet bowl. Breaths heaving, I straighten up and press the flush. My face looks back at me in the mirror, full of misery and despair. That face says, "Maybe it's best you just ditch the space suit and go home."

For a brief, tantalizing moment, I consider doing it, thinking longingly of being back at Grandma's ranch.

But just as quickly, I realize the impossibility of giving up now and going home with my tail between my legs. The die is cast. There is no going back now, only forwards.

Taking another fortifying breath, I run the water to wash my hands and rinse out my mouth. Now that my stomach has emptied, the queasiness seems to have receded a little. I look at myself in the mirror once again and put on a confident smile. I can do this.

As our ship approaches the docking bay on Mars, I breathe a sigh of relief. Our journey here has been hellish—at least for me. My skin clammy with space sickness, I'd spent my time practising my breathing, trying not to vomit what little food I'd consumed. I barely took part in any of the team activities. The others cast me looks of sympathy tinged with contempt as they went about their business while I curled up in a ball of misery.

Compounding my torment was the knowledge that the assessors on this program had noted my inability to travel well in space, and that it will be a negative mark against me when they come to select the final five. However, there's nothing I can do about it. At least we're here now, and I can attempt to make amends over the next few days as we complete the final trials before selection.

Mars is no less red and dusty than the last time I was here. However, the colony has expanded greatly, with buildings as far as the eye can see, housing a large resident as well as transient population. As we walk into the vast atrium of the indoor village, I can't help but be impressed by the human ingenuity and determination that built this massive, sprawling city on an arid planet, light years away from our home. It's a hive of activity—people going about their business, walking or skating along the internal lanes, shopkeepers peddling their wares, and a plethora of restaurants and cafés with "outside" seating, offering up all kinds of cuisines.

We're taken to our lodgings and allowed to settle in for the day before our trials begin again tomorrow. My room is basic, but comfortable. I finally get the chance to have a shower with real water, cleaning off the grime and sweat from our journey. Once I'm dressed, I send a quick message to Grandma on my communicator, telling her I've arrived safely, then decide to go out and explore the village for some place to eat.

As I step out of my room, I see Troy and Ameer, two guys on the exchange program who I've gotten to know over the past few weeks and liked.

"Hey Martha," Ameer hails me. "You're looking a lot better."

"I'm feeling like a new person," I proclaim with a cheerful smile.

"We're about to go find some place to eat. Want to join us?" asks Troy.

"Thanks. I was about to go on a very similar mission myself. What shall we pick for our first meal on Mars?"

Troy makes a face. "Something digestible. You're not the only one whose system took a battering on that journey."

"A curry?" asks Ameer hopefully.

Troy shrugs. "I could do that. How about you?"

I smile. "That works for me."

We walk along the main promenade, checking out different places until we find a bustling café that serves delicious smelling curries. I order a fragrant chicken biryani—though of course, the chicken is made from synthesized protein. It doesn't take long for our meal to arrive, and we fall on it ravenous, appreciating the taste of freshly cooked food after days of eating the bland rations on the spaceship.

As we eat, we discuss our chances of getting chosen as one of the final five.

"It sucks that I just can't travel in space without getting sick," I groan. "I'm sure that's spoiled my chance to get on the program."

"Don't be so sure," says Ameer. "I hear the next trials are going to test our aptitudes for thinking quickly in tough situations. You've got good reflexes Martha, and a great ability to think laterally. I'm confident you'll do well, unlike me."

"What is this?" Troy growls. "A pity party? We all stand an equal chance. Just have to see how it plays out."

"So says the man who's a virtual shoe-in. You know you're the only engineer on the team capable of drawing up complex schematics from memory."

Troy shrugs uncomfortably. "I have strengths and weaknesses, just like anybody."

He pins Ameer with a piercing stare. "I'm not the one who can speak eight languages fluently and pick up new dialects at the drop of a hat."

I chuckle. "We're kind of like the heroes in those old Marvel comics I used to read as a child. Each one of us has a unique superpower."

Troy smirks. "Superheroes? Yeah, I like the sound of that."

Ameer wrinkles his nose. "In that case, can anyone tell me what superpower Eliza has? I can't quite figure out how she made it so far into the program."

I huff out a quick, unamused laugh. "I could tell you Ameer, but it would make me sound like a bitch."

Ameer regards me with a frown, digesting my words. "So, it's that way is it. Who is she currying favor with?"

"My lips are sealed."

Now it's Troy's turn to laugh. "Who isn't she with? Open your eyes, Ameer. That pretty little piece with the innocent blue eyes is as ambitious as they come and won't stop at any underhand method to get what she wants. If I were a betting man, which I'm not, I'd put ten thousand dollars on her being selected."

I grimace. "I'm afraid you could be right."

The first few days on Mars go well. At least I think so. We're given a series of different trials to undertake, both individually and as teams. I'd like to believe I acquitted myself well, but time will tell. On the final day, we're presented to Ambassador Garcia at a special lunch, and she then invites each one of us for an individual interview. I've not yet mentioned to anyone my theory about the Venorians being telepathic, but in my conversation with Melinda Garcia, the opportunity finally presents itself.

We've been sitting in her office for the past twenty minutes, talking informally. Eventually, we come to the subject of her first contact meeting with the Venorians. I ask, full of curiosity, "What did it feel like to be in the same room as another humanoid species for the first time?"

She laughs. "It certainly was a unique experience."

"Were you nervous?"

"Of course. Anyone that says otherwise is a liar."

She pauses. "But along with the nerves was a sense of excitement and purpose."

"What did they smell like? Could you discern a different scent to them?" She cocks her head and smiles. "Nobody has asked me this question before. No, there wasn't an overpowering aroma, but when we touched foreheads in greeting, I detected a fragrance—earthy with a hint of musk. It was pleasant, though not a scent that felt entirely familiar."

"What did you think of their form of greeting?"

She shrugs. "All cultures have their different ways to say hello. I can't say I enjoyed having total strangers so up close and personal. It felt a little too intimate for my human sensibilities."

I hesitate, then ask my burning question. "Did you experience anything else, other than discomfort at being up close and personal?"

She raises an eyebrow. "Should I have?"

"Oh, I don't know. Perhaps a slight electric shock, or a feeling like you were being probed."

"Being probed? Where has that come from? Am I missing something here Martha?"

I look down at my hand, which I have been drumming on the fake leather surface of the sofa without being aware. I force it to be still.

"Martha?" she prompts.

I take a deep breath. "It's just something I noticed when I watched the video footage. When the female Venorian greeted one of your aides, for a fleeting second, she had a troubled expression on her face before she masked it. It bothered me, so I replayed the footage over and over again until it occurred to me that they're a telepathic race, and they use this greeting to probe the minds of the people they're meeting."

"Telepathic?" Melinda Garcia looks stunned.

"Yes, telepathic. Has no one else put forward this theory?"

She shakes her head looking bewildered, but also intrigued. "No, never. Can you show me the footage?"

I take out my communicator, linking it to the main screen, then bring up the video, scrolling to that moment where the female Venorian greets Melinda's aide. I pause it. "Watch carefully here as the Venorian female steps away from your aide. Look at her face." I play the footage.

Melinda watches intently, a frown on her face. The moment is so brief as to be easily missed. "Play it again," she demands.

I do so, and she watches it again like a hawk. Then she shakes her head. "This is very inconclusive evidence, Martha. She could be looking like that for any number of reasons. Maybe she didn't like his scent. Maybe she's not so keen on meeting humans. Who knows? It's a bit of a jump to think she must be telepathic."

I flush and bow my head. "I guess so. It's just a feeling I can't seem to shake."

Melinda smiles reassuringly. "For all I know you may be right, Martha. It's certainly something to bear in mind next time we come into contact with them."

She stands, indicating the interview is over.

"Thank you for your time," I say with a hint of despondence in my voice.

She gives me a warm smile. "It was a pleasure Martha, and good luck with the selection process. I'll see you tomorrow when the panel announces their decision."

I leave her office and pass Eliza on my way out. "How did it go?" she asks.

I nod my head, feigning nonchalance. "It went well." Then I muster a smile, "Best of luck!"

The following afternoon, we all gather in the ambassador's banquet room to hear the results. The selection panel, which includes Professor Norton, Ambassador Garcia, and three other judges, sits at a long narrow table in the center of the room, while the rest of us are seated on chairs facing the judges.

I zone out as Ambassador Garcia goes through the preliminaries, thanking us all for our endeavors and telling us how hard the selection process was. Finally, she begins to announce the winners. "Troy Summers." I clap, unsurprised but immensely pleased, as Troy stands and goes to shake hands with the judges. "Shay Smith." I clap again. Shay is a scientist who has worked extensively on the International Space Program. She's quiet and soft-spoken, but smart as a whip. I'm not surprised by her selection either.

"Diego Sanchez." Diego is a medic, involved in genetic research. Another strong candidate—and a reminder that I don't stand a chance in this race. I brace myself for the eventual rejection.

"Dimitri Woods." Dimitri is a well-known psychologist— another undoubtedly strong candidate for this mission. I clap along with everyone else, then clasp my hands nervously as the final name is announced. Ameer, seated beside me, gives my hand a quick, reassuring squeeze.

"Eliza Carmichael." So, Troy was right. And despite having prepared for this moment, I still feel a shock of disappointment. That's it. The dream is over. I clap loudly to hide my dismay, and glance over at Troy, whose lips are set in a grim line. He looks back at me sadly and shakes his head imperceptibly. I force a smile and mouth, "Congratulations," to him.

We stay a while, listening to the speeches of thanks from each candidate and clapping for them politely all over again. Eventually, we're free to go. Ameer whispers in my ear. "How about we go get drunk?"

"Good idea."

He takes my hand and leads me out. Before making our exit however, we go over to Troy. I hug him tightly. "No one deserved this more than you. Well done!"

Ameer grabs hold of his friend and gives him a bear hug. "I'm so happy for you man."

"Thanks," says Troy. "I really, really wish you two were going with me."

I shrug. "Me too, but hey, that's life."

As we're about to leave, I feel a small tap on my shoulder and turn, finding Ambassador Garcia. She smiles kindly. "I'm so sorry this wasn't the news you wanted to hear Martha. If it's any consolation, I argued in your defense, but they overruled me."

"Thanks Melinda, I appreciate it."

"Listen. The Venorians are due to arrive in the morning. There will be formal introductions with each of the five selected candidates, after which they will spend time with their Venorian exchange partners. In the evening, we'll be hosting a formal dinner party, and I've included you on the guest list. You might not get to go on the mission this time, but at least you'll get a chance to meet some Venorians and perhaps test out your theory?"

I smile gratefully. "Thank you, that was very thoughtful and kind."

Melinda smiles back. "I'll see you tomorrow."

Ameer takes my hand and walks me out the door. By mutual consent, we head towards the main village, looking for a bar to drown our sorrows in. Once we get there, we find ourselves a table in the corner. "What will you have?" asks Ameer.

"Hmm, how about you start me off with a Dirty Martini?"

"Coming right up."

I watch him weave his way around the semi-occupied space to get to the bar and order our drinks. He's a good-looking guy, with a lean muscular body, beautiful dark eyes and a sexy smile. Maybe I could also drown my sorrows in his bed. I've not been with anyone since the debacle with Trent. It's time to finally move on.

He returns a short while later with our drinks, placing them carefully on the scuffed surface of the table. We tap the glasses together. "To silver linings," says Ameer.

"And what would those be?"

"Now that we won't be working together on this mission, I can finally try my hand at seducing you."

I chortle. "Snap! I was having the very same thoughts."

Ameer grins wide. "I'm glad. I really like you Martha, and if not going to Ven means I get to spend time with you, then maybe it's a good thing I wasn't chosen."

I take a sip of my drink and sigh in pleasure. "Oh, that's good." Then I look at Ameer appraisingly. "You know, you're a shit liar. I'm perfectly aware just how much you wanted to go on this mission. No way are you happy about any of this."

Ameer's eyes turn serious. "No, I'm bummed about it. But I wasn't lying when I said I really want to spend time with you."

"I'd like that too."

We finish our drinks and order some more. As the evening progresses, our commiseration turns into subtle flirting, and then, the drunker we get, into not-so-subtle flirting. Ameer lifts a stray lock of my hair and tucks it behind my ear. "How about we take this party to my place?"

"Hmm, yeah."

In his room, we kiss and strip naked, making love unhurriedly all night long. We stroke each other to one glorious peak after another. Then we sleep, sated and content, at least for the time being.

CHAPTER 6

Martha

For the dinner party tonight, I've decided to wear the most formal gown I packed for this trip. It's a dove gray dress that cinches above the waist and flows in soft waves down to just below my knees. I ease myself into it and twirl in front of the small mirror in my room, checking out my reflection from all angles. I like what I see. The neckline is cleverly cut to give a flattering effect on my generous breasts; the loose, flowing waves of fabric soften the lines of my figure.

I've always felt self-conscious about my body. I wouldn't have minded being so tall, if I could also have been willowy and slender. No such luck. I exercise and mostly eat well, so I'm not what one would call overweight. Even so, my chest is large and my hips wide. I am not a small woman.

I step closer to the mirror and examine my face. I've styled my hair into loose wavy strands down my back and put on some light make-up. The large gray eyes that stare back at me are a striking contrast to my lightly tanned, freckled skin. Some might say they're too large—I still recall other girls in high school calling them googly eyes—but mom always thought they were my most beautiful feature.

I frown at myself. I'm coming to accept the way I look a little more the older I get. And yet I still get these occasional moments of self-doubt. *Chin up Martha, time to go.*

When I arrive at the dinner party, I'm glad I went to the effort of looking my best. It's awkward enough having to walk in all on my own into a room buzzing with the chatter of well-dressed, highly ranked people.

A passing bot offers me a glass of champagne as I walk past a wall lit with sconces, giving the room a deceptive old world feel. Sipping my drink, I weave my way through the crowd searching for Melinda and for the Venorians. It doesn't take long to spot them, towering over everyone else. I recognize the same Venorian male from the video, standing close to another Venorian, this one a female I've never seen before. As luck would have it, they're with Melinda and Troy.

I sidle up to them as quickly as I can. It's Troy who catches sight of me first. With a wide smile, he draws me close. "Martha, you're looking lovely."

"Thanks, so are you."

"So good to see you again Martha, and Troy's right, that dress is divine on you," says Melinda.

I feel the attention of the Venorians on me and my face flushes red, both in excitement and embarrassment. I look across at them, finding them watching me with polite curiosity. Melinda makes the introductions.

"This is Martha Reynolds, one of the shortlisted candidates for the exchange program. Martha, may I introduce you to Pravol—who I'm sure you've recognized—and to Treylor."

I step towards Treylor first. She's impressively tall, dwarfing my six feet by several inches. She's also stunning—large honey-colored eyes, with matching hair artfully styled into loose braids, and smooth golden-brown skin. She wears loose silky pants a beautiful shade of dark blue, teamed with a figure-hugging pink tunic that plunges at the neckline to reveal the upper contours of her cleavage. Shiny gold chains of different lengths adorn her neck and collarbone. I'm awed by her presence and flooded with happiness at the chance to meet this exotic creature.

She looks deeply into my eyes, and I could swear she reads my emotions. Carefully, she places one soft, warm hand on my cheek, then brings her forehead to mine. I feel her warmth and curious interest, then we're both stepping back. "I am so happy to meet you too," she says, her words translated and voiced by her communicator.

Oh yes, I'm sure as sure can be that she's telepathic. I never said I was happy to meet her; I only thought it. However, I don't have time to ponder this further, as it's Pravol's turn to greet me. He's even taller than Treylor, standing at around six feet seven, and incredibly broad. He too wears loose silky pants that do little to hide the thickness of his powerful thighs. A contour-hugging purple tunic completes his outfit, showing off his broad, well-defined chest. The tunic is cut at the shoulders to reveal bronzed, muscular arms. A bulging vein snakes its way from his shoulder to his wrist.

Looking up, I see his face is set in a studiously blank pose, betraying no emotion, so it's a bit of a shock when he touches his hand to my cheek, to feel a sort of vibration. As his forehead meets mine, the vibration turns into an awareness of something strong, like a rock, standing protectively.

He steps back and immediately moves towards Treylor. All at once I understand. He is protective of her. On the heels of that thought comes another. How come I could feel his emotions? Is there a telepathic feedback loop, where their ability to probe my mind allows me a momentary glimpse into theirs?

Melinda takes up the conversation. "Pravol will exchange places with Troy here. The two of them have spent the afternoon getting to know each other and preparing to step into the other's shoes. And Treylor will swap places with Eliza."

At the name Eliza, Treylor's lips curl into a slight sneer. Aha, so she isn't a fan of the devious blonde either. Speaking of the devil, there she is, looking angelic in a pale blue shift dress. "Martha," she says, looking surprised. "I didn't expect to see you here. Have you gate-crashed the party?"

If looks could kill, I'd be skewering her right now, but I respond oh so sweetly. "Well now Eliza, if I *had* been gatecrashing, then that would definitely have let the cat out the bag. Surely you weren't trying to embarrass me in front of everyone?"

She lets out a little tinkle of laughter. "Oh Martha, how funny you are. I was only teasing."

I lift the champagne glass to my lips but say nothing more. Not the best idea to be having a spat in front of the ambassador and the Venorians. Troy deftly steps in. "I was just about to go help myself to something from the buffet. You hungry Martha?"

"Starving," I say.

"Well, let's go. Please excuse us."

He steers me towards the buffet table in the back of the room which is laden with a glorious selection of finger foods.

"Thanks for the save," I say. "That got a little awkward there. My fault, I know. I shouldn't have said anything."

Troy chuckles. "It wasn't the most diplomatic thing to say, but Eliza was the one at fault there, as well you know. That woman is poisonous."

We get to the buffet table and Troy passes me an empty plate, which I heap with food. I see a dish of southern fried shrimps with garlic butter sauce, next to a another filled with smoked salmon blinis. I help myself to some sticky chicken wings and take a bite. Oh, so good, and so real!

"Wow," I say in between bites. "They've got real meat on Mars!"

"Yep, nothing but the best for this special occasion. Which is why I made sure we got here quick and loaded up."

"Good call."

I add some eggrolls and samosas to my heaving plate. As I'm doing so, I sense a presence behind me and turn. Treylor, followed by her protective shadow Pravol, is looking at the buffet table with interest. Her eyes then swivel to the mountain of food on my plate, and I see her lips quirk in amusement. "It's not often we get to eat such delicacies," I explain. "Would you like to try some?"

"I would. It smells good."

I hand her an empty plate, then give one to Pravol, who inclines his head in thanks. Treylor follows my lead, taking a chicken wing and biting into it. I watch her chew on it thoughtfully, then take another bite, concentrating on the task. Finally, she smiles. "I like it." She helps herself to some more, as well as a few other items. I watch her bite into a fragrantly spiced meat samosa and moan loudly in pleasure. "Pravol, try this," she says to her friend. She feeds him the rest of her samosa, and as he takes it into his mouth, his tongue snakes out to delicately lick her finger. Definitely more than friends, these two.

Soon we're joined by a host of other people, eager to converse with our guests and to partake of the food. I cede my place at the buffet and wander over to Troy, who is standing to one side with Shay. We chat amiably while we eat, enjoying every delicious morsel. A bot serves me another glass of champagne, which I try to sip slowly, not wanting to get intoxicated in such revered company.

Over the course of the evening, I'm introduced to more Venorians, each time sensing some of their emotions as we touch foreheads. One of them has a great surprise in store for me. Shuban, a stony looking giant with shiny black hair swept back from his brow in an intricate knot, stares at me with cool blue eyes, then he steps forward and places his hand on my cheek. *Oh my!* I feel a sudden jolt of heat. He touches his forehead to mine and then I get the full force of what he's feeling. *Desire.* Jesus! If I'm not mistaken, the alien wants to fuck me.

I step back hurriedly, my face burning. He sees my reaction and his brows crease in a frown. Was I not supposed to glimpse his mind when he probed mine? "You sensed me," he says, his tone mildly accusing.

"I-I did," I stammer. "W-was that wrong?"

"No. I am surprised. None of the other humans we have met can read our minds."

"Oh."

He smiles suddenly, and his blue eyes twinkle. "You are a beautiful woman. I hope I did not offend."

"Not at all. I'm flattered."

"Perhaps, if you are to return to Earth with us, we can enjoy each other's company."

Oh my God. The alien is propositioning me. On the back of my recent dalliance with Ameer, I feel like the barren desert of my love life has unexpectedly turned into an oasis. Should I accept? I'm young, free and single. Why the heck not?

I nod my head. "Perhaps."

He leans towards me and whispers in my ear. "I look forward to getting to know you."

I breathe in sharply. "Me too."

Then we're separated as others clamor for his attention. Chest heaving, I grab a third champagne from a nearby bot and guzzle it down, trying to calm my agitation with some liquid courage.

Oh my! Coming here this evening, I did not expect this at all. But what a night!

I've learned the Venorians are telepathic, and that I seem to be the only human that can read their minds. I've discovered they're super-hot and sexy. And I can't wait to know more about them.

CHAPTER 7

Martha

I'm woken the next morning by the buzz of an incoming call on my communicator. I sit up and grab it, pressing the respond button. It's Melinda Garcia.

"Good morning, Martha. Sorry to disturb you."

I clear my throat. "Good morning, Melinda. What can I do for you?"

"Would you be able to come into my office? There's an urgent matter I need to discuss with you."

"Yes of course. Give me twenty minutes."

"Great!"

I end the connection and hop out of bed. A quick shower later, I dress and make my way over to Melinda's office, all the while wondering what this urgent matter could be. I'm guessing it has to do with last night's dinner party. Am I in trouble over my little spat with Eliza? No, that wouldn't be an urgent matter. Perhaps it's to do with the Venorians, and my theory—now confirmed—that they're telepathic.

I arrive at her quarters and am shown into her office immediately. Melinda stands and comes round her imposingly large desk to clasp my hand, a warm, friendly smile on her face. That's a good sign. I'm not in any trouble.

"Martha, thank you for coming over so quickly." She leads me over to a small sectional sofa in the corner of her office and invites me to sit with her. "I wanted to share with you some good news," she tells me. "Firstly, you were right! The Venorians are telepathic. And a little bird told me that you have the gift too."

53

Ah, Shuban has spoken. I hope he hasn't disclosed the exact details of our interaction last night. That would be embarrassing.

"I take it you've spoken to Shuban?"

Melinda nods. "Both he and Pravol came to see me early this morning. They are intrigued by you. It is very rare indeed for them to meet someone from another species who can also read their minds. They are both adamant that you should be part of the mission to Ven. Specifically, they asked that you take Eliza's place on the program. It seems she did not make a positive impression on them—nor on me for that matter."

I'm speechless.

"Martha? This is what you wanted, isn't it?"

I try to unscramble my thoughts that have gone haywire in the last minute. "Yes. I'm just overwhelmed. This is the best news!"

Then another thought occurs to me. "Have you spoken to Eliza yet?"

"Yes, I have. Let's just say she didn't take it very well. Said some very unkind things about you. I've arranged for her return to Earth on a transport leaving within the hour, so you don't have to worry about running into her."

I heave a relieved sigh. An Eliza on the warpath is not something I want to experience.

"So, what next?"

"You'll be leaving with the Venorians on their ship at 18:00 hours, so make sure you're packed and ready at least an hour before then. Treylor will want to spend some time with you before you go. You can tell her a little more about the specifics of your life on Earth and what she should expect, living in your apartment. She'll reciprocate with more information for you about Ven."

54

"I look forward to that."

Melinda turns serious for a moment. "Martha, I'm sure I don't need to tell you just how valuable this skill you have could be. More than anyone, you'll be able to get a read on the Venorians and their intentions towards us. I'm nearly one hundred percent sure that they are a benign race that means us no harm, but there is still so much we don't know or understand about them. The intelligence you provide us with from this mission will be critical."

"I understand."

She stands to shake hands with me again. "Good luck Martha. I've been so impressed with what I've seen from you. I have every confidence in your success on this mission."

"Thank you, Melinda. I really appreciate the vote of confidence."

I take my leave and hurry back to my quarters. I'm stepping into my room just as my communicator buzzes with an incoming call from Troy.

"Guess what," he says. "I've just seen Eliza and her face is like a thundercloud."

I huff. "Yeah, that figures."

"Holy cow Martha! You're going to Ven with us!"

"I know!"

"This is fucking great news."

"Yeah. I'm so excited. Still processing though. It hasn't sunk in yet."

"Well how about this to make it more real. Treylor and Pravol have invited us over to their ship for a Venorian breakfast. Can you be ready in ten minutes?"

"Of course."

"See you then, sugar."

"Don't call me that, asshole."

"You're right. Gonna have to think of a better name now I know you're a mind reader. I'll work on it."

I shake my head. "See you in ten," then end the connection.

Shuban is the first person I see as we board the Venorian ship, which is docked on Mars in readiness for our departure later today. He comes towards me with a wry smile. "Such a shame Martha. I was looking forward to getting to know you."

I smile shyly. "Likewise. Perhaps we'll meet again on our return journey."

"I hope so, beautiful one." He looks behind me. "Ah, here is Pravol. He will take you through to Treylor's quarters. Goodbye for now."

"Goodbye."

I turn to see Pravol approaching. We exchange the customary Venorian greeting, and I get the same emotions emanating from him as we touch foreheads—protect, protect, protect. The guy must have a one-track mind. "Good morning, Martha, Troy," he says solemnly. "I hope you are both well."

"Yes, thank you," we answer together.

"Please, follow me."

We walk behind Pravol as he leads us through the gleaming corridors of the ship. I gaze curiously through a window we pass, revealing a large open space occupied by a few Venorians busily working at their consoles. As we walk, Troy nudges my arm. "What was that about earlier with Shuban?" he whispers.

"Nothing," I whisper back. "Talk later."

We arrive at our destination and enter. The room is spacious, though furnished simply and uncluttered—a sizeable circular couch and a bunk in the corner—all designed to accommodate a larger race of people than ours. I catch glimpse of a table laid with all sorts of strange looking foods, as Treylor hurries towards us. We exchange greetings. This time, I put my hand to her cheek too, and touch foreheads. *Warmth, happiness, excitement.* Same feelings as me then.

She steps back with a smile. "I am so glad to see you again, Martha."

"Me too."

She turns to Troy and greets him, then beckons us towards the table. "It is your turn to try our food this time. Come and sit."

We arrange ourselves around the table, Pravol naturally taking the seat on Treylor's side. Over the next hour, we sample a range of different foods. Some, such as the "kroot", leavened bread with a savory filling reminiscent of cheese, is absolutely delicious. I struggle to swallow the "pilat", strangely chewy meat with an unpleasantly sour tang. I wash all this food down with a warm beverage called "joh", which Treylor explains, is a staple morning drink, a bit like our coffee, though sweeter and spicier—maybe closer to a chai latte.

Treylor does most of the talking, Pravol sitting mainly silent beside her and only interjecting every now and then. They make an interesting couple. She with her outgoing and bubbly personality. Him, taciturn and solemn.

I find out a little more about Treylor. She comes from a high-ranking family with a background in the military. Her father was some kind of a general, in charge of one of the five sectors on the planet Ven. He's now retired and driving her mother crazy with different projects to keep himself busy. His latest is to learn to play a musical instrument called the "gan", but making a huge din in the process. I'll be staying in their house, but Treylor assures me I will have privacy in my own quarters.

"Do you have any siblings?" I ask.

"My older brother, Prilor. He is a somar to the Kran's son."

The Kran, as far as I understand, is some kind of monarch and spiritual leader, so the Kran's son must be like a crown prince.

"A somar?" I enquire, not having come across the term before.

"Yes. Each kran must have four somars to protect him and give him companionship. It is a lifelong commitment and a great honor for our family."

I nod, trying to understand. So, a type of bodyguard, but for life.

She smiles brightly. "You will meet Prilor and his kran. He is a very good man and very handsome." An idea occurs to her. "Let us call them now and you will see."

She takes her communicator and taps a few buttons. Seconds later, a large screen projects on the wall beside us, showing the sleepy face of a Venorian with shaggy golden-brown hair. He rubs his eyes and grumbles, "Treylor, do you know what time this is?"

"Time you should be up," she says tartly.

He sits up, showing a massive hairy chest and bulging muscles. I give a quick intake of breath. Oh my, the man is a goliath. He looks at his sister with concern in his lovely honey-brown eyes. "Are you alright?"

"I am absolutely fine," she says on a laugh. "I wanted to introduce you to Martha, who will be taking my place on Ven." She turns her communicator towards me. "Martha, meet my brother, Prilor."

The person in question scowls at me. "If anything happens to Treylor, you will answer to me," he growls. *Well, hello to you too.*

Pravol speaks up. "No, she will answer to me."

"Enough you two," exclaims Treylor, looking flustered. "You are being rude to my guest."

On the screen, I see a bronzed arm, sprinkled with fine dark hair, snake its way around Prilor's chest, then a man's face kissing him on the neck. The man addresses us with a wicked smile on his face.

"Do not mind him. He is always grumpy in the morning, is that not so Prilor mine?"

Prilor responds with a grunt. The man's smile widens. He is perhaps the most beautiful being I have ever seen. His large, darkly lashed turquoise eyes contrast with smooth bronze skin in a perfectly chiselled face that ends with the most kissable of plump lips. Raven hair, in morning disarray, frames that perfect face. I can't seem to catch my breath as I stare at this vision of perfection. My heart palpitates in my chest.

Treylor, mistaking my reaction for admiration of her brother, whispers to me, "He is handsome, yes?"

"That he is," I breathe, not certain we're talking about the same being.

On the screen, the beautiful man is fiddling with the controls on his communicator. "One moment please, let me access the voice translator," he says in a sexy, gravelly voice. Then he turns his eyes to me. "Good day Martha, we are honored to make your acquaintance and we look forward to welcoming you on Ven. I am Krantorven."

So, this is the crown prince. Treylor's brother must be his lover, as well as his bodyguard. I sigh inwardly. All the best men are always taken. Not that I stand much of a chance with this one. He's royalty, just a little out of my reach. I smile politely and respond in my best diplomatic voice, hearing his translator speak my words in Venorian an instant later. "The honor is mine. I look forward to visiting your planet." Then I remember Troy, sitting dumbfounded beside me. I turn to make the introductions. "This is my friend and colleague Troy Summers, who will also be on the mission to Ven."

Krantorven—what a mouthful of a name—inclines his head regally. "Good day Troy. I look forward to meeting you both in more formal surroundings, not when we are rumpled in bed." He looks severely at Treylor. "Next time Treylor, please send us a communication before making a call in the presence of others."

"I apologize, Krantor," she says looking a little crestfallen. "We were talking about Prilor and I so wanted Martha to see my handsome brother. I did not think."

His eyes gentle as he regards Treylor. "It is fine. Is all well with you?"

"Yes, please do not worry. All is well."

He smiles. "I am glad. And so is this grumpy giant." He kisses Prilor's cheek.

Treylor's brother looks at her and nods. "Take good care of yourself."

"I will."

They end the connection, and we adjourn to the living space, having eaten our fill. We talk some more, my turn now to fill her in on what to expect on Earth. I tell her about my friend Lulu and warn her off Trent, should he ever presume to make advances to her. Pravol growls. "He will not," he says firmly.

No, there is no need to worry about Treylor with such a protector as him. I feel a stab of envy. Nobody has ever stood up for me like this. I've never been the center of someone else's world. How nice that would be.

I look between the two of them. "So, are the two of you boyfriend/girlfriend? Engaged?"

Treylor is puzzled. "Boyfriend? I do not know this term."

"It's our way to describe two people who are together as a couple, but not married."

She frowns. "I am not sure I understand. Pravol and I are not mated, but we have plans to be in the future."

"Soon," he says. "When we come back from the Earth mission, we will mate."

"What does it mean, to mate?"

"It is a very important commitment between two people. It means we are together for life, and we cannot share our love or our body with anyone else."

"We have something like this in our culture. We call it marriage, though it's not always for life. It is possible to divorce and end the marriage."

Treylor looks shocked. "Oh, that is not good! What is a promise if it is broken?"

I smile wryly. "You may be right. But people make mistakes, and we don't consider it fair for someone to stay trapped with a person they no longer have feelings for."

"In our culture, mating is for life. That is why we only take this step after a long period of reflection. Sometimes couples are together for many sun rotations before they agree to mate. Only in very rare circumstances can a mating be terminated, by order of the Kran."

"I see. What kind of ceremony do you have when you mate?"

"First, we make a public pledge that we are going to mate. Then we have a moon rotation to prepare our bodies for the mating."

"Prepare your bodies? How?"

"We do this through deep meditation. When our bodies are ready to accept the mating, there occur changes in our physiology. I cannot explain them. It is like the cells in our bodies are preparing for union."

I nod, not really understanding. "And then?"

"There is both a public and a private mating. In public, we stand in front of our families and make our pledges. Then in private, we make an exchange of all our body fluids—our blood, the fluid in our mouths and down below." She points to her groin.

So, they kiss, have sex and make a blood vow. Ha. Interesting.

"Because our bodies have prepared for the mating, once we exchange fluids, our cells change so we become part of one another. His scent and my scent merge together to form a hybrid scent. Any female approaching Pravol after we are mated will scent it and know he is taken. And the same for me if any male approaches me."

Now it's Pravol's turn to explain. "It is not just our scents that change. Our tastes will change too. After we are mated, I will love all the foods Treylor loves. I too dislike pilat," he says, looking at me, "but once we are mated, I will love it because Treylor's taste will be merged with mine. Her mathematical ability will improve as she takes on my characteristics, and I will finally be able to sing in tune as I take on hers. This is why a mating is so important. It merges the best capabilities of two persons, allowing them to be healthier, stronger and much more skilled. Mating is the backbone of our society on Ven, and the reason for our success as a people."

I'm struggling to lift my jaw off the floor. I am in complete awe. I share a look with Troy. "Wow," he says. "That's amazing. We have nothing like that in our physiology. How lucky you are!"

Pravol nods his head in agreement. Then, it's time for us to go. We say our goodbyes and return to the village on Mars. We have time for one last bittersweet meeting with Ameer, before we go to collect our packed bags and join the rest of the team travelling on the mission. Melinda Garcia formally sees us off, then we're boarding the Venorian ship, and finally on our way to the planet Ven.

CHAPTER 8

Krantorven

The Earth female, Martha, is attractive. She has wavy chestnut hair and skin a lighter shade of bronze than ours, speckled with freckles across her cheeks and the bridge of her nose. But that is not what captures my attention. It is her eyes—clear gray, the color of a stormy sky—and the stormy, impetuous nature I sense beneath. This is no cool, calm and collected person like my mother. I sense heat and passion. Not characteristics I would want in a mate, but in bed, oh yes, that would work just fine for me.

Perhaps, when she arrives on Ven, Prilor and I should work our charms to get her into our bed for a night or two of passion. My cock stiffens at the thought. It has been a while since either of us has been with a female. I have missed the wet heat of a female cunt, the soft skin and the pillowy breasts of a woman. I pin Prilor to me and growl into his ear, "I want to fuck you hard."

He grunts. "Do it. It is that female, is it not?"

I bite the shell of his ear. "Yes. There is a fire in her. I want to slip my hard cock into her juicy cunt and fuck her as hard as I am about to fuck you. I want to spend all my precious cum into her, making her ready for your massive cock. Would you like that?"

I bite the back of his neck and he moans, "Yes, yes I would."

I grip his cock in my hand. "Then I want you to oh so slowly work your cock into her wet heat until you are buried as far as you can go, and you feel my cum around you, searing into your skin."

He's panting as he reaches for the lubrication gel, which is always placed by our bedside. I take it from him and slick my aching cock. "And then," I hiss, "you will fuck her so hard she will barely be able to walk from our bed."

I push my considerable length into his pucker, forcing my way past the initial tight ring of muscle. "You will make her spasm in release, not once, not twice, but three times, her pulsing walls gripping tight around your cock and my cum."

I start thrusting in and out of his tight hole, not gently. "Then, and only then, you will come, roaring your release and flooding her cunt with your cum so it mixes with mine."

I fuck my lover hard, imagining him fucking that Earth girl with his mighty girth. I sense the moment when he reaches the pinnacle and give one final thrust, emptying myself into him just as he roars his pleasure. I still, buried inside him, and kiss him softly, all my ferociousness gone. "I love you to the moon and back, Prilor mine," I whisper into his ear.

"I love you more, my kran."

Like clockwork, Fionbal walks in, rubbing his sleepy eyes, his cock swinging from side to side. He leans over to kiss me. "Good morning Fionbal mine," I drawl.

"Good morning my kran."

He moves over to kiss Prilor, who's collapsed on his front, my weight crushing him to the bed. "Fionbal, you will need to put some salve on him and some extra soothing salts into our bath water. I have demolished Prilor's ass today and he will be sore."

Fionbal laughs. "Consider it done."

Sometime later, we arrive on the bridge of the Phtar and relieve Dovtar, who has been on night duty. "Anything to report?" I ask.

"Not a peep, my kran," he says tiredly.

I summon him to me, and he comes over, accepting my kiss. "Go get some rest, Dovtar mine." He nods, and heads to his cabin for some sleep. Prilor takes his place, unable to mask a wince as he sits. I smirk in satisfaction. I have marked my Prilor well.

We have reached sector 5 of the Utar belt, keeping our ship cloaked, but have not seen anything out of the ordinary. This is not a busy thoroughfare. Apart from a small Driskian trading ship transporting supplies to our dorenium colony, we have not come across anything or anyone.

We continue weaving our way back and forth between the small planets and moons of this sector, on course to meet with Rivvol in one rotation's time. I'm examining data on my communicator when Fionbal calls out. "There is something moving in quadrant B6. It looks like a small ship whose cloak has been compromised."

I look at B6 quadrant on our screen. At first, I don't notice anything, then I spot it. "Are we close enough to scan the ship?"

"Yes." A moment later, he says, "It is a Klixian freighter."

What are Klixians doing in this part of the galaxy? They are a slimy race of people known for their deception and treachery. As a rule, we do not engage with them in any way. None of our other trading partners do business with them either, so there can be no innocent reason for a Klixian to be here, so far from their world.

"Prilor, edge closer until we can beam it in."

Prilor carefully manoeuvers our ship until we are within range to beam it in. As soon as it is within our clutches, I open a channel. "Klixian ship, prepare to be boarded."

A voice comes on the line. "But why? We have done nothing wrong."

"Lay down your arms and prepare to be boarded," I repeat.

Fionbal takes over the controls from Prilor, and the both of us suit up in our protective armor. A moment later, Shanbri joins us, and we all check our weapons. I look across at them before we push open the airlock. "Ready?"

"Ready."

Prilor pushes it open, and we step towards the Klixian ship, forcing open its airlock door. Holding our weapons at the ready, we enter. The space is empty. We move to the second airlock door and open it up. Two Klixians stand before us, their hands in the air.

I lower my helmet and look at them severely. "Greetings Klixians. You are very far from home."

"Our apologies. We mean no harm. Our ship has experienced some technical faults and we have stopped here to make repairs."

"Where were you headed and from where?"

"We have just been to Krovatia to trade in boral crystals and were making our way home."

A likely story. To my knowledge, Krovatians do not trade with the Klixians. I approach the Klixian and place my hand on his cheek, pressing my forehead to his. I do not get a clear reading, but my suspicion that the Klixian is being untruthful is confirmed. We will have to take them with us and wait for father. Only he will be able to read their minds and tell us what is going on.

I nod to Shanbri, who comes over to cuff their arms behind their backs, while Prilor keeps us covered with his weapon. "You will come with us for further interrogation," I tell them.

I ignore their complaints and force them around towards our ship, where they will be locked in our detention cell. Once they have been secured, we resume our journey towards sector 3.

"Fionbal," I instruct my somar. "Send a message to Rivvol telling her we have some Klixian prisoners that require interrogation. Copy father and mother."

"Understood."

It is not long before we get a reply from father.

Father: On my way.

CHAPTER 9

Martha

I'm bowled over by the planet Ven. It is beautiful, and the main city, Torbreg—named after the Kran's family of course—is magnificent. Graceful wide avenues lined with picturesque mansions and gorgeous purple and pink blossomed trees, have led us to a bustling downtown area with a large market selling colorful wares and a plethora of exotic foods. I can't wait to explore.

Our transport finally stops in front of a tall, imposing building. The walls of this grand, five-storied structure are stained a pretty color of peach, its roof comprising a glorious mix of mocha, caramel and rusty orange tiles arranged in a zig zag pattern. This, we are told, is the Interior Ministry, where all new visitors to the planet are processed.

We are ushered inside and greeted by a smart and officious looking Venorian female. All civilized societies, it seems, have their version of officialdom.

"Welcome to Ven," she says. "I am Trinar, and I will be issuing you with all the necessary documents for your stay here with us. First, though, may I ask you to come with me to our medical wing where we can give you a health check and inoculations?"

We follow her two flights up an old-fashioned circular staircase, then down a series of endless corridors, until we arrive in a pleasantly furnished room with a large sectional and several armchairs.

"Please sit, and we will call you each individually. Do help yourselves to refreshments." She points to a table with a large jug of pale pink liquid and pretty glass cups. It also has a tray with a selection of cookies and fresh cut fruit.

Troy and I approach it curiously. I pour some of the pink liquid into a cup and take a tentative sip. "It's good," I say. "Pleasantly refreshing with a hint of citrus. Would anyone else like some?"

Diego Sanchez comes over and pours himself a cup, taking a long, satisfying drink from it. "Yes, you're right. A little like lemonade but less sharp."

Troy is already wolfing down some cookies. "Hmm," he says as he munches, "these are great."

A Venorian female dressed all in white—no prizes for guessing she must be the doctor—emerges from a doorway and calls out my name. "Looks like you get to go first," Troy smirks.

I follow her into a white, clinical room, and she indicates for me to lie on a couch. She smiles reassuringly as she runs a handheld scanner all along my body. She checks the results on her screen. "Good news Martha. You are in perfect health."

"Thank you. That's good to know."

"I would like to give you a set of inoculations against local diseases which your body may not have developed any immunity to. It is a painless process, just a slight pinprick, and there should be no side effects."

"Please, be my guest."

She approaches with a large tube, which she presses into my skin. I feel a moment of discomfort, then the pain's gone.

"That's it," she says. "It is done."

"Thank you," I say as I stand to leave.

"You are welcome. Please could you send in Shay Smith to me next?"

"Of course."

Once we are all checked out, Trinar returns to take us through more winding corridors to another large, pleasantly furnished room. She presents each of us with a tablet computer displaying indecipherable text. "You must all sign this document. It is a summary of our rules and expectations of behavior while you are our guests on this planet, and your pledge that you will abide by the rules."

She sees our bewildered expressions and laughs. "Of course, you cannot yet read our language, though I hope you may learn it soon. Scroll down to the bottom of the text and you will see an English-language translation."

We do as told, and find a quaintly translated text which highlights the rules. I read through them quickly. No stealing. No sexual conduct without consent of all parties. No sexual conduct with persons under the age of eighteen sun rotations—I've learned that is the term they use for years. No littering or defacing of property. No cursing of the almighty god Lir. Proper respect to be shown to the Kran and his family. Respect when entering places of worship.

"I have no issues with any of this," I say. "Are we all happy to sign?"

Everyone agrees, and we sign the document. Next, we are issued with our own communicators and given funds in the local currency, the Litor—also named after the venerated Kran's family—so we can purchase what we need during our stay. I'm not sure what one Litor can buy, but our funds indicate we have been given ten thousand.

Trinar spends a little time with us showing us how to navigate the communicator, which is of a different design to what we are used to back home. Finally, she smiles. "That is all. Shortly, someone will come to take each of you to your designated homes. We have also planned a banquet to welcome all of you to our planet, but unfortunately it has had to be postponed as both the Kran and his son are currently off planet. If you have any questions, please do not hesitate to contact me at any time using this button here."

"Thank you Trinar," says Troy. "You have been extremely helpful."

Trinar's communicator bleeps with a message. She looks down at it then smiles at me. "Martha, your transport has arrived. Will you please follow me?"

I give the others a quick hug goodbye, suddenly feeling emotional and a little overwhelmed. That's it. I'm on my own now. Troy holds me tight. "I'm sure I'll be seeing you very soon," he mumbles into my hair. "And now we know how to use it, you can call me anytime on the communicator. You'll be fine."

I nod, then follow Trinar down to the main entrance of the building. Two people await by the door. One of them is a large bear of a Venorian with golden brown wavy hair, flecked with gray. He looks at me with kind, honey-colored eyes, and I immediately know who he is.

"You must be Treylor's father," I say. "I see the resemblance."

The man gives a loud guffaw, looking mighty pleased. "I am indeed! And you are Martha. I have already heard so much about you from Treylor." He comes towards me, and instead of the customary greeting which I have come to know, he envelops me in a giant hug. "Welcome my dear."

My eyes get misty at the warmth of his welcome and I know, at this moment, that I will be just fine. He releases me and turns to the tall woman standing quietly by his side. "Call me Senlor, and this is my beloved mate, Flidar."

Flidar bows her head gracefully and approaches me, this time for the standard greeting. We touch cheeks and foreheads. I sense cautious, but warm welcome. I step back. "I am honored to meet you both, and very grateful for your hospitality."

"Indeed, the honor is ours," responds Flidar.

"Come, let us go," says Senlor.

I hesitate. "My things," I say.

"Already inside our transport. Come, come."

I follow them out, where a large yellow drone awaits us. They usher me in, and then with a light woosh, we're up in the air and on our way to my new home.

CHAPTER 10

Shanbri

I am in that pleasant semi-dreamy state before fully awakening, lying in my bed back in our home quarters on Ven. Beside me, Dovtar's gentle snores provide a comforting rhythm to my musings. We sleep in the same bed in our room that adjoins Krantor's chamber. Fionbal has his own adjoining room on the other side.

Venorians are a race that for the most part does not like to sleep alone. From an early age, I always had someone in the bed with me. At first it was my mother, seeking mutual comfort when father was away on his military missions. Then later it was Krantor, my childhood friend, who kept me warm and cozy at night.

It was at military school that Krantor met and fell in love with Prilor. I was summarily, if kindly, replaced in the bed, and so I naturally gravitated towards Dovtar, another close friend at the academy. We have slept together ever since. What would I do without his rhythmic snores to lull me to sleep every night? I have grown so used to having him around that I hardly miss Krantor's bed, even though the dismissal stung at the time.

I give my body a stretch, enjoying the soft feel of the sheets beneath me. It is good to be back home finally after several weeks of flying on the Phtar. A spaceship has fewer comforts, and worse for me, limited cooking facilities. I look forward to spending some quality time back in my domain, the food preparation area. Perhaps I should sneak out to the market for fresh supplies while everyone slumbers. With a quiet yawn, I come fully awake and make my way out of bed, careful not to disturb Dovtar.

I walk to the ablution room where I relieve my full bladder and empty my bowels. Next, I step under the rainmaker for a quick wash of my body. Once clean, I pat myself dry on the large towelling sheet, dropping it into the cleaning chute after I'm done. Lastly, I place my lips on the open spout of the ablutenizer, and press the button to start it. A gush of warm liquid enters my mouth, followed by an automated set of brushes that—guided by a sensor—thoroughly cleanse all my teeth.

Mouth freshened, I return to our room where Dovtar sleeps on, making a rumbling sound in his chest with every other breath he takes. I smile affectionately then pull the lever to open our concealed clothes storage cabinet. I hastily pick out one of my favorite navy pants. I have several of them because they are so comfortable, draping my legs in loose-fitting silky material. At the top of the pants is a soft but supportive pouch to rest my large cock in. I pull them up my legs now and adjust myself until all feels right. I rummage through the tunics on my shelf, making a mess which Dovtar no doubt will tut about, then tidy for me. Finally, I pick out the one I want. It's a plain silvery gray, the smooth material stretching snugly over my chest and cut at the shoulders to allow my arms to be bare, for I do not like to overheat. Bending down, I slip on my sandals, and then I am ready.

A few moments later, I am out walking the winding streets of downtown Torbreg, the balmy morning air caressing my face. I breathe it in, enjoying the sweet fragrance of the blossoms on the kalso trees that pepper my path. It is the kalso season, the most beautiful time of the sun rotation. The purple and pink kalso blossoms adorn nearly every street corner, creating a charming, colorful landscape and delighting me with their sweet aroma.

Another turn, and I am at the market. Despite the early hour, it is bustling with like-minded people wanting to fill their baskets with the freshest of produce. I meander, looking for a selection of fruit for our morning repast. I purchase some ripe drias, lovely pink berries that are bursting with sweet juices.

75

I am examining some preons, sniffing them to decide whether they are ripe enough, when I notice a female about to take a bite from a blint, an attractive looking fruit that is less than attractive on the tongue—that is unless you enjoy the burn of spicy heat. In that swift perusal, I recognize that this female is not of our world. Immediately after comes the realization that this must be one of the five humans on the Earth exchange program.

"Do not!" I call out sharply, and she stops with her hand in mid-air. "You will not like it, I assure you."

She brings the hand holding the blint down. "It looks so pretty," she says in a lovely, lilting voice that I can hear beneath the translation on the communicator.

"It is very pretty, but also very spicy. It will burn the roof of your mouth."

"Oh," she says, putting the blint down. She looks up at me with large eyes the color of a lorian blossom and smiles, showing off her lovely full lips. "Thank you for the warning."

"You are on the Earth program," I murmur, for want of something clever to say. My wits have deserted me.

"Yes, indeed I am. It is a little hard for me to go incognito about town."

"Incognito?" I ask, puzzled. My translating device cannot find a matching Venorian word.

"It means without being recognized."

"Ah," I say, still tongue-tied.

"I'm Martha," she says, stepping towards me for the customary greeting. She places her hand on my cheek as I do so to hers, and we touch foreheads. Curiosity, gratefulness, and barely hidden beneath these emotions, I discern attraction. *Oh yes Martha, the attraction is mutual.*

76

She pulls back, looking flushed. In her knowing eyes, I realize she has read my mind too. How strange. I am not used to other species being able to do this. We gaze at each other in silence, our breaths coming in quick bursts. Finally, I think to say, "I am Shanbri. I work with Prilor, Treylor's brother. We are both somars to the Kran's son."

"Shanbri," she breathes. "I'm happy to meet you."

"And I you." More silence, then an idea comes to me. "Would you like to walk with me around the market? I can help you pick out some good produce."

"Thank you. I would like that."

I take out a dria berry from my basket. "This is a dria, a wonderfully sweet berry." I go to place it in her hand, but she opens her mouth, waiting for me to feed it to her. I touch the ripe berry to her parted lips, and her mouth closes around it, momentarily encircling my finger. I am electrified by the brief contact with the softness of her lips.

I pull my hand back and try to compose myself as I watch her savor the berry. "Mmm, it's good," she murmurs.

I clear my throat. "Shall we?" I ask, holding out my arm. She puts her arm through it, and we begin to walk.

I could not tell you what we say or do in the time that follows. I know we walk around the market, sample and purchase produce. But beyond that I cannot recall the details. What I can recall, in brilliant detail, is the subtle scent of her—a morning sea breeze mixed with a light floral aroma and her female musk—a scent I shall never forget until the day I die. I can recall every curve and indentation of her face and body; the changing expressions in her lovely eyes giving a hint of her impetuous, passionate nature. I can recall the soft feel of her skin under my fingers and the lilting lullaby of her voice.

Finally, I walk her back to her waiting transport. Before she leaves, I take her hand in mine and kiss it. "Show me your

77

communicator," I command gently. "I will program my contact button on it." She hands it to me, and I arrange a button in the top right corner of the screen, that she need only touch once to call me. "Call me anytime by touching this," I say.

She tries it, and immediately my communicator lights up with an incoming call from her. "See?" I show her. Then I program mine, so I too can contact her easily. "I hope I can see you again soon, Martha. I know Prilor plans to visit his parents as soon as he is able to. I will make sure to accompany him."

She smiles. "I would like that. Thank you for everything Shanbri."

I cannot stop myself from leaning forwards and kissing her lightly on the lips. "It was my absolute pleasure, Martha. Safe journey." She climbs aboard the transport, and I close the door behind her. Within moments, it rises in the air and departs. I stand for a long while, watching her go.

I never fully understood how Krantor could have fallen in love with Prilor so quickly and suddenly. Now I do. My heart belongs to this female from Earth. I know it as surely as I know I am Shanbri, son of Molbri. In that split instant, I also know that this love is doomed, for I am bound to Krantor for life, and Martha will be returning to her planet before too long.

CHAPTER 11

Martha

I'm back from my shopping expedition to the market, and have joined Flidar, my gracious host, for our daily Drekon session. It's the Venorian equivalent of yoga, a series of ever more complex poses that help the body achieve strength and flexibility. I try to follow Flidar's lead, but some of the poses are well beyond my present capability. For a woman twice my age, Flidar makes it look easy, gracefully transitioning from one position to the next.

She smiles encouragingly as she sees me struggle with the latest pose, an inverted V position with one leg and the opposite arm raised a few inches off the floor. "It takes daily practice to achieve an ease with these poses, Martha, so do not despair. You are making excellent progress."

I focus on my breathing and try to maintain the position, but lose my balance and roll to the floor. Flidar smiles serenely. "Let us try again."

And so, we continue for about another half hour, before Flidar finally calls a halt. My face is pink with exertion and my muscles tired from the effort, but I feel a sense of achievement for having gotten through the workout—more than I managed yesterday.

We find a sitting position and close our eyes to meditate, focusing on each breath as we aid our bodies to recover. My mind can't help but wander to my encounter with Shanbri earlier in the market. The Venorians are a handsome, impressive race, but even so, Shanbri stands out. Impossibly broad and tall—maybe around six feet eight—his clothes did little to mask the musculature of his physique.

Unusually for a Venorian, his hair was blond, the color of warm corn, and silky smooth. He had it twisted into a careless bun, with wavy strands coming loose at the sides. His skin was that gorgeous Venorian bronze, and his eyes… *oh my* I could have drowned in the dark onyx of his gaze. And for a while, I did. We had touched in the customary greeting, and I had immediately sensed his intense desire, a desire that was reciprocated. Shaken, I had stepped back and stared for an endless minute, my heart beating wildly.

One of the advantages of being able to sense each other's emotions in a simple greeting, is that it cuts out the cat and mouse games that we humans play. Immediately, the cards are on the table. I knew and he knew that we wanted each other. We didn't speak of it, but we jumped to a level of intimacy all in the space of a morning's walk, that would take several dates to achieve back home. Awareness of each other was in every step, in every gaze. Just thinking about him now has my heart beating rapidly once more.

"I sense your mind is elsewhere," Flidar says softly. "Will you share with me what it is?"

I take a deep calming breath. "In the market this morning, I met somebody."

"Ah," says Flidar, then remains silent. We continue to breathe in and out slowly, infusing our space with calm and serenity.

Finally, I speak again. "His name is Shanbri. You know him I think."

"Yes. He is a fine young man."

I hesitate. "He says he is a somar to the Kran's son. I'm not sure I fully understand what that means."

"It is an honor and a privilege to be chosen as a kran's somar, but it is also a sacrifice. A somar must devote his entire life to his kran and never mate. His duties are many. To protect his kran, be his companion—in all ways both sexual and non-sexual—and serve him as required. Shanbri prepares and

80

serves Krantor all his daily meals. Should there be any kind of threat or attack, Shanbri must put himself between his kran and that threat. The rhythm of his life revolves around this one person that he serves. He is not free to seek his own destiny."

A sexual companion to his kran? I feel a stab of jealousy at the thought. Ridiculous, considering I hardly know him.

"There is more," continues Flidar. "While Krantor is unmated, they are all free to have sexual relations with whomever they please, but this will all change as soon as the Kran's son finds his mate. A mating between two ordinary Venorians is a sacred vow of fidelity. When it comes to a kran, this vow includes all four of his somars. They may treat the kran's mate as their own, to bed her and even procreate with her, but they are no longer allowed to have sexual relations with another male or female. They are tied for life."

I open my eyes to see Flidar gaze at me sympathetically. "I tell you this," she says, "not to hurt your feelings, but to make you aware of the situation. Krantor could find his mate at any moment, and from that point, Shanbri will be forbidden to you. For all that he is a very fine, good man, as is my Prilor, do not give your heart to him. It will only cause you pain."

My heart sinking, I sigh. "I hope it's not too late. I really like him."

"It is never too late Martha. Attraction may be something out of your control, but who you choose to give your heart to is up to you. I love my Senlor with every fiber of my being, but before we mated, I could have chosen to love someone else. I chose him because I saw the qualities I wanted, and I saw we could build a good life together. You are a sentient being Martha, and you can make choices."

As far as empowering pep talks go, this one is up there with the best I've been given. I feel a renewed sense of purpose. Yes,

I was smitten on first meeting Shanbri. But no, I don't have to fall at his feet. Girl power and all that.

I smile gratefully at Flidar. "Thank you for your wise words."

Flidar inclines her head. "Perhaps we can find a way to distract you from thoughts of the handsome Shanbri. I meant to tell you earlier that I have invited some family friends over for dinner tonight. It will be a good chance for you to get to know other Venorians, and you will be happy to know that not all of them will be old like me."

"You are not old," I say with a grin.

"You are being kind my dear."

From a few rooms down the hall, we hear a loud, off-key clang. Flidar shudders delicately.

"Is Senlor practising on the gan again?" I ask with a twitch to my lips.

"If you can call it practising. How about we go and suggest an alternate activity for him today? I am sure Senlor would be happy to show you around the sights of Torbreg. We have many buildings of historical interest where you can learn more about our people."

"I like the sound of that," I smile.

I'm back from my sightseeing expedition with Senlor, and I have just enough time for a bath before I need to get ready for the dinner party tonight. I could have a quick shower in my ensuite bathroom, which the Venorians delightfully call the ablution room. However, I've grown addicted to the luxury of the bathing room.

Knotting a robe around me, I walk out of my bedroom and across the landing to this room of wonder. A Venorian bathing room is nothing like the functional bathrooms I am used to from

Earth. Everything here on Ven seems to be constructed super-sized, and their bathrooms are no exception.

I enter it now and lock the door behind me. On my right is a nook with a shelf filled with stacks of large, folded towelling sheets. Beside it is a long, padded bench where I can sit after my bath to dry myself and moisturize my skin with a choice of different scented creams lying in decorative pots on a side table. There is also a jug of *ploh*, which I now know is the name of the lemonade-like drink I had on my first day at the Interior Ministry. Next to the jug are cute little glasses to pour the drink into, in case I feel like some refreshment while I'm moisturizing. Bathing for the Venorians—as I've discovered—is a leisurely event.

I untie my robe and throw it on the bench. Naked, I pad over to the bathtub. It's more like a small indoor pool than a tub, sunken into the ground, with a series of short steps to climb down into it. On one side, there is a console from which I can operate the bath. Flidar showed me how to use it on my first day here. With a few touches, I program the temperature of the water—steaming hot just as I like it—and what kind of scent I want infused into it.

There are different aroma blends, depending on my mood and requirements. After an exercise workout, I can choose a blend to relax and soothe my aching muscles. If I'm feeling stressed, there's a blend to relax me. Another blend is there to reinvigorate me should I be feeling tired. The list of blends is long, and Flidar painstakingly went through all the different options with me. There is even a blend for stimulating physical arousal. I blushed as Flidar explained that I may wish to use this whenever I feel the need to pleasure myself. The Venorians are not shy talking about masturbation, or anything to do with sexuality for that matter.

My fingers hesitate on the console as I debate which blend to choose. Ever since meeting Shanbri this morning, my body has been in a continued state of arousal. Just thinking about the gorgeous Venorian has my pussy clenching with need. I haven't used the "masturbation" blend yet, but tonight feels like the right time to try it out. Decision made, I press the relevant button and all at once, a great gush of water starts pouring out of the massive spout.

It doesn't take long to fill the bath. In less than two minutes, the water level is up to my chin and the spout stops gushing automatically. I take a deep inhale of the spicy scent. *Ahh, that's good.* Looking down at myself, I notice my nipples have tightened to firm, jutting buds. I give them an experimental tweak and feel my pulse race wildly. *Oh yeah, that feels good.* I tweak them again, closing my eyes as I moan out loud.

Everywhere the water touches my body, I feel my nerve endings zing. It's almost as if the water is a set of multiple hands stroking me. My body quivers in response and my core starts to throb, begging for attention. I slip a hand down to my clit and begin to rub myself. *Oh God. Oh fuck. Oh.* I give a loud cry as my orgasm rips through me, pulse after pulse of aching pleasure. It doesn't seem to end. Aftershocks thrum through my body as I keep stroking my clit. Without warning, I'm gripped by a second, deeper wave of spasms. *Ahh.* This time, I'm screaming as sensation flows through every single molecule of my body. I've never felt anything so intense. It's almost too much.

Panting, I force my hand away from my clit and find the steps out of the tub. With an effort, I climb out and head to the bench where I collapse, not even able to reach for a towel. I lie there for a long time, until finally my breathing is under control. Sitting up, I dry my body, then pour myself a refreshing cup of *ploh*. I guzzle down the drink, thinking maybe that's why it's put there—for post-orgasmic recuperation.

Wow. That was amazing, though perhaps not something I want to experience every day. I reach for the different pots of cream and sniff them, choosing the one I want, then rub it all over my body. Once I'm done, I put my robe back on and send my used towels down the convenient laundry chute. As I pad my way back to my room, I hope against hope that the walls of the bathing room are soundproofed and that no one in the house heard my loud cries.

In my bedroom, I start getting ready for the dinner party. I decide to wear a simple navy shift dress and accessorize it with the pendant Grandma gave me. I carefully thread it on to a plain gold chain and clasp it around my neck. The pink and purple gemstones twinkle in the mirror as I gaze at my reflection. Their color reminds me a little of those lovely blossoms on the trees I saw while walking about today. I study myself in the mirror. My skin glows and my eyes sparkle from the effects of that blissful bath. I give my hair a final brush, apply a little face powder, and smile in satisfaction. I'm ready.

As I'm about to head down, my communicator buzzes with an incoming call. It's Shanbri. I hesitate for a moment, remembering my earlier conversation with Flidar. Should I ignore? No, that would be rude. I pick up. Shanbri's handsome face appears on the screen.

"Martha, you are looking well. Did you enjoy the rest of your day?"

"Yes, thank you. Senlor took me on a sightseeing trip around Torbreg. I was very impressed with the Torlant."

Shanbri's face creases into a smile. "Oh, that is one of my favorite places in Torbreg. Did you climb to the top of the tower?"

"I did, though I was quite out of breath by the time we made it up there."

He laughs, then his intent gaze takes in my outfit and face. "You look smart, and very beautiful. Are you going out?"

"No, Flidar has invited some friends over for dinner. She wants to introduce me to more Venorians."

Shanbri smiles. "If they are her friends, then you can be sure they are good people. I hope you enjoy it."

"I'm sure I will. In fact, I had better go. They're waiting for me."

"Of course, I will not delay you any further. Enjoy your evening, Martha. I will speak with you again soon."

"Thanks, Shanbri. Bye."

"Goodbye, beautiful one."

I end the connection and try to get myself composed. Seeing him again has brought back all sorts of feelings. Taking a deep breath, I walk to the staircase and down towards the large living area, from which I can hear a buzz of voices. The dinner guests must have arrived. I enter the room and Senlor immediately comes to me with a big smile.

"Martha, you are looking lovely." He clasps both of my cheeks and touches his forehead to mine. *Warmth, love, affection.* He steps back and whispers, "No need to be nervous. We are with friends." Ah, he must have sensed my nerves and perhaps a little of my earlier perturbation. It is unnerving sometimes not to be able to mask my emotions from those around me.

He takes my hand in his giant bear paw and guides me towards a group of people in the far corner of the room. I am introduced to an older Venorian couple and their daughter, who seems of a similar age to mine. She is training to be an educator of young children, so we have an interesting discussion about teaching, and the different approaches taken by our respective cultures. I'm impressed once again by the Venorian ethos. Lying and deception are anathema to these people. Why lie when that lie will be instantly sensed by the people around you?

That's not to say that people here are saints. They can err, say the wrong hurtful things, but they can't lie. Although it can be painfully awkward not to be able to hide your thoughts and emotions, as attested by my own experiences so far, it does cut out all the need for pretense and for putting on a mask. This is a society built firmly on honesty. I think back to all of Trent's lies to me during our time together. I had no idea he had applied to be a senior leader at my school. I had no idea he intended to ditch me the minute he got the job. I went along blithely unaware of his deception, making the shock and betrayal all the more painful when I finally learned the truth. None of this would have happened, had we been Venorians. I'm beginning to believe that their honesty makes for healthier relationships. No wonder divorce is unheard of here.

I'm distracted from my musings by the arrival of someone new. A tall young Venorian, perhaps in his mid-twenties, strides confidently into the room. He is greeted by the ever-cheerful Senlor and then he touches foreheads with Flidar. She lifts a hand, gently summoning me to their side. When I get close, she says, "Martha, I would like to introduce you to Senjar. His parents, now deceased, were very dear friends of mine."

Senjar steps forward, looking into my eyes, then giving me the customary greeting. As our foreheads touch, I sense curiosity, kindness, warmth. I step back with a smile. "It's a pleasure to meet you, Senjar."

He returns my smile, but then it disappears as his eyes focus on something. I follow his gaze to see him staring at my pendant. He reaches a hand to touch it. "Where did you get this?" he asks, a little abruptly.

I'm a little taken aback by his rudeness, but answer his question. "It's a family heirloom. It once belonged to my great-grandfather."

He looks at me strangely. "What was his name, your great-grandfather?"

Well really. Does he need to know this? However, good manners compel me to answer. "His name was Elijah Vane."

"Lijah," I hear him murmur. Then he composes his features and smiles. "Your great-grandfather had good taste. It is a very beautiful piece."

"Thank you."

He makes an effort to change the subject. "And are you enjoying your stay in Ven so far?"

"Very much so…" We continue to make banal chitchat, although I notice him looking at me surreptitiously throughout the rest of the evening. I push away the discomfort of his gaze and focus my attention on the others.

Dinner is a happy, convivial affair. It's amazing that I come from a planet light years away and yet I feel, after only a few days, right at home here.

CHAPTER 12

Martha

Early the next morning, I come down to the living area feeling a little anxious. My new job starts today.

As part of my life swap with Treylor, I also have to exchange jobs with her. She's a researcher at the Venorian Institute for the Advancement of Science. Now, I'm no scientist, but the people in charge of the exchange program have arranged for me to teach English as an optional class for the undergraduate students there. For her part, Treylor will be joining my old high school and teaching Venorian to the students there—the fact that I resigned from that job being conveniently overlooked by the powers that be.

I greet Flidar, who is sitting at the dining table, sipping a hot cup of *joh*.

"Good morning."

She smiles. "Good morning, Martha. You are looking well."

"Thank you. I feel well rested."

She pours me a cup of *joh*, then passes me a pale pink box with a pretty bow at the top.

"What's this?" I ask, a little puzzled.

"It came this morning from Shanbri. He baked cakes for you."

"He bakes?"

She laughs. "Oh yes! He is very gifted at food preparation."

I open the box eagerly and find a beautifully presented little oval cake with cute looking pink icing. Next to it is a swirly-shaped pastry with some kind of red jelly topping on it. It all looks amazing and—taking a sniff—smells delicious. I admire this offering for a moment longer, but then my hunger takes over. I pick up the cake and bite into it, not sure what to expect.

Oh. My. God. So good. I moan in delight as I cram another bite into my mouth. The cake is light and moist, its sweetness offset by the lemony-tasting icing. I take another delicious bite. Who would have thought it? That large muscle-packed man is a wizard in the kitchen.

Flidar watches me in amusement as I finish my mouthful of cake and say on a happy sigh, "This is fantastic." Then, I remember my manners. "I'm sorry. I forgot to offer you some. Would you like to try this lovely looking pastry?"

She smiles as she shakes her head. "No, my dear. This is all for you. Enjoy."

I sip on my *joh* before picking up the pastry. If anything, it tastes even better than the cake, the crust wonderfully flaky, the red jelly on it sweet and tart all at once. It's made of dria berries, I realize—maybe those same berries he picked at the market yesterday. I'm suddenly overcome. That gorgeous, sweet man made all this for me. I touch a hand to my heart, feeling it flutter.

Flidar observes me, her gaze full of understanding. "Shanbri is a wonderful man," she says, "and he obviously is very taken with you. But Martha, do not forget of what we spoke last rotation."

And just like that, my high comes down a notch or two.

"I won't. I have to thank him though. Will you excuse me while I go up to speak to him?"

"Of course."

I sprint up to my room and take out my communicator. Sitting myself comfortably on the bed, I call Shanbri. He answers straight away.

"Martha, good morning to you."

"Good morning Shanbri, and thank you so much for the cakes. They were amazing!"

Shanbri beams at me in pleasure. There's the sound of laughter and then a face appears behind him. The man—presumably another somar—grins at me and says, "Our Shanbri woke up extra early to make them just for you. Then he spent an age decorating the box to please you. What magic spell have you put on my friend?"

A flustered Shanbri shoos him away. "Enough Dovtar, leave us in peace." His friend chuckles and does as instructed.

Face flushed, I mumble, "I don't know what to say. I'm so flattered, but you didn't have to go to all that trouble."

Shanbri fixes me with his brilliant dark eyes. "Yes, Martha, I did, but it was no trouble. On the contrary. It brings me great pleasure to craft a food offering for you. Please know that I will send you a gift every morning from now on."

Is he for real? One quick gaze into his eyes and I know he's sincere. My heart can't seem to stop fluttering. With an effort, I try to inject some rationality into the conversation. "That is so sweet of you Shanbri, but really, there's no need."

"Perhaps not, but, Martha, please do not deny me this. I want to bring you a gift of joy every morning. You do not know how much it means to me that you start each rotation with a smile as you think of me."

Oh, my beating heart. "Thanks Shanbri," I breathe. "I shall treasure every offering."

We talk for a while longer. He asks me about my plans for the day and I tell him about starting my new job today. "I'm a little nervous," I say.

He smiles encouragingly. "I am sure you will be fine. You have planned your lessons, yes?"

"Yes, but I'm not sure how well they will go down."

"I imagine the students will be very excited to meet a person from another planet, and they will have many questions for you about Earth. Do not worry too much about it. I am certain it will turn out fine."

"I hope so. Anyway, enough about me. Tell me about what's ahead for you today."

So, he tells me a little of what he'll be doing. First, he'll be sparring with Fionbal—that muscular body of his requires daily workouts to maintain—and then he'll be assisting Krantor on a detective mission to find out why some unfriendly aliens have been flying in a zone of space called the Utar belt, which apparently, they're not allowed to enter. I'm fascinated to hear the inside track on the political goings on of this planet.

Eventually, we reluctantly end our call. In a slight panic, I look at the time and grab my purse. I have to get to work.

Thankfully, the journey to the Institute takes no more than ten minutes in the drone, and I manage to arrive without being grievously late on my first day. I'm met by an officious looking Venorian female who introduces herself as Mivsar. She shows me around the place and gives me my schedule. The Institute is a lovely period building set in large ochre-colored bricks, with high vaulted ceilings on the inside. Walking through the endless corridors, I'm grateful for the map I've been given—painstakingly transliterated into English for me.

We get to the room I've been allocated. Mivsar opens the door and politely invites me to enter ahead of her. After a few more instructions and a reiteration that I should contact her if I need anything further, she takes her leave. Alone in my new domain, I look around. It's a cosy space, dominated by a large desk and one of those fabulous Venorian chairs that adapt ergonomically to your body, ensuring maximum comfort and support.

I sit myself down on the desk chair and test it out. *Very nice.* I swivel it round and gaze out the window. Below me is an open space, with picnic benches and resting pods for the students to hang out in during their leisure time. I spend some time observing the young Venorians in their natural habitat. Two girls are sitting under the shade of a tree, kissing passionately. A young, nerdish looking male Venorian is sipping on a hot beverage while he reads something from his communicator. Another group of students are chatting animatedly and laughing. I smile. It seems, young people have similar pursuits whatever world they're in.

I glance at the time. My first class is in half an hour. Just enough time to settle in and try to ease the nervous flutters in my stomach. I log in to the system, as instructed by Mivsar, and load my lesson slides. Then it's time to go. As I get to my feet, a message arrives on my communicator from Shanbri.

Shanbri: Break a leg.

Me: Thanks. Where did you pick that up?

Shanbri: Krantor was just on a call with your ambassador from Mars, and I gathered the courage to ask her what is best to say in your language when you want to wish someone good luck. She said, "Break a leg". Was it right?

Me: Yes, Shanbri. I'm so touched, thank you.

Shanbri: Although you know, you will not need luck because you will be fantastic no matter what.

Me: You say all the right things mister.

Shanbri: I mean them. Go now, I will not hold you up any longer. I will call this evening to ask how it went.

Me: Thanks :-)

Shanbri: What is the meaning of these symbols?

Me: Look closely. It's a smiley face.

Shanbri: :-)

Grinning, I head out the door. Using my map, I navigate my way to the lecture theater, only getting lost twice and making it there with five minutes to spare. I consider that a win. The room is empty, so I go to the computer console and set up. A moment later, the door opens, and a set of students walk in. They observe me curiously, then go to find seats right at the back. I suppress a smile. Some things never change.

CHAPTER 13

Krantorven

The information elicited from the Klixians has thrown little light on what the Saraxians are up to. Father interrogated them using his special mind reading skills. It turns out they were telling the truth about their ship experiencing technical faults. They had been due to rendez-vous with the Saraxian ship in Sector 8, but the sensors on their ship broke down and they ended up in Sector 5 instead, and much too late for their meet up with the Saraxians.

It is still not clear why the Saraxians wanted to link up with the Klixians, and why they arranged to do so in the Utar belt. All the Klixians could tell us was that they were to meet the Saraxian ship at the appointed time with a shipment of boral crystals which they had procured from Krovatia using underhanded methods. We confiscated the crystals and sent the Klixians on their way.

Having spent some time with Rivvol finetuning our defense strategy, there was nothing further for us to do but return to Ven. Since then, my somars and I have been racking our brains trying to work out the boral crystals connection. Why would the Saraxians need them?

The crystals are plentiful on Krovatia, but because of their importance to the spiritual beliefs of its inhabitants, they are not traded with outsiders. In fact, I have never myself come across them before, although they are well known in Krovatia and used for prayer in all their temples. That's about all I know, but we are making it our business to learn more.

This morning, we are all sitting in a circle in our work quarters, the boral crystals we confiscated from the Klixians laid on the table before us. We have debated the possible reasons why the Saraxians might want them. Our latest theory is that they plan to pass them off as vlor stones, and sell them to unwitting customers at a profit. The crystals glow a pretty pink color, though not as deep a pink or purple as our vlor. To the untrained eye, however, they could be mistaken for our own precious stone.

Nevertheless, I think we should investigate a little further. There is a renowned scientist called Hontar who works at the Institute for the Advancement of Science. I believe it is best to let him make a thorough forensic analysis of the crystals before we return them to the Krovatians. I want to know everything we possibly can about them.

I yawn and stretch lazily. My sparring earlier this morning must have worn me out. Getting to my feet, I conclude things. "Good. Then it is decided. Please could one of you take the crystals to Hontar."

At this Shanbri sits up. "I will go!" he announces.

"Thank you, Shanbri mine."

I am unsurprised that it is him who has volunteered. Dear, precious Shanbri—always wanting to serve.

He stands and gathers the crystals up into a pouch. "If there is nothing more, I will take them right away."

"Please do, Shanbri, and then you may take the rest of the rotation to provision and prepare our meals. Dovtar and Fionbal, please continue your work on our security upgrades." I smile tenderly at the giant somar next to me. "Prilor mine, let us attend to the meetings we have scheduled."

CHAPTER 14

Shanbri

I have been staring blankly at the boral crystals in front of me, my mind elsewhere, as it has been for the last three rotations since I met Martha. Love is a curious thing. It makes your entire world shift on its axis. Your mind becomes preoccupied with thoughts of your loved one. What is she doing right now? How is she getting along in her new job? Are her lessons going well? Did she enjoy the cake I baked her this morning? Thoughts of her make my heart beat with added excitement and joy.

I hear Krantor say he wants to send the crystals to a scientist at the Institute for the Advancement of Science to do some further investigation on them.

The Institute for the Advancement of Science?

I shake myself out of my stupor and sit up. "I will go!" I say quickly before anyone else. I collect the crystals into a pouch and stand to go. Krantor very kindly gives me the rest of the rotation off to provision and prepare our meals. *Perfect.*

First, I slip into the food preparation area and put together a basket of food. As I'm placing a freshly baked loaf of *kroot* in the basket, Dovtar comes up behind me.

"I am guessing there is a reason for your eagerness to make the journey to the Institute— something to do with the Earth female. Am I right?"

I do not answer straight away. Carefully packing my basket, I eventually reply, "I am most eager to be useful to my kran, Dovtar, but I will also take this opportunity to check in on Martha."

"And have a picnic lunch with her?" he asks wryly.

"We must all eat a lunch repast, so why not do it together?"

"Naturally."

He places a hand on my shoulder and kisses my cheek. "Enjoy your repast with her Shanbri, but please have a care of your heart. I do not wish to see you get hurt."

I stroke a hand to his cheek. "Thank you, Dovtar. I am afraid it is much too late for that. She has already captured my heart."

He squeezes my shoulder. Through our contact, I sense his emotions. *Concern, sadness, worry.* I place a hand over his on my shoulder and murmur, "Love hurts, but it also brings much joy, Dovtar. Let us focus on the joy right now and not worry about the future."

He nods his head, kisses me once more, then goes back to his work with Fionbal. I finish preparing the basket, and a few moments later, climb aboard our drone.

I arrive at the Institute a short while later and make my way to the administration office. At my knock, a female sitting at her work console looks up at me enquiringly.

"Greetings. I am Shanbri, son of Molbri, and somar to Krantorven."

"Welcome, Shanbri. How may I be of assistance to you?"

"I am looking for a scientist named Hontar, with whom I have business to conclude on behalf of my kran."

"Of course. You will find Hontar in his laboratory on the second floor of the building. I will send you the directions." She taps her console and sends a map of the building to my communicator.

"There is one other thing," I say.

"Yes?"

"I also need to visit Martha, the Earth female. Is she teaching a class right now? If so, in which part of the building?"

She taps away at her console to check. "Yes indeed, Martha Reynolds is teaching a class, which has only just begun. It is taking place in lecture hall 5 on the third floor."

"Thank you for your help. I appreciate it greatly."

"It is my privilege."

I take my leave of her and quickly find my way to the laboratory, wanting to get my business done and out of the way. I hand over the boral crystals to Hontar, explaining what we require of him, then bound up the steps to the third floor, looking for lecture hall 5. I find it without too much difficulty and open the door quietly, not wanting to disturb the flow of her lesson. I slip into an empty seat by the door and observe.

Martha is standing at the front, showing slides with images of her home planet. The picture behind her shows two humans holding hands, the female wearing a long white garment and the male dressed in a black suit. Martha speaks in a formal, teacherly tone, which I immediately find very sexy and alluring. "When two people want to make a commitment to each other, they have a wedding ceremony, something similar to your mating on Ven. We have different traditions across our planet, but in my culture, the female—also known as the bride—wears a white gown. Something like this."

Someone puts their hand up to ask, "What does the ceremony involve?"

"It involves the saying of vows in the presence of witnesses and the exchange of rings. After that, the two people become a married couple. The female is known as the wife and the male as her husband."

The lesson continues as I watch Martha explain further aspects of her culture and field questions from the students. She does this with an air of competence and confidence that belies the nerves she was feeling beforehand. I listen in fascination, hungry for as much knowledge about her and her world as possible.

Finally, the lesson comes to an end. Most of the students file out of the lecture theater, though a few hover around her, wanting to ask more questions. For a while, I watch her patiently address their queries, but then I stand and make my way down to her.

She catches sight of me, and my heart gladdens at the look of pleasure on her face. "Shanbri! What a lovely surprise."

I smile at her and hold up my basket of goodies. "I have come to take you out for a lunch repast." Addressing the remaining students in her vicinity, I say, "Perhaps you could save your questions for another time."

They nod and smile, walking off to leave the two of us alone. I put my basket down and step close to Martha, placing a hand on her cheek for the customary greeting. She brings her hand to my own cheek, and we touch foreheads. I read her emotions. *Happiness, excitement, desire*. I am not alone in feeling the way I do.

We pull apart, gazing into each other's eyes. "Where shall we go?" she asks.

"We can take a walk in the gardens of the Institute, and I am sure we can find a peaceful spot for us to have our repast."

"That sounds like a good idea," she smiles, picking up her communicator. "Let's go."

I guide her out, saying, "I much enjoyed listening to your lesson and learning about the customs of your people, Martha. You are a good teacher."

"Thanks, Shanbri, but I'm not so sure about that. This is all new to me, you know. I haven't taught adults before; my old job was working in a school. Add to that the fact that I'm from a totally different planet..."

"Well, from what I saw, you are doing just fine."

"How long were you there? I didn't hear you come in."

"I arrived shortly after the start of your lesson but did not want to disturb you, so I sat to one side and listened. I found it interesting that despite our planets being light years apart, there are still so many things we have in common."

"Yes, I've been struck by that too! Although of course, there are differences as well."

"That is what makes it so interesting—finding the commonalities and the areas of divergence."

By now, we have reached the gardens, and I steer Martha towards a bank of trees overlooking a large, picturesque pond. "How about we sit over here in the shade of the trees?" I ask.

"That sounds good."

I take out the blanket I had tucked into the basket and lay it out on the soft green grass at the foot of a tree. Taking off my sandals, I place them carefully on the edge of the blanket, and Martha follows suit. She goes to sit at the other end, but I stop her. "Why do you sit there, so far from me?"

She regards me, puzzled. "Where else do you propose I sit?"

I lower myself to the ground with my back against the trunk of the tree, spreading my legs wide. "Come sit here and lean your back on me," I say, pointing to the space between my legs. She seems undecided, so I add. "I want to feed you with my own hands, sweet Martha."

She approaches me hesitantly. "Is that a Venorian custom?"

I chuckle. "Well, we do very much like physical contact, so yes it is in a way a custom. But more than that, I want to hold you. Will you let me?"

She nods shyly, settling herself down between my legs. I envelop her in my arms, holding her close to me. I am struck by just how right it feels to hold her like this. I bury my nose in the fragrance of her hair, breathing her in. Her thoughts fly at me. *Oh so right. We shouldn't.*

"Why should we not?" I say out loud.

"The day I met you, I had a conversation with Flidar. I asked her what it means to be a somar and she explained."

"I see."

"It sounds like an impressive job… but it also made me a little wary."

"Martha, I have never had a single regret about becoming Krantor's somar. Not until I met you."

I feel her heart quicken at my words, but then she says, "So, I know there is this attraction between us, but it would be wrong to pursue it."

I sigh, running a gentle hand down her arm. "I understand. But please, do not shut the door on me completely. While you are here on Ven, consider me your friend."

"I do, Shanbri."

"Good. If you are ever in need of anything, come to me. Please."

"I will."

She rests her head against me in silence for a few perfect moments. All is right with the world when she is in my arms. I hold my precious love, never wanting to let her go.

I know the exact instant when she senses the hardening of my cock. I may have agreed to only being her friend, but my body has other ideas. I take a deep breath in and try to control my arousal. I do not succeed.

"We said, just friends."

"I know, and I will abide by your wishes, Martha. However, I cannot stop my body from being attracted to you. Please try to ignore it while I feed you."

I delve into the basket and pull out the loaf of *kroot*, breaking it in half. "Have you tried *kroot* before?" I ask.

"Hmm, yes. I love it."

"Try this one I baked just this morning."

I pass it to her and watch her savor each bite. Once she is done, I take other items out from my basket, feeding them to her one by one. I feel such happiness at her sighs of pleasure as she tastes the food I prepared for her. Feeding the people I love is something I have always enjoyed. Martha picks up on the thought. "You're such a great cook. Did you never think about pursuing it as a career?"

"I did. My secret desire was to apprentice in culinary school."

"Secret? Why couldn't you?"

"My life path was mapped out for me before I was even born. You see, I come from a distinguished line of people who have served the Tor family. My grandfather was somar to the current Kran's father. That makes me the Kran's nephew through the maternal line, and Krantor's cousin. It was always expected that I would become one of his somars."

"Oh. Was it not possible to just decide not to follow that path?"

I breathe in deeply, remembering that time. "Yes, it was. The Kran was aware of my wishes and gave me the option to follow my own desires."

She stirs against me, turning to look into my eyes. "So, why didn't you?"

"It would have meant disappointing Krantor. I could not do that."

I sense her unease. "Do you love him that much?"

"I do love him very much, but that is not the only reason why I chose to dedicate my life to him."

"What other reasons are there?"

"It has to do with things that happened to me long ago. When I was five sun rotations old, I lost both my father and mother. Father was killed in battle during the last war with the Saraxians and mother, distraught at losing her mate, chose not to continue living. My uncle, the Kran, kindly took me in and raised me as his own."

"Oh Shanbri. I'm so sorry. That must have been hard."

"It was a very difficult time, Martha, but I am grateful to the Kran and his mate. They gave me so much love and helped to ease the pain of my loss. And Krantor too. He and I are of the same age, and we became inseparable. When it came time for him to attend the military academy, there was no question I would go with him. We did everything together. I could not abandon him."

She snuggles into my arms, thinking through what I have said. Eventually, she murmurs, "I lost my parents too, but not in the same way as you. I was already an adult, in college, when it happened five years ago. They were killed in a drone accident."

"Oh Martha, I am so sorry. My heart hurts for you."

"The worst of it is, I blamed my grandparents. They wanted us to be together for a celebration called Thanksgiving, and Grandpa paid for my parents to fly out to see them on a new drone that was supposed to halve the time of travel. I didn't go with them because I'd already made plans to spend the holiday with my boyfriend. The last time I spoke to Dad was when he called me just before they left. I didn't have a good feeling about this drone, but I didn't say anything. I wish now I had."

"Oh my love." I kiss the top of her head and gather her close. "It is hard to live with regrets. If we look back on the past with the knowledge of the present, we always see things we could have done differently. But it is no use, for we cannot change the past."

"I know. It's taken me a long time to accept that. I went to see my grandparents just before coming out here, and we made our peace."

"I am glad for that."

Martha's communicator chimes and she picks it up. "I have to get back. I have another class in ten minutes."

"Of course." I hold her to me one final moment more, then help her up. With quick, efficient movements, I tidy everything up and place it back in the basket. "Come, let me escort you back."

Hand in hand, we walk towards the Institute. Once there, I kiss her goodbye. "I hope to see you again soon, Martha."

"I hope so too. Thank you so much for the lunch, Shanbri."

I smile, "My pleasure."

CHAPTER 15

Martha

The next few days pass in a whirl of activity as I settle into my new routine at the Institute. In addition to my new job, I've also signed up for lessons in Venorian with a tutor recommended by my hosts.

A date has finally been set for us five humans to be presented to the Kran in an official function at his palace. It's due to happen at the next gray full moon—which I've worked out is in a fortnight's time. The Venorians have two moons, a red one and a gray one, which they use to mark their calendar. It takes me a while to convert their dates into the format of days, weeks and months that I'm used to, but I'm getting there. I'm looking forward to finally meeting Shanbri's boss, Krantorven, and of course to meeting the head honcho, the actual Kran—especially after hearing so much about them.

As promised, Shanbri sends me a daily treat, each more delicious than the other. Every morning, I wake up excited, wondering what new delight is coming my way. Every bite I take has me falling further and further under his spell. Nevertheless, I'm sticking firm to my commitment to be just friends, even if my heart may be having other ideas. I am a sentient human being that can make rational and sensible choices.

A week after our picnic lunch finds me lying in bed, telling Shanbri about my day. "So, I had my first Venorian lesson today."

He grins. "Tell me something in my language."

Hesitantly, I enunciate, *"Mor ta noshli."*

I see him hide a smile. "And good evening to you, my sweet. You have very nearly got it right. It should be *mor ta nothshali*. Try again, please."

Unfortunately, my adult brain is not the knowledge sponge it used to be as a child, and I'm finding it difficult to get my head around the different sounds and intonations of the Venorian language. However, I try once more. "*Mor ta nothshali.*"

He beams. "That is it. Well done!"

I bask under his praise. We talk some more, then he gives me the good news. "Krantor has finally released Prilor to come visit his family next rotation. I shall accompany him."

"That's great news!" I enthuse.

Although they have been back for some time from their off planet mission, Krantor has kept them so busy that this is the first opportunity Prilor will have to see his parents. I know Flidar and Senlor will be excited to hear this news. I'm focusing on the fact that I'll be seeing Shanbri again. Of course, we're just friends, but I'm still allowed the simple pleasure of enjoying his presence in the flesh, appreciating his fine, fine form, and inhaling his delicious musk. There can be no harm in that surely.

They arrive promptly the following evening, and Prilor walks straight over to his mother, enfolding her in his arms. Shanbri holds a dish of cakes he has baked, but he puts it down so he can stride over to me. We greet each other as is customary. My hand trembles on his stubbly cheek, and then I press my forehead to his. *Heat, desire and—love?* I linger there a fraction longer than necessary, probing his mind again just to be sure. *Love. Oh.* There and then, my heart unfurls like a new leaf, and a warm feeling grows in my chest. Foreheads still together, I respond with the same emotions. *Heat, desire, love.* We step back, our burning gazes fixed on each other.

107

The moment is broken as Senlor approaches and greets Shanbri. I look up to find myself observed by Prilor. Stiffly, he comes forward to greet me. We touch foreheads and I sense caution, distrust, worry. I step back. "Prilor, it's good to finally meet you."

He nods his head but doesn't speak. "My people mean yours no harm," I burst out. "Treylor will be fine."

His eyes spark at this. "How can you be sure?" he asks in a gruff voice.

In truth, I can't be absolutely sure. I'm not privy to the decisions and discussions of the higher ups in my world, but we have no reason to want to pick a fight with the first alien civilization we have come across in our space explorations. It wouldn't make any sense.

As I'm in Ven, the planet of honesty, I respond, "I can't be sure. All I know is my own personal feelings and intentions. Before coming here, I too had my fears and suspicions about your people. But now, having gotten to know you a little better, I admire your people and your world. I want to learn from you and form a lasting friendship between us."

Shanbri places a hand on my arm. "Stop badgering her, Prilor. She is telling you the truth."

Senlor cuffs his son on the shoulder. "Of course she is. Be nice to my guest please, Prilor."

With perfect timing, Flidar comes in to call us to dinner. We move to sit around the large circular dining table, Shanbri to my right. All through the meal, I sense his presence and his barely suppressed desire. This friendship thing is really, really not going to work. I'm about to combust. Under cover of the table, he takes my hand and traces circles around my palm with his finger. I shiver in excitement. My core tightens, dripping my arousal into my panties. Whatever self-control I thought I had is well gone. I want him. To hell with the consequences.

I'm amazed that no one else can sense this maelstrom of emotions. I look across to Flidar, and find her observing us dispassionately. Yes, she knows, but she has already given me her advice and won't intervene further. If I insist on this foolishness, then it will be on my head. I squeeze Shanbri's hand and stand to make my excuses. Then I hurry up to my room and enter the attached bathroom. My flushed face stares back at me in the mirror. The eyes looking at me are wild, unfocused, undone.

My bathroom door opens, and I know who it is. I throw myself at Shanbri and then I'm kissing him like there is no tomorrow. He tastes like every forbidden sin in the universe. He tastes like perfection. My hands are buried in his silky hair as our tongues tangle and lap at each other. I hear his mind loud and clear, "*I need. I need.*"

My mind calls out the same response. Without unlocking our lips, we speak to each other. He knows and I know what we're about to do.

My hands frantic, I push down his pants and free his enormous cock. He bunches up my dress and rips my panties down my leg. His hand returns, cupping my pussy and feeling my wetness. Our lips are still on each other, drawn together like a magnet, unable to prise apart. Suddenly he's lifting me up as if I weigh no more than a feather—which I don't—and pressing me against the bathroom door. Frantically sucking on his tongue, I wrap my legs around him, opening myself up to his probing length. Then he's pushing inside, filling me up as I've never been filled before. I gasp into his mouth, but he doesn't let me go. In, in he goes, until he's buried to the hilt.

Impaled on his giant cock, I breathe deeply into his mouth. I hear his thoughts. "*Mine. So good. I need.*"

My mind responds, "*I need too.*"

That's all the green light he requires. He begins to fuck me hard against the door. My tongue against his, my legs wrapped around his hips, all I can do is hold him tight and feel. Oh God how much I feel as he buries himself deep inside me over and over again.

My core tightens. *"I'm about to come."*

His thoughts rush at me. *"Me too."*

Our lips still joined, we moan our release into each other's mouth. Spasm after spasm rips through me. He pulses within me for an eternity, drenching me with his cum. My gasps and moans are swallowed by his hungry mouth.

Finally, he stills inside me, his breaths still mingling with mine. I hear his mind, *"I never want to let you go."*

I telegraph my response, *"Me neither."*

We stay like this, clutched tight, mouths locked, his length still buried inside me. Eventually, reality intrudes. Everyone must be wondering where we have disappeared to. Reluctantly, he pulls his lips away and lets my legs drop to the floor. His softening cock slowly pulls out of me. As it does, a woosh of liquid drips down my leg. "Let me clean you," Shanbri says.

He finds a washcloth and wets it, then he kneels before me and carefully wipes me clean. He finishes his ministrations with a gentle kiss to my core. "You will be sore. I am sorry."

"I'm not!"

He stands, smiling sweetly. "I am not sorry for what we did, just sorry that you will hurt."

"It was worth the pain."

We straighten up our clothes, and I gaze at myself in the mirror, adjusting my hair and make-up. "It is no use, my heart. Everyone knows what we have done."

He's right. Deceptions are not possible in this society. Oh well. "Shall we go?" I ask.

He takes my hand. "Let us go."

We walk down the stairs together, my pussy throbbing. We find everyone sitting comfortably in the main room, sipping on warm *joh*. Their eyes scrutinize our joined hands, but they say nothing. Prilor wears his customary scowl. Quite clearly, he does not approve of his friend consorting with the enemy.

"Would you like some *joh*?" asks Flidar, ever the perfect host.

"Yes, please."

She pours us each a cup, and we sit next to each other, sipping the warming drink. Prilor glances at his communicator. "We must return. Krantor needs us." He stands.

Shanbri addresses him. "You go ahead to our transport. I will be with you shortly."

With a nod, Prilor walks out. Shanbri pulls me to standing and says his farewells to Senlor and Flidar. Taking my hand, he walks me to the front entrance of the house. His hands stroke my face lovingly. Once again, he seems to read my thoughts perfectly, as he answers my doubts. "It is done now, Martha. There is no going back, only forwards." He gazes deeply into my eyes. "I cannot promise you a future, but please know that my heart will always be yours. I would very much like if we can make the most of the time we have and be together as often as we can."

"Yes."

"I cannot always get away, but I will try to come to you as much as I can."

I touch his cheek. "Shanbri."

"I know. There is no need for words." He kisses me lightly. "Goodnight my love."

"Goodnight."

CHAPTER 16

Martha

I wake up a little later than usual the following morning. The soreness in my core reminds me of yesterday's events, as if I could ever forget. I have never had sex like that before, where both mind and body communed as one. I touch my aching pussy. I have never been filled quite like that before either.

Then comes an unwelcome thought. We didn't use any protection and I'm not on any birth control. Could a pregnancy be possible between our species? I try to remember where I am in my monthly cycle. My old communicator would have told me that information, but I had to leave it behind on Mars. We were not allowed to bring any of our technology to Ven with us. I do a mental count and sigh in relief. No, the likelihood of pregnancy is low. However, I shall have to sort out some birth control soon if we're to have regular sex.

I bathe, dress and go down to look for Flidar. I find her sitting at the dining table, sipping a hot drink of *joh*. "Good morning."

She raises her eyes and smiles. "Good morning."

I help myself to some *joh*, which I have grown to like, then I join her at the table. I take a few sips, not speaking straight away. Then, "So, quite clearly I didn't take your advice."

She looks at me in amusement. "Quite clearly not."

"I had every intention not to act on my desires, but then I couldn't stop myself."

"Martha, you had a choice and you made it."

"You're right. I have very poor self-control when it comes to Shanbri, so I've discovered."

"I hope for your sake your heart will not be hurt too badly."

113

"Oh, it will hurt, but I'm trying not to think about the future too much and just take things day by day."

"That is a good way to be sometimes."

I sip my drink some more. "There's something I need to ask. Is there a possibility of a pregnancy? I don't know if our species are compatible that way. I'm not on any birth control, so if there is a risk, I should see a doctor and get myself protected right away."

Flidar stares at me speechless.

"I seem to have shocked you. I apologize."

"I am not shocked, only surprised. Your species needs protection from pregnancy?"

"Yes of course. Isn't that the way for all species?"

"No, not with the Venorians."

"I don't understand. Clearly you have procreation between your males and your females. Surely a pregnancy will result unless they have protection?"

"No, it will not."

Now it's my turn to be speechless.

Seeing my confusion, Flidar explains. "As you know, what marks us out as a species is our ability to read minds, but that is not all we can do. We can also control our fertility through our minds. A pregnancy will only occur if both the male and the female consciously decide they want it to and instruct their bodies accordingly."

Huh.

"So how does it work? Is it something each person has to prepare their body for through meditation, or can it be a spur of the moment decision?"

"No preparation is required. During the sexual act, the person has to make a conscious decision to want a child. That thought is transmitted to the sexual partner and in that moment, he or she must decide if they want a child too. If the answer is yes, they make it known in their thoughts, and their bodies will respond by becoming fertile."

Wow. There is no end to the ingenuity of the Venorian race. Imagine that. Only having pregnancies when both partners spontaneously instruct their bodies to procreate.

"So, I guess there's no need for me to get on birth control."

"You will only get pregnant if Shanbri expressly wills his body to be fertile."

"Good to know."

I finish my drink and I'm about to pour another when the chime rings, indicating someone at the door. Flidar frowns. "Are you expecting someone?"

"No."

She stands and checks her communicator. "It is Senjar. I wonder why he is here." She presses the buzzer to let him in. A moment later, Senjar walks into the living area, his eyes finding us straight away.

Flidar approaches him with the standard greeting. "I was not expecting you," she says as she touches foreheads with him. She steps back with a frown.

Senjar turns to me, and it's my turn to greet him. *Worry, excitement, nerves.* "What is it Senjar?" I ask quietly.

"There is an important matter I wish to speak with you about, Martha."

"Is it the reason why you kept staring at me the other night?"

"Yes, it is that reason."

Flidar interjects. "Please have a seat Senjar, and explain yourself."

We all sit around the table again as Flidar pours a cup of *joh* for him.

"Last time I saw you Martha, you were wearing a piece of jewelry."

"Yes. It belonged to my great-grandfather."

Senjar takes a deep breath. "I recognized it immediately. I have seen it in photographs and videos of my ancestor's mating ceremony. My great-great-grandfather presented it to my great-great-grandmother as a mating gift. There are many pieces of jewelry with vlor gemstones out there, but this one is distinctive. The arrangement of the stones is in a pattern that spells our family name—Jar—in our language."

I look at him nonplussed. "That can't be right," I say, "because the pendant comes from Earth. I didn't purchase it in the market here. It's an heirloom that belonged to my family back home."

Senjar shakes his head. "No Martha, there can be no mistake. If you recall, I asked you your great-granfather's name and you said it was Elijah Vane. I have a great-uncle who was killed on an off-planet mission and his name was Laijar, or to give his name fully, Laijarven. It is the same name as your great-grandfather, but adjusted to fit your language."

My heart beats wildly. *Can it be? No!* "I'm sorry Senjar. It must be one of those strange coincidences one hears about, but you must know how impossible it is that my great-grandfather and your great-uncle are the same person."

"Believe me Martha, I had the exact same thoughts as you. How could it be possible? So, I decided to do some investigations into Laijar's death. It has taken me several rotations to dig through layer after layer of bureaucracy, but I discovered some important information that you may not be

116

aware of. Martha, our species have known about yours for many centuries. We did not make contact with humans because we determined that you were not technologically advanced enough. However, we kept an eye on your planet, checking for developments and waiting for the day when it would be appropriate to make contact."

Fucking unbelievable! Oh shit, what if it's true?

Senjar continues his tale. "Around eighty sun rotations ago, we noticed a strange occurrence on your planet. Our sensors told us that flight activity had ceased, with most of your airships grounded. Looking through the history records from your planet, I learned that around that time, there was a pandemic on Earth called Covid-19, and that your people's response was to stop human contact as far as possible and isolate in their homes. This now explains why air traffic ceased, but at the time, we did not know. We were curious about this development, so we decided to send a small mission to Earth to find out more. Laijar was on that mission, but he never made it back. It has always been presumed that he was killed there, but now we know that was not the case."

I put my face in my hands, shaken to my very foundations. If this is true, that would make me part-Venorian. Oh shit! Maybe that would explain why I can read minds just like them. But no! It can't be true.

I feel a gentle hand stroke my back. Flidar speaks softly in my ear. "Do not fear Martha. We will get to the bottom of this. It will be fine." She soothes my back with calming circular strokes, then addresses Senjar. "Pull up some photographs of Laijar on your communicator and show them to Martha. Perhaps she will recognize him."

I sit up as Senjar swipes his communicator a few times. He hands it to me. Looking at me from the screen is a man—a Venorian—who I indeed recognize. I've seen plenty of video footage of him at my parents' wedding and of him holding me as a baby. It's him, no doubt.

"It is your great-grandfather, is it not?" asks Senjar.

I nod. "Yes, it is."

"We can also do a genetic test on you Martha to fully confirm the truth, if you are willing."

"Yes, I need to know for sure."

Senjar smiles approvingly. "I have taken the liberty to arrange this test, if you will come with me now."

I hesitate. "Could I ask one of my colleagues, Diego Sanchez, to come along too? He is a geneticist, and I would greatly appreciate his input."

"Of course."

I pull out my communicator and contact Diego. His face immediately appears on the screen. "Martha, everything alright?"

"Yes, I'm fine, but something has come up and I'd like it if you could come over to check on some genetic tests that are going to be done on me."

Diego looks puzzled, but says, "Sure, no problem."

"I'll send you the coordinates straight away. Can you get there as soon as you can?"

"Of course."

I end the connection and without my asking, Senjar sends the coordinates to Diego. Flidar is also busy on her communicator. I hear Shanbri's worried voice. "What is it Flidar? Is all well with Martha?"

She turns the screen towards me, so he can see me. I smile. "I'm well, but something has happened that could be important. Can you get away just for a short while?"

Eyes serious, Shanbri responds immediately, "I will come."

Flidar interjects. "Not to my house Shanbri. Senjar will send you the coordinates. We are going to have Martha genetically tested."

I sense Shanbri's confusion, but he simply nods his head and ends the connection. Senjar stands. "Shall we?"

We all troop into Senjar's transport, and within minutes, we arrive at our destination, a graceful building on the edge of the downtown area. Diego is already there, waiting, and as we walk up the ornate steps to the main door, I hear a woosh as Shanbri's drone lands behind us. Moments later, his arms are wrapped around me. No words are exchanged, but his mind transmits comfort, worry, love.

Senjar leads the way into the clinic, where we are met by a gray-haired female Venorian wearing white. Senjar introduces us. "This is Mivtal, who will conduct the tests."

Mivtal smiles. "Please, follow me."

She leads me to a couch and gestures for me to lie down. Shanbri sits by me, holding my hand in his while Mivtal takes out a tube with a sharp needle at its end, similar to what we have on Earth for taking blood tests. She smiles kindly. "This will only hurt a little," she says.

Shanbri squeezes my hand, but I say, "That's fine. I've had blood tests before."

With nimble fingers, Mivtal takes my arm and pricks the needle on the inside of my elbow. Seconds later, a red flow of blood rises up into the tube. It doesn't take long. Within moments, she's removing the tube and pressing a small pad on the wound. "I will need some time to analyze your blood. Senjal, I will also need a sample of your blood for comparison."

He nods his head in agreement and takes the space on the couch which I've vacated. Shanbri draws me close. "Come, let us sit in the next room and you can tell me what is going on."

We walk out to the adjoining room, where Flidar awaits us. She calmly offers me a drink, and I sip the refreshing *ploh*. While I drink, Flidar fills Shanbri in on the latest developments. He sits close to me, stroking my arm gently as he listens.

"It is making sense," he finally says. "The way you can read minds like Venorians. Your height, which is not usual for Earth females, I think. Also your eyes. They are the same color as Senjar's. The Jar family are known for that distinctive eye color."

"If it is true, that would only make me an eighth Venorian. Surely, that should have diluted a lot of those Venorian traits?"

Gabriel, who has joined us in the room, shakes his head. "Not necessarily. Not if the Venorian gene is the dominant one, as seems to be the case here. Even if you are only an eighth Venorian, that eighth is more dominant than the rest of your human genes. It explains a lot of what has perplexed me about your telepathic abilities."

"Grandma must have known. She gave me that pendant for a reason. Why did she never tell me?"

Gabriel snorts. "What, that you were partly alien? That would have sounded crazy, especially in those days before we made first contact."

"But even after, and when she knew I'd applied to the exchange program, she never said a thing."

He shrugs. "A long-buried secret like that is hard to disclose. She gave you the pendant, knowing it would be recognized over here and you would find out the truth."

Shanbri kisses the top of my head. "This is good news, my heart. It means you have kin on this planet. Perhaps even a reason to stay."

Senjar, leaning against the door he has just come through, laughs. "You do have kin, and they will be very keen to meet you once I tell them the news, especially my great-grandfather—that would make him your great-uncle."

I look up at him. "He's still alive?"

"Alive and well. He lives on the family farm just outside the city. The Jar family are farmers going back many generations."

Now it's my turn to laugh. "And great grandpa continued that tradition on Earth. He owned a ranch in Colorado, which he passed down to my grandma."

We're interrupted by Mivtal entering the room. She addresses me directly. "My analysis is complete, Martha. The tests confirm that you are indeed a genetic relation to Senjar. You have distinct Venorian genes, which are combined very interestingly with your human genes. Perhaps you would like to see?"

I'm reeling in shock, but I manage to nod and follow her to her lab, where she has the analysis projected on to a large screen. I listen to Mivtal going through her findings, pointing things out on the screen, but most of the technicalities go over my head. All I can think about is that I am part-Venorian, and I have family here. Shanbri holds me close, nuzzling my hair.

After a while, when there is a lull in the discussion, I ask, "What does this mean for me?"

Gabriel replies, "For all intents and purposes, it means you are genetically a Venorian, as that gene trumps all the other human ones you have. You're in perfect health, so quite clearly, the mingling of human and Venorian genes has done you no harm. In terms of what it means for you, well, I think most of it will be psychological rather than physical. You're going to have

121

to adjust the way you think about yourself, and it may take some time for you to accept these changes. It helps that you found out about this here on Ven, and not on Earth. I suggest you take time to visit your new family and get to know them. You may also want to start some therapy sessions with Dimitri. As a psychologist, this is his area of expertise. I'm sure he can help you come to terms with all of this. I'll contact him and fill him in on what's happened."

Flidar adds, in her soothing calm voice, "We will give you all the help you need to adjust, Martha. Gabriel's advice is sound. Take time to explore this new reality, and we will support you as best we can."

I nod, overwhelmed, and unable to speak. Shanbri, still holding me close, reads my thoughts and acts as my mouthpiece. "She is very grateful to all of you for your kind advice and support. But now, she needs a little time alone to come to terms with this news. I will take her back home."

Shanbri guides me out of the room, making our farewells. In a daze, I let him lead me to his transport. In seconds, we're up in the air and on our way back to the house. We don't speak—at least not in words. In our thoughts, he sends me love and comfort.

Once back in my bedroom, he strips us both naked and gets us into bed. I cling to him, revelling in the feel of my naked skin on his. He holds me to him, stroking his hands all over my body, gentling me. I feel his great erection nudging my abdomen, but he makes no move to ease his sexual tension. I'm glad. Apart from the fact that my pussy is still sore from yesterday's exertions, I'm too emotional right now for sex. I need his soothing touch to help me calm the churning sea of my thoughts.

He strokes me for an endless time, and slowly, I feel myself return to an even keel. I kiss the firm wall of his chest and nestle my head there, idly stroking his skin and the soft blond hair that covers him.

Eventually, he speaks. "Now that I know you are Venorian, I wish more than ever that I had not committed myself to being Krantor's somar. If I were free, I would make you mine—but it is too late for that. Now all I can hope for is that Krantor does not find his mate for a very long time."

I sigh and echo his thoughts.

CHAPTER 17

Krantorven

After our stint patrolling the Utar belt, we are finally catching up on some of our official duties here on Ven. Tonight, we will be holding a function to welcome the five humans that have come to our planet as part of the exchange program. My mind recalls that delicious looking Earth girl, Martha, and my cock twitches in anticipation. Fionbal, who is cleaning my body in the bathing pool, looks up at me, his eyebrows raised. I smile. "No, it is not your gentle touch doing this to me, Fionbal mine. I am just thinking about the beautiful Earth woman, Martha, who we shall be meeting tonight. Prilor and I have designs upon her, do we not my love?"

Prilor shrugs uncomfortably. "I am not sure that is a good idea, my kran. She has become very close to my mother, like a daughter to her, and it would not feel right for me to seduce her."

I am surprised. He had seemed extremely aroused when I had voiced my dirty thoughts about her that day when I fucked him hard. Something is going on that he is not telling me. He will—when I have him alone—for Prilor keeps no secrets from me.

I sense some tension in the bathing pool. Looking around at my somars, I see where it is coming from. Shanbri. He has been acting a little strange lately. I must speak to him and get to the bottom of this mystery. But not now, for we have to be at the banquet hall very soon to welcome our guests.

I stand, allowing Fionbal to dry my body. My cock is still standing to attention. Fionbal looks at it hungrily. "Would you like me to pleasure you my kran?" he asks hopefully.

I look at Shanbri. "It is a long time Shanbri since you have tasted my nectar. Would you like to do the honors?"

Shanbri lowers his eyes. "I thank you my kran, but I see that Fionbal is very much wishing to drink from you. I would not take that pleasure away from him."

How like Shanbri to put others' needs before him, but there is something else I can sense too. My determination to get to the bottom of this goes up a notch. "Very well, Fionbal, please go ahead."

Fionbal needs no second invitation. Quickly, he kneels before me and takes my cock deep into his mouth. I push gently until I am all the way inside, the tip of my shaft dipping into his throat. He takes it, breathing through his nose. Then I start to fuck him, watching him struggle to take me in, but never giving up on his duty, like the good somar he is. His eyes stare at me with devotion as I extract my pleasure from him. Ah, it feels so good. It is not long before I come, gushing my sweet nectar into his welcoming mouth. Fionbal swallows me down, his face transformed in ecstasy. At the same time, Prilor puts his lips to Fionbal's cock, giving it only a few sucks so that he too spurts his pleasure. Sated, we all go to dress and get ourselves ready for the function tonight.

◆◆◆

The palace is a vast sprawling set of interconnected buildings in the heart of downtown Torbreg. It is a mixture of private quarters and official spaces such as the banquet hall where tonight's event will be taking place.

When I returned from the military academy, a fully-grown Venorian with four somars, I was granted my own quarters in the palace. The space we inhabit includes all our sleeping rooms, our living and working areas, the extra-large bathing room—large enough to fit myself, my somars and my eventual mate—and the food preparation area, where Shanbri reigns.

Presently, we make our way along a winding corridor towards the official spaces located in the central section of the palace. On the other side of the banquet hall lie another set of corridors, one leading to the guest quarters where visitors to the palace are invited to stay, and another leading to my father's private quarters, which was also my home until I became an adult. My sister Sonlar still has her own chamber there, which she uses whenever she is in town.

When we arrive, the banquet hall is thrumming with the buzz of happy chatter from the guests, a selection of the highest-ranking officials on the planet and representatives from our oldest and most noble families. Father sits beside mother, decked out in his splendid purple gown which he wears for such occasions. I sit to one side, surrounded by my beloved somars.

The humans arrive, and one by one, they give the customary greeting to my father and mother. Father addresses them in a speech expressing our welcome and our hopes for a fruitful exchange of information between our peoples. However, I pay little attention to what he is saying, for my eyes are on Martha.

She is exceptionally beautiful tonight, in a gray gown that mirrors the stormy silver of her eyes. Oh yes, we are going to fuck her, Prilor and I. He will have to get over whatever scruples are holding him back. She is too delicious to forgo. I smile in anticipation of that pleasure.

Then the speeches are over, and the humans come over to greet me. I touch cheeks and foreheads with them, as is expected, but it is the last one, Martha, whom I am most interested to read. She steps towards me, and our eyes meet. My heartbeat picks up speed and I feel my face flush with heat. I am dimly aware that my cock is standing stiff.

Then I place my hand on her cheek and nearly cry out at the scorching heat of her. She gazes at me in surprise before placing her hand to my cheek and I sense instantly that she feels the same hot heat I do. We stare at each other, cheeks flushed, the palms of our hands burning. Then we bring our foreheads

126

together. An explosion of sensation. Heat, arousal, possession. *Mine, mine, mine.*

I step back abruptly, breaking the contact. My breaths are coming short and choppy. It cannot be. Surely it cannot be. A human! My mate cannot be a human. The universe has made a mistake; played a silly joke on me. I glare at her, my face like thunder. Then with all the regal imperiousness at my command, I turn away and dismiss her.

I hear whispers as the humans are led away to meet with other dignitaries, but I tune them out. Prilor places a hand on my arm. "My kran?"

"Not now Prilor," I say through gritted teeth. Forcing deep breaths in and out, I turn to face my somars. Shanbri is eyeing me with a wrathful expression on his face. I have no time for whatever petty grievance is making him cross. Not right now.

Gathering up all the composure I can summon, I say, "Let us circulate and speak with our guests." I walk towards a group of Venorians standing before me, smiling amiably at them. With all the skills honed over many sun rotations of doing my duty as the Kran's heir, I make my rounds, listening and responding to the various people I meet. I studiously avoid the humans, not daring to allow myself close contact with that female again. In fact, I consider the possibility of banishing her from my planet and sending her back to where she belongs.

Next to me, I feel Shanbri and Prilor stewing. One for an unknown reason, the other because he has picked up on my distress, but I ignore them and keep going, smiling and playing the good host. Of course, the people I greet sense that all is not well, but they are too polite to speak of it. On and on I continue with the social niceties until finally, it is over, and people begin to take their leave. From the corner of my eye, I see the humans make their way out of the banquet hall. She looks up and for an instant, our eyes meet again. Hers looking hurt and confused.

Mine probably still looking enraged. From across the room, I read her thoughts clearly. *"Why?"*

I transmit back. *"Just go."* Head bowed, she complies, turning to leave the room. I sigh in relief as I watch her go.

The crowds thin out as more and more guests start to leave. I see father walk towards me. Once he gets close enough to speak, he grits out, "In my quarters, all of you. Now!" He turns to go, and we follow him.

He strides towards his quarters, Dranlar opening the door for us as we approach. Once we are inside, he shuts it behind us and father turns to face me, his expression grim. I begin to speak but he holds his hand up to silence me, and I feel him probe my mind. He stays focused on me for several moments, then lets out a breath. "So that is it. You have found your mate."

"No! It cannot be father." I start to pace the room. "She is a human. No kran has ever mated with another species. It must be a trick. Maybe they are in cahoots with the Saraxians."

"It is no trick Krantor. She is your mate."

"How could that possibly be?"

Father glances at Shanbri, who, if possible, is looking even more furious than before. His hands are fists at his side, his face set in a growl. "Tell him Shanbri."

He takes angry breaths in and out, trying to calm himself before he manages to spit out, "She has Venorian blood. She is a descendant of Laijarven who went missing on Earth eighty sun rotations ago."

I reel back in shock. "How do you know? Why did no one tell me? And why the fuck are you so angry?"

He does not respond, but continues to stare at me, his breaths heaving. It is Prilor who speaks and surprises me. "Because he has fallen in love with her."

128

CHAPTER 18

Shanbri

For the first time in my life, today I have felt real anger towards my beloved Krantor. In the bathing pool, when he talked about seducing my Martha, I very nearly punched him. And then the way he rudely cut Martha during their introduction made me want to hurl ten thousand insults at him. All this anger, however, is nothing compared to what I am feeling now.

My Martha is his fated mate. She is his to take. Why, why does the universe play these cruel games? Have I angered Lir in some way that I am being paid back so painfully? My Martha, now his. I want to scream. She is mine!

And so, when Krantor demands to know why I am so angry with him, I cannot speak. I can only transmit my fury through my eyes and thoughts. It is Prilor who reveals the truth to him. "Because he has fallen in love with her."

Krantor looks at me uncomprehendingly for a few moments, then sinks down on the couch, his face in his hands. I sense Dovtar behind me. He places a calming hand on my shoulder. It says, "Hold back. Do not say anything to your kran that you will regret." I heed my friend's thoughts and maintain my silence.

Finally, Krantor looks up at me. "Shanbri, I am so sorry. I did not know."

I incline my head, but still do not speak.

Krantor addresses his father. "What now?"

The Kran replies, "She must be told. All this must be explained to her."

Krantor glances at me. "What about Shanbri?" he asks.

My uncle regards us with a hard expression that I have not seen on him since we got into trouble for placing itching powder on our annoying history tutor's undergarments. "This is not about Shanbri," he says firmly. "This concerns our planet and its future. We are only given one fated mate in our lifetime, Krantor. Do not let her slip through your fingers. Do I need to explain to you that without a mate our line is finished, and you can never gain the powers necessary to fulfil your role as the Kran?"

Krantor looks down at his hands. "No," he mutters.

"Good. Then you must use all your powers to convince Martha to agree to mate with you. She must come to you willingly. Nothing, and I mean nothing, is more important than this right now." This last, he says with a stern look at me. "Tomorrow, send Prilor to bring her to the palace. Explain everything to her, then seduce her as only you can do. The mating bond will ensure that she is extremely attracted to you. I could sense the sizzling heat between you from across the room tonight."

Pain lances through me. The Kran focuses his gaze on me. "Once she arrives, ensure your somars are out of the way. Neither Prilor nor Shanbri can be close by as you and she explore your mating bond. I do not care what your hearts tell you. The mating bond takes priority over any love attachment that any of you feel. Do I make myself clear?"

We all nod.

"Good. Now everyone leave except for Shanbri. I need have words with him."

Krantor glances at me ruefully but follows his father's instructions. They all walk out of the room while I stare in silence at the Kran.

He comes over to me, sighing heavily. "Shanbri, sit yourself down. Let us talk."

I sit on the couch and the Kran lowers himself beside me. "Shanbri, I am going to speak to you now as your loving uncle, not as your kran."

I nod, my eyes glistening as he continues. "Beside my mate and my son, I love you more than anyone in this world. Believe me when I say I want your happiness. But right now, you are letting your jealousy of Krantor cloud your judgement."

"How so, uncle?"

"Just think, Shanbri. If you love Martha, then what is the only way that you can be with her?"

I sigh as the truth begins to sink in. "That's right, Shanbri. Only as Krantor's mate can Martha also be yours. It will be a compromise as you will have to share her with him, and with the other somars. Ask yourself this. Would you prefer not having her in your life at all, or having her but not entirely to yourself? I know it is a hard truth to swallow when one is in the throes of young love, as I see you evidently are. Sometimes we cannot have what we want in its entirety, but we can have enough to make us content."

"You are right uncle, but it hurts."

He runs a gentle hand along my arm. "I know. It will hurt less in time. But for now, my beloved son, I must ask you to step back and keep your distance from Martha. I could sense how strong her feelings are for you, and having you around her during this time will cause her more conflict and distress. Stand aside and let Krantor become her mate. Give me your word, Shanbri."

I swallow the painful lump in my throat. "I promise," I say hoarsely.

CHAPTER 19

Martha

I'm agitated on the journey back to the house, reflecting on the strange happenings of the evening. There is no way I could be mistaken. Krantor was angry with me, and he wanted me to leave. But why? What did I do wrong?

Could it have something to do with the sensations I felt when we touched for our greeting? That inexplicable burning heat and that intense physical desire? I feel shame now as I remember how I drenched my panties on contact with him. He's an extraordinarily beautiful man, but that's no excuse. What kind of person does that make me, that I can betray Shanbri so easily?

And Shanbri too was angry. I saw the fury in his eyes. Does he know about my shameful reaction to his kran? Did he somehow sense, standing so close by, that I very nearly had an orgasm at Krantor's touch? God, this all so fucked up.

My transport drops me in front of the house, and I let myself in using the code Flidar gave me. Up in my room, I kick off my shoes and drop down on the bed. Should I call Shanbri? I hate feeling distance from him. I pick up my communicator, but just as I'm about to call, it buzzes with an incoming message from him.

Shanbri: My heart, I am not angry with you, just at fate. Tomorrow, Prilor will be coming to fetch you for a meeting with Krantor. All will be explained to you then. For now, I must keep away from you—on the Kran's orders. But please remember that I love you now and always.

I press the button to call him, but he rejects the call. Instead, he sends another message.

Shanbri: Please darling no. I cannot speak with you, and I must keep away for now. You will understand soon. Goodnight.

Me: Did I do something wrong?

Shanbri: No my dear. You have done nothing wrong. Goodbye for now.

I throw down my communicator, frustration eating at me. What in the heck is going on? Why would Krantor want to see me when he so clearly wanted me to go earlier on? Nothing makes sense. Why did I feel such intense physical attraction for him? Is that a normal reaction to meeting a kran? Or just something to do with me? All will be explained tomorrow, but dammit, I want to know now!

With a huff, I stand and take my dress off, then get ready for bed. It's a very long time though before I get to sleep.

◆◆◆

Prilor arrives early in the morning, just as I'm pouring my fist cup of *joh*. His mother looks up in pleased surprise. "Prilor my dear. This is an unexpected delight."

He comes over to embrace Flidar. "It is always a pleasure to see you mother. However, this is not a visit. I am here on Krantor's orders to take Martha to him." He looks at me stiffly. "Martha, are you ready to go?"

"Am I in trouble?" I ask.

"No, of course not. Krantor would like to see you urgently."

I gulp down my drink and place it on the counter. "Alright. I'm ready." I bid a frowning Flidar farewell and follow Prilor to the door. He opens it and ushers me out to his waiting transport. I try again once we are out the door. "Can you tell me what this is about?"

Prilor purses his lips. "I cannot. Please, let us go."

He refuses to talk or even look at me throughout the journey to the palace. Once there, he takes me through a set of corridors to a different section of the palace, presumably Krantor's private quarters. We enter a pleasantly furnished, brightly lit room, and he motions for me to sit down on the circular couch. Unlike human couches, which are mainly designed for people to sit and watch a big screen, Venorian couches are massive ring-shaped receptacles that you can sink your entire body into. They're designed for resting—I've had many a peaceful nap on Senlor and Flidar's couch, often with them beside me—and for socializing with others while in a state of deep relaxation. I don't know how relaxed I can be though, in my current predicament.

I take off my shoes, as custom dictates, and ease my body on to the couch, feeling it adjust to my shape and enclose me comfortingly. Prilor disappears down the hall and I wait, full of anxiety despite his and Shanbri's insistence that I'm not in trouble. Something is going on, that's for sure.

I'm not kept waiting long. I hear light footsteps and look up to see Krantor entering the room. I get to my feet awkwardly, not knowing what kind of reception he's going to give me. Will he still be mad at me?

He comes to stand before me, and stares into my eyes. I feel myself flushing and my heart pounding. Hesitantly, he comes forward and places a careful hand to my cheek. He removes it almost instantly, as if scorched. "Holy Lir!" he exclaims. Then, he touches my cheek again, keeping his hand there this time. I follow suit, placing my hand on his cheek. I feel an instant burn of heat. I look at him in confusion, but he simply brings his forehead forwards to touch mine. A kaleidoscope of sensation assails me. Arousal so intense, my core throbs; my heart pumping like a bullet, the ricochets pounding in my ear. And his voice repeating over and over in my head, "*Mine.*"

We step apart, breathless. "Wh–what's happening?" I stammer.

He stares at me. "I have just met my mate," he says.

"What?"

"You are my mate."

The pounding in my head is reaching a crescendo, making me dizzy. I whisper, "I don't understand."

He takes my hand and presses it to his groin. *What the fuck?* His massive erection juts against my fingers, rock solid and hot. "This is what one touch from you does to me. And I do the same to you. If I put my hand to your cunt, it will be soaking wet, will it not?"

I gasp in shock and pull my hand away from his raging hard on as if burnt, but my face betrays me. He gives a satisfied smile. "You are wet for me Martha."

I take a deep breath. "What is this? Some magic voodoo a kran can do to unsuspecting females?"

"It is the mating bond, and it is just with you that this happens, nobody else."

"I don't understand."

He sighs. "Please sit, Martha. I will explain."

I climb back on to the couch and he lowers himself beside me, but not too close. He's silent, choosing his words. Finally, he says, "There is something that only happens in the male line of my family. Each of us has a mate destined for us. We do not know who it is until we meet her. On first contact, our senses tell us we have met our mate. It is that hot sensation we felt on touching each other, the pounding heart, the intense attraction, the feeling of possessiveness. I have never felt this with anybody else Martha, only you. You are my destined mate."

"Why does this happen? What does it mean?"

135

He shrugs. "I do not know why fate sends each Tor male a mate. I simply know it for a fact. Once we are bonded as mates, things change between us. We become as one. Our minds meld, joining together all our memories. We will be able to read each other's thoughts, even when apart. There will be no secrets between us. I will know everything you know, and you will know everything I know. It is a unique bond not experienced by ordinary Venorians, only by the males in my family. But not only this. By mating, I unleash my full telepathic abilities. I will be able to read in detail the thoughts of all individuals around me—and so will you. It is because of this gift that my family has been given the responsibility of being the krans of our planet."

"This is madness Krantor. I can't be your mate."

"Yes, you can. You are mine."

I shake my head impatiently. "You don't understand. I'm in love with someone else. I can't join my life to you, no matter what impossibly crazy reaction I have when I'm near you."

"You love Shanbri."

I gaze at him, shocked. "You know?"

He nods. "You and Shanbri are in love with each other, just as I am in love with Prilor."

"Then you see how impossible this is."

"No, it is not impossible. It is the way it will be. We will be mated and share a bond with each other for the rest of our lives. We will love each other—how can we not when we will be part of one another? But we can also love others. By loving you Martha, I will not love my precious Prilor any less. Your loving me will not take away any of your feelings for Shanbri. It can, and it will work, I promise."

This is all just too much and too crazy to contemplate. Someone please wake me up from this bizarre rabbit hole I've fallen into. I pinch myself hard on the arm, and Krantor looks at me in confusion. "Why did you do that?"

"To see if I'm dreaming."

He laughs, genuinely amused. "It is true enough, Martha."

"So, you think we can all live together as one happy family, do you? Let me tell you, in my world we have a saying. Two's company, three's a crowd. I can't even begin to imagine what four would be."

"Well to be accurate, it would be six because of Dovtar and Fionbal."

I give my head an ironic slap. "Of course! How could I forget there are four somars. So, you expect me to have a relationship with each of them too?"

He smiles smugly. "One big happy family, Martha."

I can't help but laugh at the ludicrousness of it all. Then I turn serious again.

"So how would this work? Fill me in on the logistics of how you see this big happy family functioning. Would I sleep with you, or with Shanbri, the man I love?"

He lifts his head and eyes me imperiously. "I am the kran, so of course as my mate you will share my bed." A pause. "But also, we will share it with Prilor. I cannot sleep without him."

I eye him right back. "Would I share my body with him as well as my bed?"

"Naturally. He will be your mate too." He gives a wicked smile. "In fact, we had been planning to fuck you together, even before I found out who you were. We saw you on the ship with Treylor, and we wanted you."

I take a sharp intake of breath, aroused despite myself. "And what about Shanbri? Where does that leave him?"

He thinks for a moment. "We can come to an arrangement. Maybe you can sleep in his bed every full red and gray moon."

So basically, I get to be alone with my love twice a month. I snort. "Lucky him!"

He fails to hear my sarcasm. "Yes, he will be very lucky to have the woman he loves in his bed."

"And what if I say no, and refuse to be your mate?"

His face becomes serious. "I cannot force you to mate with me, Martha. You must do it willingly. However, I want you to understand that your decision has repercussions for everyone on this planet. I have only one fated mate—it is you. If I do not mate with you, then the Tor line comes to an end, and I do not become the Kran after my father dies. I would not have the special abilities required to fulfil the role. This planet would be left without a leader."

"Oh, so no pressure then."

"The stakes are extremely high, Martha. But the rewards are high too. Just think. As the Kran's mate, you would lead this planet with me, a position of immense power and privilege. You would gain incredible abilities. Imagine being able to communicate with me through our minds across galaxies. Imagine being able to read the minds of the people you meet and know exactly what they are thinking. You would share a bed with two virile men who would make it their mission to pleasure your body to ecstasy each and every night. You will have the man you love near you and share his bed from time to time. And there are another two men who will be devoted to you, serving you as they serve me. Will you really turn your back on all this?"

I have no answer for that.

Krantor moves closer to me on the couch and his nearness sends my pulse racing. "Your body does not lie, Martha," he breathes. "I can feel your response. You ache for me. One touch of my finger and your cunt will spasm in release. Shall we see?"

He slides his hand into my pants, skilfully finding his way under my panties to my achingly wet core. One tap of his finger to my clit, and I explode, my core pulsing over and over again. A moan escapes my lips. As the spasms subside, he brings his face close to mine. "Just think what pleasure I can bring you, Martha mine," he murmurs. Then he removes his hand from my pussy and brings his wet finger up to his lips, licking my essence clean. His eyes close on a moan as he tastes me. "So good." He opens them and gazes at me intently. "You were made for me, Martha."

I'm powerless to respond. I simply gaze back at him entranced. After a while, he pulls away, and I regain my ability to think.

"I need time to think this over," I say.

He inclines his head.

"And I want to speak to Shanbri. I won't make a decision without him."

He hesitates, then nods his head once again. "I will send him to you now." He stands and walks out of the room.

CHAPTER 20

Shanbri

I find Martha lying on her side with her head in her hands. On hearing my footsteps, she looks up.

"I can smell him on you," I say gruffly.

She looks stricken. "I'm so sorry Shanbri. Something happens to me when he gets close. I can't control it."

I huff out a frustrated breath and come to recline beside her. "Do not apologize. It is the mating bond doing this to you. There is nothing anyone can do about it."

"Are you mad at me?"

"Never!"

I reach out and place my hand on her cheek. She touches mine, and then we bring our foreheads together. *Love, confusion, worry.* "Do not worry, my heart. It will be fine," I tell her as we pull apart.

"How can you say that Shanbri? It's all fucked up!"

My Martha has a way with words.

I sigh. "You are right, it is fucked up as you say, but… it is what it is. We cannot change the way things are."

"You sound remarkably calm if I may say so."

I laugh, unamused. "You should have seen me last night. I was hissing with fury. Then the Kran spoke to me and made me see things a little more clearly."

"What should I do, Shanbri?"

"I cannot make that decision for you, Martha. It has to be yours."

"But tell me, what do you want me to do?"

"It is not about what I want. I cannot have what I desire. I want you as my mate, not his."

"It's what I want too."

I draw her close to me and heave a long, sad breath. "It is not to be, my love."

"So, what's Plan B?"

I gaze at her, puzzled. She smiles at my confusion. "Sorry, these translator chips work so well that I sometimes forget we're speaking a different language. Plan B is a term for the backup plan, what you do if you can't go for your preferred option."

"I see. Plan B is that you mate with Krantor."

She stares at me, hurt in her eyes. "You'd be ok with me pledging myself to another man?"

"I cannot contemplate it without feeling great pain, but it is the only solution."

"What about if I refuse to mate with him, and we continue our relationship as we have now?"

I shake my head sadly. "That would not work for many reasons. Firstly, once it is widely known that you rejected Krantor as a mate, you will be shunned in Venorian society. You would have to return to Earth, where you would find yourself also spurned for having Venorian blood—and we would be galaxies apart from each other. There are no easy roads to follow, my darling heart."

I take her hand and place it on my chest. "There are other reasons too. Think about what will happen to this planet and to our people if Krantor is unable to mate. It is unthinkable. It could lead to much civil strife that would weaken us and make us vulnerable to our enemies. And there is one more thing. The intense physical reaction you feel in Krantor's presence will only get stronger the longer you two go unmated. There is no getting away from the mating bond. It is something more powerful than any of us."

She thinks about this for a long time, then she says, "Krantor expects me to share a bed with him and Prilor once we're mated. However, he says he'll allow me to sleep with you on the nights of the full moons."

"That is generous of him. As your mate, he could demand that you be with him every night."

She snorts. "That doesn't feel generous to me! And then there's the matter of the other somars. It's expected I'll have relations with them too. You don't know how hard this is for me to get my head around. In my culture, people are exclusive. Polyamory is rare."

I stroke her hair comfortingly. "In my culture too. My father did not share my mother with anybody else. This situation is unique to the Kran's family. It is a long-established tradition here that krans have four somars who they are intimate with. When you mate with Krantor, you will also be mating with the four of us. In fact, we will be saying vows to each other in the ceremony."

She looks at me surprised. "You mean I'll be exchanging vows with you too?"

I smile. "Yes, my heart."

"Oh."

Then her look of wonder disappears. "That means I'll also be exchanging vows with Dovtar and Fionbal, who I hardly know."

"You will have time to get to know them before the ceremony. Believe me when I say you will grow to love them as I do. They are the very best of men. And I promise they will love you devotedly too."

"You're close to them?"

"Very close. In fact, I sleep to Dovtar's snores in my ear every night."

She frowns, and I sense her jealousy. "No Martha, please do not feel like this. We Venorians rarely sleep alone. We like the warmth of Venorian contact when we sleep at night. Dovtar is my closest friend, and I have shared his bed for years. I love him dearly, but not in the way I love you."

"But you have sex with him?"

"Sometimes I do. We are men with sexual needs. Who else would we turn to but the people who are closest to us to relieve such needs?"

"So, on the nights I would be sharing your bed, Dovtar would be there too?"

"No my heart. If you wish it, Dovtar can bed in Fionbal's chamber on those nights. Perhaps it is selfish of me, but I would like to have you just to myself whenever it is possible."

Martha nuzzles into my neck. "That's what I want too," she says on a sigh. We hold each other close, inhaling the rich, sustaining fragrance of the other. After a while, she shifts and huffs in frustration, "God this is all so fucking crazy. I don't know if I can go through with any of this."

"Take some time to adjust. You do not need to decide right away. I know there have been so many changes in your life lately. Why not see the other human, Dimitri, and talk things through with him to get a different perspective." I pause. "In the meantime, I am to keep my distance from you. The Kran has been very clear on this. Spend the next moon rotation getting to know Krantor better, and his other somars. Think and reflect about which path you wish to take for your future. And although I will not see or talk to you, know that my thoughts will constantly be with you."

She stares at me, her eyes bright with impending tears. I lean forward, intending to gently kiss her lips in goodbye. The moment we touch, those intentions shatter into a million pieces. She parts her lips, and I cannot stop myself from plunging my tongue into the warm delight of her mouth. We lick and suck each other's essence hungrily.

"*I love you. I need you.*" I read her thoughts loud and clear as our mouths devour each other.

My mind responds, "*I love you too. You are all I want.*"

Her tongue clings to mine. My hands in her hair pull her closer to me, even as I transmit, "*I have to go.*"

She bites my bottom lip. "*Not yet.*"

I bite her lip in return. "*I must.*" I suck her stinging lip, then withdraw my mouth with a light pop. I force myself to pull away and stand. "Goodbye my love," I breathe softly. Then I quickly walk out of the room before I can change my mind.

CHAPTER 21

Martha

"So, you see what a fucked-up situation this is."

I'm lying on a makeshift therapist's couch in Dimitri's living room, having just told him of my impossible dilemma. I'm not convinced he can do much to help me out, but it did feel good to unburden myself to a fellow human. He takes a moment now to consider, steepling his fingers in the good old-fashioned way therapists do.

"It is certainly a unique situation I have not come across before, but we may still approach it the way we would other problems we face on Earth. The mistake many people make, Martha, and which causes them unhappiness in the long run, is to believe that there are only binary choices to make in life—yes or no, friend or foe, stay or go. Life is more complex than that and the decisions we make are usually based on a choice of three rather than two possible outcomes, as expounded in Wakeford's Theory of Three, if you've heard of it. It was penned by a 21st century theorist, so a little before our time. It argues that in most cases our choice lies in deciding which two out of three outcomes are the most important to us. As Meatloaf, a 20th century artist I like to quote, once said, 'Two out of three ain't bad.' Let us apply this theory to your problem and decide what your two out of three desirable outcomes are."

I'm doubtful about all this, but I'll play along. "Ok, shoot."

"Your first desirable outcome: you want to be with the man you love. Am I right?"

"Yes, I definitely want that."

"Your second desirable outcome: you want to be accepted for who you are and loved. Am I still on the right track?"

I shrug. "I guess so. Now that I know I'm part-Venorian, it explains a lot about why I've sometimes felt out of place back on Earth. I think people there will struggle to understand and accept me once they know I have alien blood and I'm telepathic. I don't want to be on the outside of the circle, so yes, it's important for me to feel accepted and loved for who I am."

Dimitri smiles. "And rightly so. Whatever decision you make will have to take that into account."

"So, what's the third desirable outcome?"

"The third outcome is this: you want to be in an exclusive relationship."

I laugh. "Don't we all?"

"Not necessarily, but I see it in your case. You don't want to be in a threesome or a quad, or even a sextuple. You want to be a couple, just the two of you."

I sigh. "Yeah."

"So now, we come to the hard part. You can't have all three of these outcomes, so which two of these are most important to you?" He ticks them off on his finger. "Be with Shanbri. Be accepted and loved. Be in an exclusive relationship."

"Well, I can't have one and three. I can't be with Shanbri and have an exclusive relationship with him."

"No, not here on Ven. I don't know the ins and outs of his vow to Krantor, but it seems to be a binding contract, so in order for him to commit to you exclusively, he would have to break his vow and possibly leave his home planet. Admittedly, not one of your most viable options."

"So that only leaves me with one and two. Be with Shanbri, be accepted and loved, but not be exclusive."

"That is one possibility, yes, but you have missed out another."

"Such as?"

"You could go for two and three. Be accepted and loved and be in an exclusive relationship, but be with someone else, either here on Ven or back on Earth—someone you have yet to meet perhaps. You talk of going back to Earth as if you'll be an outcast because of your Venorian heritage, but it could also open up some interesting doors for you there. Who knows who you might meet as a result of having been on this exchange program? I guess what I'm saying is this. If it's that important for you to be exclusive, maybe you should start looking elsewhere and not at Shanbri or Krantor."

I'm quiet as I digest this. I've fallen so deep under Shanbri's spell that it's easy to forget I've only known him for a few weeks. I hadn't even taken into account the possibility that he might not be the one for me, that there could be another love out there in my future. Or maybe someone from my past. I think of Ameer and that one night of passion we had on Mars. It pales in comparison with what I've experienced here on Ven with Shanbri. No, my future does not lie with Ameer, of that I'm sure. How about someone I've yet to meet? My heart squeezes painfully at the idea of moving on from Shanbri, but it's something I must consider.

Choices, choices, choices.

I sigh. "Thanks Dimitri. You've given me fresh perspective. I'm going to need to sleep on it and reflect."

He smiles. "Good idea."

I stand to go, and he walks me to the door. He looks at me sympathetically and says, "You have difficult decisions ahead Martha. I really don't envy you. Just remember though, you still have choices. And whatever you decide, we'll all support you."

I kiss his cheek. "Thanks Dimitri, you've been a good friend."

The following morning, I'm woken early by a call from Krantor. He smiles winningly at me on the screen and says, "Good morning, my mate."

Yawning sleepily, I mutter, "Not your mate yet, remember?"

He grins. "Only a matter of time, Martha. And how are you this morning?"

I eye him grumpily. "Sleepy."

"I see you are not a morning person."

"Correct. I like my sleep and I could have had fifteen minutes more had you not woken me up."

He looks genuinely contrite. "Then indeed I am sorry." He turns to his somar beside him. "Prilor, remind me the correct time to call Martha in future." He returns his gaze to me. "Now that you are awake, perhaps we can make use of those fifteen minutes by talking. I want us to get to know each other better."

I shrug. "What shall we talk about?"

He ponders the question. "Hmm. I do not want to ask the standard kind of questions. I want to get to the heart of what makes you, you."

I wait while he thinks. "Let me see. Ah, yes. Martha, what is the thing you value most in a person?"

After my experience with Trent, I don't have to think about this one. "Two things. Honesty and loyalty. I hate lies and I don't want someone who will jump ship the moment things get rough."

He nods in understanding. "Well, honesty is a given in our society, as it is practically impossible for mates to keep secrets from one another. You will know everything about me, Martha, and have access to all my thoughts. If I am annoyed about something, you will know it straight away. I hope this will be a welcome change to what you have experienced with your fellow humans on Earth."

"I hope so too. I had a bad break up with my ex just before coming here, and it has made it difficult for me to trust."

"What did he do, if I may ask?"

"Behind my back, he applied for a job as a leader at the school where I worked, knowing it would cause a conflict of interest between him being my boss and him being my partner. He planned to dump me if he got the job, which he did. He went from telling me he loved me one day, and the following asking me to leave our home."

Krantor is indignant on my behalf. Even Prilor is scowling. "The scheming lowlife! What a piece of scum! If I ever get my hands on him—"

I put my hands up. "No need Krantor, it's all past history. I've moved on. I just wanted you to understand why loyalty and honesty really matter to me."

He glares at me. "What is this unfortunate person's name?"

I snort. "What's the point in telling you? He's light years away on Earth."

"The point, my dearest Martha, is that your honor demands he pay restitution for the wrong he did to you. When we visit Earth, as I am sure we will in due course, I will personally handle this matter."

"What do you propose to do? You have no jurisdiction on Earth."

He smiles devilishly. "I have my ways. Never fear, I will make sure justice is served on the scoundrel."

I smile back, charmed despite myself. It's nice to have a knight in shining armor come to the rescue every now and then.

"In any case," Krantor goes on, "I will find out his name once our minds meld. I will know all that you know. Rest assured the matter will be dealt with. Hmm, I look forward to finding out all the juicy details of your past life, Martha. You interest me greatly."

"Yeah? Well it works both ways. I will get to know all the juicy details about you too! And I bet there's far more interesting stuff in your past than in mine."

He looks amused and exchanges glances with Prilor. "Well, I have not lived the life of a holy person, so there will be quite a few, shall we say racy episodes in my life that you will find out about."

I grin. "I can't wait."

His smile widens. "I do believe, Martha mine, that you have just admitted you will become my mate."

"I have not!"

"Well, you just said you cannot wait to find out all the racy details of my past—which you will when we mate."

Oh. I did.

"Never mind, forget I said that."

He tries not to look smug but fails. "If you insist, Martha mine."

"Well, our fifteen minutes are up. I have to get going."

"Very well. I wish you a pleasant day, Martha. Expect my call tomorrow morning—at the correct time."

"Bye now."

"Goodbye."

Two weeks go by, and I'm still undecided about whether or not to mate with Krantor. I speak to him every day now, our calls replacing the daily conversations I had got used to having with Shanbri.

As promised, Shanbri has kept away, though he continues to send me fresh cakes and pastries every morning. They're his love letters, each one different and meticulously made, telling me in ways other than words just how much I mean to him. I treasure them. *God, I miss him.* I rub my aching heart and try not to dwell.

By mutual consent, I've not met Krantor in person again. The physical pull of our mating bond is just too strong to allow me to think clearly in his presence. I've chosen to get to know him at a distance, through our communicators. Prilor is usually there when we speak—I've begun to think of him as Krantor's shadow. The gruff giant is warming towards me, though I still detect a touch of possessiveness at the idea of him having to share his precious kran with me.

In our call today, I'm telling Krantor about my impending visit to meet Poljar, my great uncle, at the family's farming estate. Senjar has broken the news to him about what happened to his brother, my great grandfather Elijah. He's very keen to meet me, and I him.

Krantor smiles. "I hear the Jar estate is magnificent. They grow a vast variety of staple crops as well as breed grivs."

"Grivs?"

"Ah, not an animal you have back on your home planet. Prilor will send you a picture of a griv so you know what it looks like. It is a large four-legged animal which our ancestors used to ride to get from place to place. Of course, now we have transport drones, so we only ride grivs for pleasure."

"I see. A little bit like the horses we have back home. I loved riding them at my grandma's ranch."

151

"Then I'm sure you will love to ride a griv. There is also something else. Grivs have two massive wings on each side, so not only can you ride them, but you can also fly on them."

"Fly them? Oh wow."

Krantor smirks proudly. "I do not wish to belittle your home planet Martha, but from the sounds of it, what we have here on Ven is infinitely superior."

I try to hide my amusement. As befits a person of his exalted social stature—a person who is waited on hand and foot— Krantor has a tendency to be arrogant. I've come to see that it's not necessarily his nature to be so, but just a trait that has developed as a result of the circumstances of his life. Digging under the regal imperiousness and arrogance, I've seen glimpses of a genuinely caring and loving man. I see it most when he looks at Prilor. Those two are so in love. It makes me wonder, uncomfortably, what place I could carve out in their lives. It's yet another thing that makes me hesitate about this proposed arrangement.

On screen, Krantor is smiling wryly. "I feel you mock me, Martha."

"Me? No!"

He chuckles. "Very well. I will make a deal with you. Go to your great uncle's farm and ride a griv. Then when you return, tell me truthfully whether or not it's infinitely superior to riding one of your horses from Earth."

"And if I do?"

His gaze turns heated. "Then, my love, you will have to pay a forfeit."

"What kind of forfeit?"

"The mating bond has deprived me of the chance to be with you in person, but I'm still craving you, Martha. So, this is the forfeit I propose. Next time we speak, and you admit a griv is superior to a horse, I want you naked on your bed. I want to watch you pleasure yourself."

My heart pounds in excitement and guilt. *What about Shanbri?* Krantor reads me like an open book. "Martha, if we are to be mates, I will become intimate with every part of your body and your mind. There will be no barriers between us. Shanbri has accepted this—or he will come to accept this in time. Show us your beautiful naked form and how you pleasure yourself. It is but a small part of what we shall do once we are mated."

I think quickly. He's right. This would be a taste of what's ahead of me if I agree to become his mate. If I can't even go through with this, then I might as well pack up my bags and return to Earth.

"I have two conditions," I say.

"Name them."

"No word of this is to reach Shanbri. It would hurt him too much."

"Agreed."

"I want the both of you naked as well, and I want to see the both of you pleasure yourselves too."

A wicked smile springs to Krantor's lips. Even Prilor is grinning. "You have yourself a deal." He pauses. "Another thing. I would like Fionbal and Dovtar to escort you on your trip tomorrow. It will put my mind at rest to have them protecting you, and it will be a chance for you to get to know them."

"Why would I need protection? Am I not safe?"

"You are safe, and I do not want you fearful. However, rumors are flying about town that you are my fated mate. As a future kran's mate, your safety has become a top priority. You will perhaps not have noticed, but I have had you followed by some of my security officers since the night we met."

"Oh. I didn't know."

"Do not worry. I will send Fionbal and Dovtar to you first thing tomorrow with the delivery of Shanbri's cakes."

"You know about that?" He raises his brows. "Of course you do."

"Goodnight, Martha mine."

"Not yours yet. Goodnight."

Dovtar and Fionbal arrive promptly the following morning as I'm sipping a cup of *joh*. Both are tall, powerfully built and impossibly handsome—I have yet to meet a Venorian that isn't attractive. Maybe it's to do with the way they mate, sharing the best of each other's characteristics. Does that filter out the less attractive traits? I need to remember to pick Gabriel's geneticist brain about this one day.

Dovtar is lean, darker skinned than the rest, with thickly lashed almond-shaped eyes the color of melted caramel. He's reserved, talking very little. On touching foreheads, I sense warmth, curiosity, attraction. I can't help remembering that he's the one who sleeps beside Shanbri each night and feel a pang of jealousy. As we step away from each other, his eyes narrow. Oh shit. He knows. Damn this stupid telepathic link.

Fionbal seems to be the more outgoing of the four somars, with curly brown hair and bright green eyes that twinkle with humor. I like him immensely on sight. We touch foreheads next and again, I sense curiosity, attraction, warmth. As I step back from him, he produces a beautifully wrapped box—Shanbri's gift. I take it with a smile and open it eagerly. Today's offering from my lover is a fluted cake a dark shade of plum with swirls of multicolored icing. Shanbri's art is not just in crafting delicious cakes but also in making them so pleasing to the eye. Next to the cake is a pastry in the shape of knot, sprinkled with Venorian nuts.

I pick up the cake first and take a bite. Oh my! Could this be the best one yet? Moist and velvety, the flavor of it is somewhere between chocolate and coffee, and something else uniquely Venorian. I moan in pleasure as I finish it. Shanbri is a fucking genius. I wish I could tell him, but he's been strictly incommunicado since the last time I saw him at the palace. I pick up the pastry and bite into its nutty, flaky goodness. Mmm, yes. So good. I gobble it up, my eyes dreamy as I think of Shanbri making it for me. As I'm chewing the last bite, I sense eyes on me and look up. Both Dovtar and Fionbal are unashamedly staring. What? Have they never seen a woman enjoy her food?

"In my world, it's rude to stare," I say with a hint of snark.

Dovtar looks contrite. "I am sorry to make you uncomfortable. I could not help it. You looked so happy." He smiles reassuringly. "I will pass the message on to Shanbri that his food offering was well received."

I nod. "Please do. Tell him I treasure his gifts immensely."

"I will. I know he is eager to hear news of you. He misses you greatly."

My eyes well. "I miss him too." Oh *fuck, fuck, fuck*. I'm about to cry. I try to hold the tears at bay as Dovtar and Fionbal's gazes turn worried. I blink and fan my eyes. "I'm fine," I say, voice wobbling dangerously.

Suddenly, I find two strong pairs of arms wrapped around me like a sandwich. Dovtar holds my face to his broad chest while Fionbal nuzzles my back, raining soft kisses on the top of my head. The kindness is my undoing. I begin to cry in earnest as both men soothe me with their hands and their thoughts. *"Martha, please don't cry."*

"Martha, you will see him again soon."

"We care about you, sweet, sweet Martha."

155

Wrapped in the warmth of their embrace, I finally bring my tears under control. We stay like this for some time, nobody moving to let go. I feel... cherished. Is this how it will be to be mated to Krantor and his somars?

Dovtar intercepts my thought and responds, "Yes, Martha. We will cherish you. I promise."

I finally pull away and wipe my face with the back of my sleeve. Dovtar's eyes are warm and bright as they gaze down on me. I feel silly now for my jealousy earlier. I smile shakily. "Thank you, both of you."

"No thanks are necessary. Would you like to go refresh yourself before we leave?"

I nod. "Give me a minute; I'll be right back."

A short while later, they escort me to their transport and we're on our way to my ancestral home. The journey takes just under an hour. We fly over the colorful roofs of the city until we reach the outer edges of Torbreg, leaving it behind. The drone swoops gracefully over undulating hills and a small forest nestled at the foot of a mountain—Mt Tormas—named unsurprisingly after the Kran's revered family. Beyond the mountain, we fly over a valley covered in a wide expanse of cultivated fields, though I couldn't tell you the name of the crops I see. Finally, we begin our descent, and that's when I catch sight of a large, magnificent looking house.

It stands proudly in three distinct, zigzagging blocks, each a slightly different shade of peach. The house is three tall stories high, with large domed windows framed in a dark russet color—the color of the earth. Beyond the house I see a familiar set of outbuildings, much like what we have at Grandma's ranch, but bigger. My heart pounds in anticipation as we land with a gentle thud a moment later.

Dovtar jumps out of the drone first, looking around before holding his hand out to me. I take it and step down to the ground, followed closely by Fionbal. Someone emerges from the house and starts walking towards us in brisk strides. I recognize Senjar. He beams in welcome as he approaches me. "Martha, I cannot begin to say how happy I am to see you here." He places a hand to my cheek and touches his forehead to mine. I read happiness, excitement, pride. We step back and Senjar greets the two somars by my side. "Please," he says, "follow me."

We walk with him towards the house, climbing a set of grand steps to the main entrance. It's there I see an old man, standing proudly, his stance powerful despite his advancing years. This must be Poljar, my great uncle. I stop before him and he examines me silently, his face stern. He observes me with icy gray eyes, the color of a sea storm. I see the resemblance to my great grandfather, and to me. Silently, he beckons me to him. I put my hand to his cheek as he does the same to mine, and we touch our foreheads to each other. *Love, pain, longing*. His hand on my cheek tightens as he chokes back his emotion. He steps away, and I see tears glisten in his eyes. In a rough voice he says, "Welcome home, dear girl."

"Thank you. It's good to be here."

He eyes Fionbal and Dovtar. "And who have we here?"

Fionbal steps forward respectfully. "Fionbal, son of Marbal. I am a somar to Krantorven." He exchanges the customary greeting with my great uncle, then Dovtar follows suit.

"Dovtar, son of Sentar. I am also a somar to Krantorven."

Poljar grunts. "So it is true what the rumors say. You are to be mated with the Kran's son."

"I haven't agreed to it yet," I say defiantly.

Poljar chuckles. "That's my girl. Keep them on their toes." Then he becomes brisk. "Come along, let us not dawdle endlessly at the door. Come inside and have some refreshment. Senjar, tell your sister to come down and greet her cousin."

157

Senjar nods. "I am messaging her now. She will be down shortly."

We follow Poljar into a massive living room with high beamed ceilings. It's a little rustic, but warm and inviting. We sit on a large couch just as a young girl, no more than sixteen or seventeen years old, comes rushing in, bearing a tray with drinks and snacks. She puts it down on a side table and comes to me, smiling shyly. "Welcome," she says. "I am Treyjar."

This must be Senjar's younger sister. I smile and give her the customary greeting. *Excitement, nerves, joy.* "It's good to meet you, Treyjar," I respond as I step back.

Over the next hour, I get to know my long lost family a little more. They share photo-videos going back generations and tell me stories about my great uncle, Laijar, and the wanderlust that led him far away from his home—a curious symmetry with the spirit of adventure that brought me all the way here. While we talk, Dovtar and Fionbal sit silently at my side, strong and protective.

Then Poljar suggests I go out and explore the farm. "You must also pass by the griv enclosure and see our magnificent animals."

Senjar jumps up. "Good idea. Would you like to take a look around?" he asks me.

"I would love to."

With Dovtar and Fionbal trailing behind, we make our way outside. Senjar leads me to the nearest outbuilding. "This is where we house our grivs. We have reared them in our family for many generations."

We reach the massive structure and enter it through a large wooden door. I'm struck by the familiar smell of hay, animal sweat and dung. Sunshine streams through a large side window, illuminating the interior, where I spot a half dozen giant animals that I can only describe as a cross between a horse and a dragon. They snuffle and shake their heads at the intrusion. One of them, a tall creature with a shiny coat of a rich brown, watches me closely. Suddenly, it gives a loud whinny, and shuffles over to me. Heart beating wildly, I try not to show any fear as it nudges me gently.

Its eyes fix on me mournfully as it whinnies once again. "She recognizes you," Senjar says softly beside me.

I look back at him, surprised. "How so?"

"Grivs have the ability to pass on their memories from mother to child. This griv is called Saila, and she is the great granddaughter of Sonla, who was your great uncle's favorite. She recognizes your eyes and your scent. She knows you are his kin."

I'm bowled over by this knowledge. I look again at Saila's expressive eyes, that are watching me with keen intelligence. I lift a hand to stroke her large, gleaming head, and she whinnies softly, nuzzling into me. *Oh my. I think I've just fallen in love.*

"Would you like to ride her?" Senjar asks beside me. "You do not need to be afraid. She will take good care of you."

Dovtar lays a gentle hand on my shoulder. "I will ride her with you, that way you will feel safe, especially when we leave the ground."

I smile at him gratefully. "Thanks, Dovtar. I would like that."

"In that case, let me lead her out," says Senjar cheerfully. He cocks his head to the side, and the griv understands him, following him out of the barn without any further instruction. Outside the building, she comes to a standstill, then bends down to the ground. Senjar quickly throws a large saddle on her back and ties it with efficient movements, handing me the rein. Hesitantly, I climb on, swinging my leg around to the other side. Beneath me, the griv feels massive, powerful and incredibly warm. An instant later, Dovtar settles on the saddle behind me. He places both arms around my waist protectively. "How do you feel?" he asks.

"Fine, I think. Just keep holding me as Saila stands up."

"I will," he promises.

Senjar makes a clicking sound with his mouth, and Saila begins to get back on her feet. I clutch the rein tightly, feeling Dovtar's protective arms around me. Saila rises to her full height, which is considerable, and I look down to the ground which seems a very long way away. My heart pounds in excitement and fear.

"Do not worry," Dovtar murmurs into my ear. "You will be fine."

Saila starts to move, a gentle canter at first, then gradually picking up speed. The endless expanse of fields pass us by as we start to gallop. The fresh breeze whips my cheeks. Nestled in the warmth of Dovtar's embrace, I start to enjoy myself. I don't know how fast we're going—but it's faster than I've ever ridden before. Field after cultivated field whizzes by as we gallop. I feel free.

Dovtar whispers into my ear. "Are you ready to fly?"

"Yes," I breathe.

He makes a strange whistling sound through his teeth and suddenly, great wings unfurl at each side of Saila's flank. She flaps them once and we lift off the ground, whooshing up into the air. Her wings move up and down slowly, gathering height and speed until we're cruising, high up in the sky. *I'm flying.* I shout it out with glee.

I hear Dovtar laughing behind me, sharing in my joy. He holds me tight, nipping at my neck, and communicating with his thoughts. *"Best feeling ever."*

I respond, *"I know. I love it."*

On and on we fly, zooming in a wide circle around the entire estate. Eventually, it's time to head back. My stomach plunges as we begin to lose altitude, swooping lower and lower until, with a light thud, Saila's hooves touch the ground. We gallop towards the farmhouse, slowing down to a light canter as we get close. Saila comes to a stop directly in front of the barn and bends her limbs to allow us to dismount. On shaky legs, I step on to the ground, Dovtar right behind me.

I turn to him. "That was amazing!"

He grins. "Yes, it was."

With efficient strokes, he unstraps the saddle from Saila's back, and she rises, walking calmly back to her home. Before she does so, she gives me one last friendly nuzzle. I watch her go enraptured. As Dovtar shuts the door to the enclosure, I'm aware of one thought. I owe Krantor a forfeit.

CHAPTER 22

Martha

I'm back in my bedroom, the events of today whirling in my mind—Dovtar and Fionbal's affection when I cried, the emotional meeting with Poljar, and of course, that amazing flight on Saila. I come back to the same question I have each night. Should I agree to mate with Krantor?

I've formed a little spreadsheet in my head of arguments for and against the decision. In the plus column, there's Shanbri, and the fact it's the only way I can be with him. That's a big, big plus. But there's more. Today at the farm, I felt loved and accepted by a family I hadn't known about until recently. Ironically, I felt this most when Saila came to nuzzle me, recognizing my face and scent. I feel like I belong here. Today, Dovtar and Fionbal made me feel cherished and protected. Ok, so I'm a modern woman that can stand on my own two feet. I don't need to be protected, but it felt kind of nice.

Some more positives. The more I get to know Krantor, the more comfortable I am with him. I don't love him—at least not the way I love Shanbri. I am fond of him though, and of Prilor. I imagine once the mating bond sets in and our minds meld, this fondness will morph into love. And there's no denying the physical pull of attraction between us. My pussy throbs and floods whenever I'm in Krantor's vicinity, and my mind turns to goo. I can't help but feel shame about it, even though I know it's because of the mating bond, a powerful elemental force over which I have no control. I'm told the overwhelming physical pull between us will settle once we're fully mated, though the intense attraction will always be there.

And then I come to the negatives. Number one, I'll be living far from my home on Earth. I won't see Grandma or Grandpa, or my friend Lulu. Another negative. I'll be the third wheel in Krantor and Prilor's relationship. Will there be times when they start to resent my presence in their midst? That really is my sticking point. How can I commit myself to a man who's madly in love with someone else? Krantor seems to think we can all love each other without creating any conflicts, but I'm not so sure.

And then we come to another sticking point. Even though I'm physically attracted to all of them, fundamentally I'm built for monogamy. I want one partner in life, not five. If I had to choose that partner, it would be Shanbri. It's him I love and want by my side. Or am I fooling myself? Could Shanbri also be a passing infatuation? My heart clenches whenever I think of him—whenever I eat one of the cakes he gifts me every day. No, I'm not going to double guess myself on this. My feelings for him are real. I do love him.

So, what do I do?

My head hurts from having to think about it all. I don't feel ready to make life-changing decisions just yet. Whatever happened to girl meets boy, girl dates boy, girl moves in with boy, until finally girl marries boy?

I suppose that could still be an option for me if I returned to Earth. Every time I think of it though, I reject the idea. I hate to admit it, but Krantor's right, damn him. Earth pales in comparison with everything I've experienced on Ven. If I'm truly honest with myself, I know that I want to stay here. I love this place, its people, and the family I've newly discovered.

So, maybe I should just embrace this bizarre new situation and enjoy having five gorgeous men at my beck and call. Isn't that the fantasy touted in all those romance books I secretly like to read? I just have to let go of the shame and let go of my Earth conditioning that tells me a woman sleeping with five men must be a slut. Nobody here is going to judge me, that's for sure.

An incoming call on my communicator interrupts my musings. Speak of the devil. It's Krantor, wanting his forfeit. It's the moment of truth. Can I go through with this or not?

I pick up.

CHAPTER 23

Krantorven

Once upon a time, I dreamt of a mate who would be cool, sensible and wedded to duty just like my mother. Fate had other ideas for me. My Martha—for she is mine, no matter what she thinks—is nothing of the kind. She is passionate, impetuous and does not put duty above all else. Now that I know her, I would not want her any other way.

We have not met in person since that time she came to the palace. Had we done so, we would have ended up in bed and not left it for several rotations. I crave her body. Every time I speak to her on my communicator, I get hard thinking about her scent and her delicious taste. The unfulfilled mating bond pulls more strongly at me with each day. She must become my mate. I cannot imagine what will become of me if she says no.

Prilor, bless him, has become accustomed to my raging arousal whenever I speak to her. At the end of each call, his mouth is on my cock without my asking, sucking me to completion. Today, however, is different. I made a little deal with Martha, and I fully expect her to pay the forfeit. In anticipation of this, Prilor and I are already naked on the bed as I tap my communicator to call her.

She answers straight away, her face flushing as she sees us unclothed, though our cocks are not in her field of vision yet. We are both rock hard already.

"Martha," I say. "Are you ready for your forfeit?"

"Aren't you getting ahead of yourself? You don't know yet if you've won."

I hold back a smile. "Martha, is riding a griv infinitely superior to riding one of your Earth horses?"

She grimaces and mumbles, "Yes it's superior." Then she adds, "But maybe not infinitely so."

"Oh Martha, semantics!"

"I guess."

"So, my love, here is what I want you to do. Unbutton that pretty shirt of yours slowly, button by button. Then I want you to remove any undergarments you are wearing beneath it. Look me in the eyes while you do."

She hesitates a little longer. My Martha's Earth morality gets in the way of what she knows and feels she must do, but the pull of our mating bond is stronger.

I sense the moment she gives in to that pull. Fixing her eyes on mine, she begins to comply. I do not let my eyes stray from hers. I want to see and feel her emotions as she bares herself to us.

The shirt comes off, then her undergarments. I know the exact moment her breasts are naked, even though my eyes stay on hers. I hear Prilor's intake of breath. My hand touches his cock. As I suspect, it is leaking.

Taking my time, I let my eyes travel from Martha's face down to her chest. Holy Lir, she is perfect! Delightful orbs, substantial enough to fill my big hands, stand upright before me. The skin on her breasts is pale, nearly the shade of the mother's milk that will flow out of them one day. And at the summit, erect and pointing straight at me, are beautiful pinkish brown nipples.

"Touch yourself," I growl.

She brings a hand to each breast and tweaks her nipples. I hear her moan. Fuck! I want to bite them and suck them. My cock engorges even more. I take it in my hand and give it a tug.

"Take off your pants. Get naked now," I grit.

With hands that shake, I see her pull down her pants and undergarments in one go. Finally, I glimpse the delicious cunt I have been dreaming of. Unlike the females of our world, it is totally hairless, with a plump, dimpled mound. She is breathtaking.

"Open your legs. Show me your cunt."

She does as told, no longer hesitating. Oh my fucking great lord! My eyes drink in the soft folds of dewy pink skin, dripping with her arousal. I ache to lick her.

"Touch yourself."

"Let me see you too," she pants.

Prilor shifts the angle of my communicator so that it reveals our leaking hungry cocks.

"Oh," she gasps, her eyes taking us in.

"Go on. Touch yourself," I grate harshly, as I begin to stroke myself to the delicious sight of her. She brings two fingers down to the pleasure nub above her slit and begins to rub it in a circular motion. Her breaths come in and out sharply. I know she is close. And fuck so am I.

I grip my cock hard, jerking it to a fast rhythm. Jerk, jerk, jerk. Her fingers moving on her cunt echo my rhythm. Rub, rub, rub. That's it my girl. With a cry, she reaches her climax, just as Prilor and I spurt jets of cum onto our bellies. I groan my release, my heart racing.

Then, I look back up at her with all my raging unfulfilled need. "You. Are. Mine." I bite the words out, then end our call. I let my head fall back on the bed and close my eyes. *Mine.* She had better fucking admit it soon.

I sense Prilor get up and return a moment later with a wet washcloth, which he uses to clean us up. Then he's lifting up the sheets and tucking us under the covers, his arm wrapped tight around me.

"I need her," I murmur.

"I know."

"I love you Prilor."

"And I love you. Go to sleep now."

He kisses the top of my head and I drift off to sleep.

Next morning is a morning just like any other. I wake to Prilor's strong arms around me and to his pleasuring of my cock. Our moans rouse the sleeping somars next door, who troop in one by one for their morning kiss, before we all make our way to the bathing room. In the water, which today has been scented with a blend to raise our spirits, Fionbal runs a washcloth all over my body. Theoretically, I am well capable of washing my own body, but I find the gentle hands of my somar on me infinitely soothing first thing in the morning. I lay my head back and enjoy, closing my eyes with a sigh.

From the drying bench, I hear the sound of my communicator calling. Shanbri jumps out of the bath and goes to fetch it. His face as he looks down at the screen tells me all I need to know. It is Martha. Handing me the device, I tap to answer.

"Martha mine, good morning to you."

She smiles nervously. "Good morning Krantor." Then a pause. I wait patiently for what I know she is about to say. She is finally ready to admit the truth. "Krantor," she begins again. "I've got some conditions before I agree to becoming your mate."

"What are they Martha mine?"

"First of all, I would like your promise that within the next year—your sun rotation—we will visit Earth and see my grandparents. They are old, and I don't know how much time they have left. I want to see them again."

"Very well, we can work in a diplomatic mission to Earth."

"Thanks. There's more."

"Speak, Martha. I am listening."

"I want to be clear about the role I'm expected to take on as a kran's mate. I know your mother commands a spaceship and that she spends a lot of time off planet. That is not something I'm willing to do. I don't like space travel and I don't like the idea of not being permanently based in one place. That's just not for me Krantor."

Her eyes plead for understanding, but there is no need. I already know that Martha is going to forge a different path to my mother's. Gently, I say, "I know. I do not expect you to undertake duties off planet. However, I would like it if you could be involved in the strategic planning and decision making for our planet by attending the weekly council meetings. I would also want you to be my consort for official functions. Would that be agreeable to you?"

"I think so, though I'm not sure how much use I would be."

"Do not forget, you will have access to all my knowledge. I also know that you have abilities which will be of great use to us, for you had to go through a very rigorous set of tests in order to be chosen for the exchange program."

She nods. "Perhaps. I'll do as you say, but I also want to have time to pursue my own interests. Back on Earth, I was an educator with a specialism in linguistics. I'm hoping to continue working in that field by teaching Earth languages to Venorian children—perhaps even setting up a small school where humans and Venorians can be educated side by side."

I beam at her. "That is an excellent idea, Martha mine. It will build greater understanding between our peoples."

She smiles in relief. "I'm glad you like the idea."

"I do, very much. Is there any other condition?"

"Yes, a few more."

"Please go on."

She hesitates. "I don't know how to say this without causing offence. I know that in becoming your mate, I'll also become a mate to your somars. However, I'm not ready to become intimate with them, at least not until I've had time to develop long lasting feelings. With the exception of Shanbri of course, would they agree to wait until I'm ready before we develop a sexual relationship?"

I look around at my somars, raising my brow in question at them. Dovtar, looking grave, immediately speaks up. "Martha, I will never impose myself on you, no matter what vow we make at the mating ceremony. I will wait as long as you need. Please be assured of that."

I turn to Fionbal. "And you?" I ask.

Fionbal does not hesitate. "Martha, I am very attracted to you and want to bed you, but I agree with Dovtar. It can only happen when you are ready. I will wait as long as you need."

Then Prilor chimes in. "It is the same for me too, Martha. You already know how attracted I am to you, but I will never force myself on you. Nothing happens until you are ready."

I feel Shanbri's burning gaze on my mate. I turn to Martha and say, "I suppose your final condition involves Shanbri. Am I right?"

"Yes." She looks at him longingly on my communicator screen. "I want to spend more time alone with Shanbri. I love him, just as you love Prilor, and I need more than just the nights of the full moons to be with him."

"Martha, I am willing to consider this request. However, I do not know how it will be with us once the mating bond has settled. There will always be that pull between us, and that primal need to fuck. The mating bond is an elemental power

170

that cannot be dismissed easily. Let us see how it goes, and we can then discuss a change to our sleeping arrangements."

"What do you think?" she asks Shanbri.

Shanbri clears his throat. "My heart, Krantor speaks sense. We cannot know how it will be between the two of you once you are mated. However, I would like to spend as much time alone with you as possible. I will treasure every moment."

"I miss you," she says, with a trembling voice.

"And I miss you, my sweet love."

Then, Martha gathers herself and comes to a decision. "In that case, Krantor, I agree to becoming your mate."

Thank fuck.

CHAPTER 24

Martha

My decision has unleashed a rollercoaster chain of events. Before I can become Krantor's mate, I'm required to become a Venorian citizen. The process is laborious, in the best of bureaucratic traditions. First, I must have two Venorians vouch for my good character—for this Flidar and Senlor kindly did the honors.

Then I'm required to establish due justification for my being awarded citizenship. Using a notarized statement from Grandma back on Earth that I am indeed the great-granddaughter of Laijar, a statement from Mivtal confirming my lineage through her genetic tests, and an affidavit from Poljar, my elderly great-uncle, that he acknowledges me as his kin, I am finally able to convince the authorities that my citizenship is justified.

In the meantime, I have had to prepare my body for mating through a series of meditation exercises. Flidar, bless her, has acted as my mentor, guiding me through the long daily practices that are teaching me to exert greater control on my body through the use of my mind.

At first, I found them impossible to do, but I had a little breakthrough today when I was able to visualize the cells in my body and the individual genetic strands that make me who I am. It is these strands that are going to change because of my mating. Once Krantor is my mate, part of his DNA will imprint itself within me—through the sharing of our bodily fluids—and I will take on some of his genetic characteristics. Our scents will mingle to create a hybrid Martha-Krantor scent. Some of my genetics will imprint themselves on Krantor in the process. He's hoping I'll pass on to him my rapid observation and response skills that helped me ace through the selection tests for the exchange program. I'm hoping he'll gift me with his exceptional eyesight, which allows him to read things from over sixty feet away.

If that's not enough to keep me busy, I'm being outfitted for a mating ceremony gown—not the white that tradition dictates in our culture, but a beautiful shimmery gown in pink and purple, the colors of Ven's precious gemstone, the vlor. Krantor's sister, Sonlar, is designing the dress, as well as a wardrobe of outfits I will need for my new position as a kran's mate. I've been getting to know my prospective sister-in-law during the regular appointments with her to try out and adjust the outfits she's making for me. She's friendly and extremely talented, creating designs that flatter and show off my tall, slightly voluptuous figure.

And last of all there are the tattoos. Krantor and each of his somars have selected small individual designs that will be imprinted on the inside of my thigh, just below my pussy. The intimate positioning of the tattoos is intentional. They are for my mate and somars to admire when they, ahem, go down on me, and act as a reminder that I belong to them. They have each thought deeply about what they would like to imprint on me.

Shanbri has picked a cute drawing of my favorite cake that he's baked for me. I'll have a little Shanbri cake an inch below my pussy. Prilor has picked a small drawing of a stormy sky, because he says that's what my eyes remind him of. Fionbal has chosen to adorn me with a lovely drawing of pink and purple kalso blossoms which were in bloom on the day he met me. Dovtar has gone for a simple drawing of a heart inscribed with his name. And what about Krantor? Well, he has imaginatively decided that I shall be etched with the word "MINE" in pride of place at the top of my thigh.

However, this is not one-way traffic. Oh no. For each of the five men who are to join their lives with mine will be getting an intricate etching of my Venorian name—Marthajar—on their groin, right at the base of their cock.

173

We are all to go today to have the tattoos done. A buzz on my communicator tells me that my men—what else can I call them—are awaiting outside. I call out a quick farewell to Flidar and hurry to open the door, filled with excitement. It will be the first time I see Shanbri in the flesh since that day I spoke to him at the palace.

It's him I see first, standing before me as I open the door, looking massive and tall and incredibly handsome. "Shanbri!"

He grins and opens his arms. I fly into them, holding him tight. Oh God, it's so good to see him again! I nuzzle his neck, inhaling his intoxicating musky scent, and planting hundreds of little kisses. *"I need you."*

He buries his face in my hair. *"I need you too."*

We might have stayed this way for hours if it weren't for a loud clearing of a throat nearby. I glance up to see Dovtar's amused eyes watching us. "Come on lovers, it is time to go."

I let go of Shanbri, a little embarrassed. "My apologies. It's been so long since I've seen Shanbri."

Dovtar smiles. "No need for apologies, but let us be on our way."

Shanbri takes my hand and leads me down to the transport, where Krantor, Prilor and Fionbal are observing us with varying levels of amusement. I decide to brazen it out. I climb into the drone airily and ask, "Are you all ready to be branded with my name?"

Krantor laughs. "More than ready. I'm especially looking forward to seeing you branded as mine."

I squeeze Shanbri's hand as I feel him tensing beside me. I bury my face into his neck. *"Let it go."*

He strokes my hair gently. *"I am trying."*

Our journey doesn't take long. In a few minutes, the drone is landing beside a three-storied building overlooking a small park. As we walk towards the door, it opens and a beautiful Venorian female with jet black hair and aqua eyes comes to greet us. I touch foreheads with her first and sense curiosity and warmth. Once all the greetings are done, she leads us into her studio where I shall be having the tattoos inked. It's a large, functional room, with pictures of her designs adorning most of the walls. Each and every design is beautiful, and I feel a shiver of anticipation at the knowledge that I'm going to be the recipient of such incredible artwork on my body. With a polite smile, she asks me to undress from the waist down and lie on the couch.

I hesitate. Shanbri of course has seen me naked, so have Krantor and Prilor. The others, however, have never observed my body without clothes. I expect them to do the gentlemanly thing and turn away, but no such thing happens. I suppose nudity is not as big a deal for the Venorians as it is for humans.

Krantor taps his foot impatiently, wanting me to hurry up. It's Shanbri that comes to my rescue. He comes over and places his hands on my cheeks. *"What is it?"*

We touch foreheads. *"I'm embarrassed to be naked."*

He strokes my cheek. *"There's nothing to fear. We are all your mates."* I breathe deeply, still unsure. *"How about I undress you?"*

I kiss his cheek. *"Please."*

Shanbri gets down on his knees and removes my shoes, then slides my pants down my legs. Dovtar steps forward to take them from him. Gently, Shanbri takes hold of my panties and pulls them down. He presses a kiss to my mound before coming to stand. Taking my hand in his, he leads me to the couch and helps me get comfortably situated. He doesn't leave me, going to sit at my side, my hand in his, as the tattooist comes over to begin her work. She parts my legs gently and cleans the area to be inked. I feel the eyes of all the others on my exposed pussy. Shanbri leans his head towards mine. *"You're beautiful. Don't worry."*

The tattoo artist begins her work, inking each of the five designs on the inside of my thigh. It's a sensitive area and the needle stings, but Shanbri holds me tight, incanting words of love and comfort into my mind. Finally, it's done, and she steps back. Krantor comes close to inspect her handiwork, placing his hand on my thigh. His proximity starts the mating bond working, making my heart pound madly and my core clench. In full sight of everyone, my pussy starts to leak juices, giving away my arousal. Krantor says softly, "Not long now," and touches my wet clit with his knowing finger, detonating my climax. I hear Shanbri's sharp intake of breath as he feels me orgasm beside him. The other three somars' eyes are glued to me as they watch my pussy pulsing and leaking.

"Prilor, come and lick her clean," Krantor says in a commanding voice.

His somar approaches, and looks me in the eyes, heat evident in his gaze on me. I know he's awaiting permission, despite Krantor's command. My aching pussy makes my decision for me. I give a slight nod. Carefully, the giant Venorian lowers himself between my legs, avoiding the newly inked patches, and starts to lick my wet pussy with gentle, delicate strokes of his tongue. At his touch, I feel myself come apart, as yet another climax rips through me. Shanbri captures my mouth, swallowing my moans and sighs in a searing kiss as I pulsate in pleasure at Prilor's touch.

All too soon, the moment ends. Shanbri releases my mouth, still keeping a hold on me. He levels his gaze on Prilor as the big man sits up, his short beard coated with my cum. Krantor growls, "Let me taste her on you." He pulls Prilor to him and kisses him hard, licking the seams of his lips and my wet juices off his beard. The sight of these two impossibly attractive men kissing to the taste of me is incredibly arousing. *"That's hot,"* I telegraph to Shanbri.

"I know."

The tattoo artist approaches once again and places a sterile pad on my newly inked skin, then indicates I can go. Dovtar approaches with my clothes. Reverently, he pulls my panties up my legs, careful not to nudge my bandage. Then he helps me with my pants and brings me my shoes. "Thank you Dovtar," I say.

He smiles. "It is my pleasure."

Fionbal brings me a cup of *ploh* to drink, and I smile my thanks. I'm beginning to enjoy being waited on hand and foot. I finish my drink and hand the cup back to him. "So," I say, "which one of you big boys is having my name branded on him first?"

Shanbri stands to attention. "I will."

He quickly undresses, unveiling his magnificent cock. I sense the tattooist's admiring gaze on him, and I can't help my possessive response. I give her a sharp tap on the shoulder, my eyes flashing a warning. "Sorry," she mumbles, and gets to work. I watch in fascination as she inks Marthajar on Shanbri's groin. *I've marked him. He's mine.* My satisfaction is intense.

One by one, each of the somars get their tattoos done. Fionbal's cock is thick and long, though not quite as big as Shanbri's. Dovtar's cock is the slimmest, but it has a strange beauty of its own standing over plump and full balls sacks. And then I see Prilor's cock. Oh my! It's even more massive in the flesh! How the heck am I ever going to fit that into my vagina? I watch in strange satisfaction as the grumpy, prickly giant who has been so resistant to my charms, has my name inked on his groin. He senses my gaze and looks up at me. I press my lips together, trying to stop my grin, but he sees it, and to my intense surprise, his face breaks into the most beautiful smile I've ever seen. My heart skips a little beat.

Finally, it's Krantor's turn to be inked. Fionbal deftly undresses him—does the man never do a thing for himself? Krantor's cock is large and beautifully formed, the smooth skin gleaming a shade of bronze darker than the rest of his body. That pesky mating bond pulls me to his side, my gaze fixed on his proud member which has risen to attention at my proximity. "See what you do to me?" growls my mate.

Shanbri puts his arm around me and pulls me out of the way so the tattooist can begin her work. "He's beautiful, isn't he?" he whispers into my ear.

"Yes," I sigh.

He kisses the top of my head. "There is no need to feel guilty about appreciating the sight of your mate."

"Is it wrong of me to feel that I might like some parts of this arrangement?"

"No Martha. I want you to be happy. Take your pleasure without guilt. Do not forget, I love him too."

I turn in his arms and kiss him gently. "I love you."

"And I love you."

"We'll make this work."

"We will."

I burrow into his massive frame, seeking the comfort he gives so freely. It's finally now, that I start to believe things are going to be alright.

CHAPTER 25

Martha

The day of my mating has arrived. I'm feeling a jangling of nerves and anticipation, just like any Earth girl on her wedding day. Last night, I moved into the palace, sleeping in a set of private guests' quarters. My family—the Jar clan—are here with me in full force. Senjar is sitting beside me, cheerfully demolishing a tray of pastries recently delivered from Shanbri. Even today, my lover bakes for me. I'm savoring one of them slowly, thinking of him with every bite I take.

Beside Senjar sits his younger sister Treyjar, and from her I sense barely repressed excitement and wonder. The palace is a far cry from the quiet life she lives out on the family farm. To my right, completing the picture, is my great-uncle Poljar, who sits quietly reading from his communicator. Later today, he will be doing the equivalent of walking me down the aisle and giving me away. I'm awed and incredibly touched at the thought of having a caring family supporting me on my big day.

Footsteps sound behind me, and I look round to see Flidar and Sonlar arriving. I stand to greet them, feeling comforted by the warmth and love they project on contact of our foreheads. Sonlar immediately sits and helps herself to one of Shanbri's pastries. "Mmm," she says as she bites into the flaky crust. "No prizes for guessing who baked these lovely things." Her eyes twinkle in amusement.

"Are you ready my dear?" asks Flidar.

One would think I'd be allowed a pass on my Drekon workout and meditation practice, seeing as it's my wedding day, but that's not the case. "Yes," I mumble, and follow her to the next room which has already been prepared with mats on the floor. Patiently, she takes me through the different poses, helping me center myself and prepare my body for what's ahead.

What's ahead…

I've had the ceremony explained to me. I've learned the vows I will be making to Krantor and to each of his somars. I know that at some point today, Krantor and I will become one, melding together our DNAs and memories, and that this will require an exchange of our bodily fluids. Yeah, no big deal.

My heart begins to palpitate. Flidar places a gentle but firm hand on my knee. "Calm yourself, Martha, and focus on your breathing exercises." I take a deep breath, and return to my meditation.

When our session is over, Flidar guides me to the bathing room, where a large, scented bath has been filled in readiness for me. I undress and step into its warmth. "I will leave you now and return in a short while," she says. I smile my thanks and lie back, closing my eyes. My body feels weightless, my joints as pliable as butter. I think of Shanbri. What is he doing right now? Is he thinking of me? How strange that on the day of my wedding—ok my mating—I should be thinking about someone other than my mate.

Flidar returns and helps me to wash my hair. Her fingers massage my scalp, lulling me into a deeper state of relaxation. She reads my mind. "You are thinking of Shanbri," she says softly.

"Yes."

She continues to rub my head soothingly. "You have a difficult path ahead of you Martha, but I believe with patience and love, you will find your way through."

"I hope so. I worry how Shanbri will feel today, watching me mate with Krantor."

"He will feel many things. Pain, yes. But also love, desire and joy. Do not forget that by mating Krantor, you will also be tying yourself to Shanbri."

"Yes. I have the vows memorized. I can't wait to say them to him."

"It will be fine Martha. Just trust in whatever deity you believe in that there is a plan and that it will begin to make sense in time."

"Thank you Flidar, for everything."

"It is my pleasure, Martha dearest."

She helps me out of the bath and wraps me in a large towel. "Come. Let us get you ready. Sonlar is impatient to see her beautiful creation on you."

An hour later, I step out of my quarters dressed in my loosely flowing mating gown, and walk the short journey to the walled courtyard where the ceremony will be taking place. My great-uncle is at my side; the rest of the family follow behind us. As we emerge into the late afternoon sunshine, I see the many guests seated, facing a small rectangular altar where an elderly Venorian female in a pale pink gown awaits us. I know she is the holy priestess, who will be leading the ceremony. The courtyard has been decked with flowers and garlands— naturally in the purple and pink colors of Ven—which shimmer in the orange glow of the setting sun, lending a surreal quality to the sight before me.

On the priestess's right, stands Krantor and his family, surrounded by his somars. My gaze finds Shanbri, standing tall in a dark purple cloak, his hair for once groomed impeccably into a topknot on his head. Our eyes meet for a long, feverish moment. Then he smiles slightly and looks down at his feet.

I continue to walk along the moss covered path on my bare feet—shoes, it seems, are not part of the wardrobe of a Venorian bride—until I reach Krantor, who gives me an admiring smile.

The priestess addresses us in a calm, but commanding voice. "We are here on this joyful occasion to witness and bless the mating of Krantor and Marthajar. Please all kneel for our prayer to the bountiful god Lir."

I carefully get down on my knees and bow my head. The priestess begins a long and soulful prayer, which I try to follow, but find my mind meandering. Eventually, we are called to stand again. The priestess speaks once more. "Krantor and Marthajar. Today is a day of union, not just of your souls and bodies, but of your two families. From this day forward, the Tors and the Jars will be as one. Members of the Jar family, please face the Tors and repeat after me. Tors, you are now kin of my kin. I bestow on each of you my love and undying loyalty. We are now one." I repeat the words, along with Poljar, Senjar and Treyjar who are standing behind me.

"Now the Tors, please repeat after me. Jars, you are now kin of my kin. I bestow on each of you my love and undying loyalty. We are now one." Krantor and his family, including his somars, face us and repeat the words. My eyes meet Shanbri's as he says the vows.

Then the priestess resumes her speech. "Krantor, you are joined in a holy vow to your four somars, Prilor, Shanbri, Dovtar and Fionbal. Today, they will also join you in making a holy vow to your mate. Somars and Marthajar, please approach the altar. The rest may step back and be seated."

We walk to the altar. The priestess smiles at me kindly. "Marthajar, turn around and face away from the altar. Somars, take your positions."

Prilor comes to stand facing me, around two feet away. Shanbri stands to my right, Dovtar and Fionbal to my left. All of them except Dovtar unlace their cloaks and, holding the edges with their fingers, spread their arms wide, forming a protective circle around me, shielding my body from view. Beneath their cloaks, they are naked. Dovtar approaches me

182

and gently unties the laces that hold together my gown, until it falls away, leaving me naked as the day I was born. He takes the dress and places it carefully on the altar, then stands aside.

"Prilor, begin your vows," instructs the priestess.

Prilor's heated gaze takes in my naked body, starting from my toes up to my face. His eyes, burning with emotion, lock on mine as he begins to speak. "Marthajar, I stand here unclothed and unadorned, to pledge myself to you today. I vow to be faithful to you, my kran and his somars. I promise to love you, serve you and protect you until my dying day. Will you accept my pledge?"

I step towards him. "Yes Prilor, I will. Today I stand unclothed and unadorned to pledge myself to you. I vow to be faithful to Krantor and to you, his somar. I promise to love, cherish and honor you until my dying day. Should you so wish, Prilor, I promise to bear a child to you. Will you accept my pledge?"

Prilor responds hoarsely. "Yes, I will."

The priestess speaks. "Now seal your pledge with a kiss and a meld of your minds."

I place my hands on Prilor's massive, hairy chest, feeling the warm heat of him and his heart pumping under my fingers. I raise my face to his and accept his sweet, gentle kiss. Our foreheads meet and I read his mind, *"I love you, beautiful one. I will protect you always."*

My mind responds, *"I think I love you too, my big grumpy giant."* Then I step back.

"Now Fionbal, begin your vows."

I turn to face Fionbal, and we say the same vows, sealing them with kiss. After that, it's Dovtar's turn and then, last of all, I come to Shanbri. His face is damp with a sheen of sweat; his body fully aroused. As he makes his pledge to me, his voice shakes with emotion. I place both of my hands on his firm chest, and gaze up at him with love as I say my vows. My voice catches on the last sentence. "Should you wish, Shanbri, I promise to bear a child to you." I feel his heart skip a beat, and an image comes to my mind of a little boy with Shanbri's blond locks. I realize the image has come from Shanbri's mind, projected to mine. I transmit back, *"Soon, my love."*

"Now seal your pledge with a kiss and a meld of your minds." The voice of the priestess interrupts our private conversation. I bring my hands up around Shanbri's head and pull him to me for a fierce, passionate kiss. I hear his raging thought, *"You're mine."*

I tangle my tongue with his. *"I'm yours."*

I step back, breathless. The priestess addresses us again. "Now it is time for you, Krantor, to come and make your pledge."

I am still enclosed in the protective circle of the four somars' arms, their cloaks hiding my nakedness from general view. Prilor briefly lowers his arm to let Krantor enter the circle, then brings it back up again. My mate faces me, unlacing and removing his cloak to reveal his perfect naked form. My face flushes; my heart pounds a mile a minute.

"Speak your vows Krantor," prompts the priestess.

Krantor repeats the same set of vows, his eyes never leaving my face. "Will you accept my pledge?"

"I will."

Then it's my turn to say the vows and his turn to respond. "I will."

"Approach the altar and place your hands on it palms up," commands the priestess.

We do as instructed. "As fated mates, you must seal your pledge with an exchange of your body's essences. First, with your blood." She takes a sharp vlor stone and quickly makes a shallow incision on each of our palms. Blood immediately oozes from the wounds. "Face each other, palms together." I turn to face Krantor and place each of my palms to his. As we make contact, I feel a sizzling heat where our blood mingles. "Now kiss, to exchange your mouth fluids." Krantor's lips touch mine for our first ever kiss.

Nothing prepares me for the explosion of sensation on contact with his mouth. I feel the most intense arousal I've ever experienced in my life, and I orgasm spontaneously, pulse after pulse of my core leaking juices down my leg for all to see. Krantor's tongue plunders my mouth and I suck on him, drinking in his incredible taste. My heart beats so fast I think it might burst from my chest. A myriad images come to my head. The strands of my DNA, unfurling and welcoming his intrusion. My cells pulsing with new life. His memory bank depositing into my mind. My memories flying into his.

I'm lost to the sensation, no longer aware of what is around me, only of him, and of him becoming part of me. I scream his name in my head. *"Krantor!"*

He responds. *"Yes, Martha mine. We're one."*

We continue to kiss, devouring each other, our hunger insatiable. Our hands are still trapped together, our blood still mingling. My core clenches in desperate arousal. *"I need you. Now."*

Krantor lowers us to kneel on the ground. *"Mount me"*.

With no thoughts to my surroundings, only a desperate primal urge to mate, I shift forwards until my pussy comes into contact with his straining erection. Slowly, I lower myself down onto it, letting him fill me completely, the tip of his shaft touching my cervix. *"Oh fuck that is good! Bring your legs around me."*

I do as he instructs, my mouth and hands still attached to his. As soon as my legs squeeze around him, I feel him start to thrust up into my pelvis. Each thrust delivers delicious agony, delicious sensation. *"Oh God. I'm going to come."*

He thrusts even harder. *"Come for me!"*

His next thrust sends me over the edge. I pulsate around his length, groaning my ecstasy into his hungry mouth. I feel him spurt hot jets of cum into me, and an immediate blazing heat as his essence mingles with mine. My lust is partly sated, but I still need more. He responds immediately. *"I know."*

With our mouths, hands and groins in a continuing tight embrace, Krantor pushes me down onto my back, his cloak cushioning my descent onto the mossy ground. *"I'm gonna fuck you hard."* He begins to plunge into me, his cock having magically never softened. I sense his amusement at my passing thought. *"Yeah, that's me. The love machine."* And he thrusts into me again.

"Hey! You were thinking in English just now."

I feel his internal smirk. "Darling, I know all you know. Now shut up and let me fuck you." And for a while after that, my thoughts go blank as he does indeed fuck me to within an inch of my life. He brings me to two more earth-shattering orgasms before releasing a second gush of hot cum into my womb. I feel its scorching heat as it melds into my being, marking me with his genetic code as no doubt I must be marking him.

Finally, we collapse in an exhausted heap. Several things happen at once. I feel our hands being gently unclasped, cleaned and bandaged. A warm wet cloth is brought to my aching pussy, cleaning up the excess mess. I feel Shanbri's pain and envy, mixed with his arousal, but there's nothing I can do about it right now. I feel Prilor's pain too. I hear a multitude of voices and thoughts. The priestess standing behind the altar,

"Holy Lir! I never imagined that a joining of fated mates would be like this!"

Troy, sitting in the crowd, *"Jesus, I can't believe they just fucked!"*

And Dimitri next to him, *"I hope she doesn't regret this."*

Gabriel's excitement, *"This is fucking amazing! I hope they let me examine the changes to her DNA."*

Sonlar's amusement, *"God my brother is loud when he fucks."*

Krantor laughs into my head. *"If she thinks that's loud—"*

And then a stern voice, Krantor's mother, *"That's enough now you two. You'll have plenty of time to explore your new powers, but would you please hurry up and get dressed. Your father is hungering for that roasted prot."*

Krantor and I look at each other in horror. *"Oh shit. Mom and Dad can hear us think."*

The Kran's amused voice, *"Oh yes, my dears, we hear you loud and clear. Now give the love machine a rest and let us eat."*

I flush to the roots of my hair. *"I can't believe my father-in-law just heard us fuck. This is so weird."*

The Kran responds in amusement, *"You've just joined a unique club, Martha. Get used to hearing lots of things you shouldn't."*

Krantor sits up and gives me a hand to help me stand. Dovtar rushes to drape my gown around me, fastening it with careful hands. I smile at him. "Thank you."

He kisses me softly on the lips. "It is my honor to serve you, Marthajar."

He then gives Krantor's soiled cloak a hasty wipe and drapes it around his kran's shoulders. With our modesty restored, the other somars break their circle around us and step back, lacing up their cloaks once again. I stand with Krantor, hand in hand, as the priestess bestows her final blessing on us. "May Lir bless your union with health, happiness and fecundity. Go forth now, your mating is complete."

The crowd bursts into applause as Krantor pulls me to him for another kiss. *"Let's eat quick and get back to our room. I'm still hungry for you."*

I let myself savor the sweet taste of him. *"Oh yes, good thinking."*

Our happy thoughts are interrupted by the Kran's voice in our heads. *"You'll leave when I say you can and not before. Now get moving. You are not the only hungry ones."*

Krantor pulls away ruefully. *"This telepathic thing can have its downsides."* Yet we do as we're told and lead the way to the banquet hall.

CHAPTER 26

Shanbri

She is beautiful. As we say our vows, I am overwhelmed with emotion. I pledge myself to her, promising to love, serve and protect her until my dying day. In the eyes of everyone, she may not be my mate, but right this moment, she feels like mine. We seal our pledge with a kiss—a passionate kiss that has me burning with desire—and my mind calls out to hers. *"You're mine."*

I hear her response loud and clear in my head. *"I'm yours."*

Then of course, the moment is gone, because Krantor steps forward to begin making his vows. Krantor. The man I love most in the entire universe. I did not take the decision lightly to become his somar. There were other things I wanted to do with my life than to be a somar, but I did this for him. I have loved him all my life. At first, he was the exciting and fun cousin I got to play with on visits to the palace. Then, when I was orphaned and alone, he became my everything. I basked in his affection. I followed him into every adventure, every prank, every sexual awakening. I had no doubt in my mind that I wanted to devote my life to this wonderful creature, even after he fell in love with Prilor. I knew I still had an important place in his heart. Even now, I know this.

And yet it pains me greatly to watch him mate with my Martha.

Always in my life I have been the one giving, the one thinking of others, the one serving. Then Martha came along, and I wanted her all to myself. Of course, I could not have what I wanted. Krantor has to take precedence. I understand this. I care for the wellbeing of my planet and my people, so I know he must mate with Martha. It is ordained by fate and by Lir, our all-knowing, all-powerful god. I know I must accept this, but by all that is holy, it hurts!

I know the exact moment when Martha is no longer mine. I see how she is flushed, her eyes smoky with desire as they make their vows to each other. And then they kiss. Palms together sharing their blood, they kiss, and both forget the existence of the world around them. They lose themselves in the kiss, hungrily sucking each other's essence. Being so attuned to her, I sense when she climaxes, her cunt dripping her release down her thigh.

In that moment, I am seized by a powerful desire to rip her from his arms and take her—to make her mine again. My cock is rock solid. I feel a desperate urge to ram myself deep within her warm tight cunt and be the one to make her climax in ecstatic pleasure. I almost do it, but Prilor grips my hand tight. *"Do not!"* More than anyone, he understands. His glittering eyes seek mine, imparting a second warning. *"Do not!"*

I force myself to breathe deeply and recall my sanity. With a frantically beating heart, I watch Krantor and Martha sink to the ground and mate in animalistic passion. Once the mating is complete, Dovtar gently bandages their wounds. He is the one to wipe Martha's cunt clean and to dress her once again in her mating gown, while I watch, a part of my heart broken.

At first during this ceremony, her eyes had sought mine constantly. Now Krantor is all she sees. She is no longer mine.

For the rest of the evening, I perform my duties as somar on autopilot, my heart frozen in pain, but my cock still throbbing and aching for her. Finally, we return to our quarters, escorting Martha and Krantor to their chamber, then closing the door behind them. We will not see either of them again until the mating bond has established itself.

By mutual agreement, all four of us drift to the bathing pool, wanting to wash off the sweat and tension of the day. Fionbal has made sure it is filled, and put soothing fragrant salts into the water. I shed my cloak and dive underwater, letting the heat soothe my unhappy body. I emerge to find Dovtar beside me, watching me with his deep, soulful eyes. "Dovtar," I mumble then stop. I cannot find the words to say how I feel.

He places both hands on my cheek. "I know," he says. "Come here my love. Let me ease your pain." He puts his mouth to mine, kissing me softly and sweetly.

I part my lips and feel his tongue seek contact, tasting his familiar, comforting aroma. I kiss him back, transmitting my emotions. "*I need.*"

He deepens the kiss. "*I know. Take me.*"

We pull apart breathlessly and I twist his body around, pushing him down to lean on the edge of the pool, his ass up in the air. Fionbal is there, slicking my rigid cock with lubrication. He slips a lubricating finger into Dovtar's ass, then another, preparing him for me. I am a large man, so it is rare for me to fuck his ass, but tonight, he gives himself to me. I watch with impatience as Fionbal stretches Dovtar, stroking my slicked cock in rising excitement and anticipation. Finally, he is ready. As slowly as I can manage, I push my aching cock into Dovtar's tight hot channel. I hear his agonized moan as my massive member stretches him impossibly. "Do not stop," he cries raggedly.

"I cannot," I groan. I thrust once more and this time I manage to plunge all the way in. Oh the heavenly bliss. The feeling of his tight ass choking my huge cock is exquisite. My hand flat on his back, I start to fuck him, fast and hard. Each thrust brings greater ecstasy. I ram him mindlessly and desperately until I reach the precipice. "Ahh," I roar, and find my release, pulsing my hot cum deep inside Dovtar.

As the pleasure recedes, my body is racked with sobs. I collapse on Dovtar's back, still intimately joined, and cry my pain. Hot tears flow like a raging waterfall from my reddened eyes as I let out all the feelings that have been bottled inside me ever since I learned that Martha was Krantor's fated mate. I feel soothing hands on my back, stroking me gently. Instinctively, I know it is Prilor. That great big bear of a man with an even larger heart, who is himself hurting, comforts me as best he can.

Finally, when I have no more tears to shed, I stand and slip my cock out of Dovtar. I am dimly aware of Fionbal cleaning me up and Prilor holding me in his massive embrace. Dovtar stands, wincing in pain, but smiling. "Thank you," I grunt out.

"It is my honor and pleasure to give you what you need, dearest Shanbri." He kisses me softly.

Then Prilor is leading me out of the bathing pool. We dry our bodies, drink our nightly tonic, and go to bed.

CHAPTER 27

Krantorven

I come awake slowly, becoming aware of my limbs entangled with hers and my arms draped around her soft belly. I breathe in the fragrance of her hair, feeling my cock getting hard. It has been like this for the past several days. Funny, I think in terms of days and weeks now, not in moon or sun rotations. I've taken on so much of her language, that I sometimes forget to think in mine.

We have been voracious in our hunger for each other, barely leaving the bed at all. We fuck until exhaustion sets in, then sleep, eat and fuck again. Father explained it would be like this for the first week, while the mating bond establishes itself. During that time, we've been unable to be apart, even for a few minutes to go relieve ourselves in the bathroom.

I slide my hand down to her well-used pussy and begin to stroke. I feel her immediate response as she comes awake. *Krantor*. She calls my name silently. We've found that we've had very little need to use our voices when we can communicate just as well—sometimes even better—through our minds. *"Martha mine, I need you."*

She stretches. *"Give it a lick to get me ready."*

I kiss the top of her head. *"My pleasure."*

I ease down the bed to where her legs are already parted for me. I lower my mouth to her pussy—what a great name for a cunt—and start to lap at her eagerly. I can't get enough of her taste. It's the most delicious flavor in the world. I lick and suck, feeling her juices begin to flow. Her core throbs. I feel it as if it's my own body. I know just the moment she's about to climax, and I give her clit a light nip, sending her over the edge. In an instant, I'm on her, my cock plunging into her pulsating depth and pounding her into a second release. We come together—as we always do now—and collapse on the bed, spent.

I fall to my back and slumber lightly for a while, but not for long. *"Martha mine."*

She shifts next to me. *"What?"*

I run a finger down her smooth back, making her shiver. *"I think our mating bond has settled. I do believe I could go to the bathroom without having you come with me."*

She turns and observes me in amusement. *"Go for it."*

I stand and take a few paces away from the bed. That's about as far as I've been allowed to stray from her this past week. I wait for the pull, forcing me back, but I don't feel it. With a satisfied smile, I continue on my way to the bathroom and have a much needed evacuation. Oh, it's good to have privacy for such things again.

"I can still hear you!"

Ok, well some semi-privacy. I wash my hands and return to the bed in fine spirits. I jump on top of my mate and ravish her with a kiss, then pause and sniff. *"You smell."*

She sniffs me right back. *"So do you."*

I collapse by her side with a laugh. I guess it's past time we had a bath.

"Yes, it is."

I get serious as my thoughts turn to seeing Prilor again. We haven't seen or spoken to any of our somars since the day of our mating. Shanbri has left us trays of food each day, but we haven't emerged from our room to speak to any of them. A vital part of the mating bond setting in is to have complete alone time with no interruptions. I wonder how Prilor has fared without me.

Her thoughts echo mine, "I wonder how Shanbri has been."

I trace my finger down her straight nose and lovely plump lips. "I know you do. Hey, I never knew the two of you met in the market. How romantic, him stopping you as you were about to bite into a blint. That's a story to tell our children."

She runs soft fingers along the hair on my chest. "Yeah, it was pretty romantic. He made me feel… well, you know how."

I smile. "Yeah, I know. It's the same for me with Prilor."

I lean across her and reach for my communicator, calling Fionbal. His sweet face smiles back at me. "Good morning Fionbal mine!"

"Err, actually, it is good afternoon."

I bark out a laugh. "Ah. Well, good afternoon then. Fionbal mine, we are ready for our bath."

He grins. "I will start it now. It will be good to see you again, and Marthajar too."

"Tell me Fionbal, how is Prilor?"

He hesitates, but I read his mind. "I see. Well, I will talk to him when he gets back from his physical training."

Fionbal looks at me strangely. "I forget you can now read our minds without even a touch."

I smirk. "That's right Fionbal mine, no more secrets."

He huffs. "I have never kept any secrets from you."

I smile at him fondly. "I know my love. Now hurry up with that bath. I warn you, we both smell."

"Yes, my kran," he says, and ends the connection.

A short while later, he knocks and peeps his head through the door. "Bath is ready, my kran."

"Excellent."

I jump out of bed and hold my hand out to Martha. She stands and follows me to the bathing room, smiling shyly at Fionbal. I'm amused to read his thoughts. *"Oh my, look at the state of her. What must they have been doing?"*

Martha reads him too and flushes bright red.

"Oh Martha mine, this mind reading business is going to land us in some embarrassing situations."

She shrugs and dives into the pool, submerging her body. I feel her delight at the soothing and refreshing embrace of the water, and decide to follow her straight in. We frolic for a while, splashing each other in our joy while Fionbal observes us curiously. When we're done, we approach the edge and allow my somar to clean us with his washcloth.

As Fionbal is patting us dry after our bath, his communicator bleeps with an incoming call from Shanbri. He picks up. "What is it Shanbri?"

Shanbri's serious face appears on the screen, and I immediately know something is wrong with Prilor. I snatch the communicator from Fionbal's hands.

"What happened to Prilor?" I snap. I'm too emotional to read his thoughts.

"We were sparring, maybe a little too energetically to get rid of our tension, and I... I am sorry my kran, I accidentally speared him in the foot."

I'm filled with irrational fury towards Shanbri. How dare he hurt my Prilor! Martha's hand on my arm infuses me with enough calm to be able to spit out, "Send for emergency transport. Get him to the clinic and I'll see you there."

"Transport is already on its way my kran."

"Good." I end the connection and storm to our chamber. Absently I notice Dovtar has already replaced our soiled sheets and placed fresh garments for us to wear on the bed. In a mad rush, I dress and stride outside to find our transport. Martha trails behind me, not saying anything, but sending soothing vibes through our mind connection. In no time at all, we reach the small clinic that is used by our family and other important dignitaries. I'm led up to a room where I find Prilor prone on a bed, a bloodied bandage on his foot. "My heart!" I cry.

His pained face clears as he catches sight of me. I clutch him in my arms and use my senses to check out his level of injury. I'm relieved when I find the spear has not caused any permanent damage, although it is aching greatly. He needs more pain relief. Before I even get the chance to speak, Martha is calling the doctor and insisting on increasing Prilor's pain medication. She speaks in fluent Venorian to the thunderstruck medic, who stares at her in shocked surprise. "Hurry!" I roar. He jumps, and rushes into action.

I hold Prilor to me, kissing his cheek and stroking his shaggy hair. "Oh Prilor mine, what have you done to yourself? It's clear you cannot take well enough care of yourself when I'm not around. Tonight, you sleep in our bed."

Martha speaks to me silently, *"Maybe it's best I sleep with Shanbri tonight and leave the two of you alone."*

I turn to her and nod. I stay by Prilor's side as they administer his pain medication, and watch over the medic as he patches up his foot and places a fresh bandage on it.

I turn to instruct Fionbal to get us back home and for Shanbri to prepare a soothing broth for my love, but Martha has already spoken to them. I transmit my thanks, immensely grateful for this mind connection we have. Fionbal and I carefully manoeuver Prilor on to a wheelchair—no easy task as he's a big man—and set off for our transport. I hold Prilor close to me the whole journey home, whispering words of love and comfort to him.

After much effort to avoid causing him pain, we finally settle him on our bed. Seeing Prilor here again causes my heart to clench painfully. This is his bed, and for a week, he was exiled from it. Even knowing that it was unavoidable, I feel terrible guilt. No more, my Prilor. From now on, you sleep here with me every night.

Shanbri brings in a tray with some steaming broth. I read his sadness and worry, and I suddenly feel shame at having vented my fury on him. Before he turns to go, I call him to me. "Shanbri mine, come."

He approaches hesitantly. "I am so sorry for my carelessness my kran. I wish I could go back in time and not have had this happen."

I kiss him lovingly. "We cannot change the past, Shanbri, but I wish to apologize for my anger at you. It was uncalled for."

He strokes my cheek and kisses me back. With a wry smile, he says, "It seems like forever since we have kissed. I have missed you my kran, as well as Martha."

"I know. Tonight Shanbri, she will bed with you."

"Thank you Krantor."

He turns to go, but Prilor reaches out a hand to stop him. He pulls him back to his side, and kisses him softly. "Do not fret, Shanbri. I shall soon be back on my feet and trouncing you in combat again. Thank you for this fine smelling broth." They touch foreheads, transmitting the feelings they cannot put into words, then Shanbri leaves us alone.

"Eat, my love," I say to him.

He finishes the broth, and then I settle him by my side. I sniff his glorious musky scent and stroke my fingers through the hair on his burly arms. "I have missed you, Prilor mine."

"No more than I have missed you."

I arrange the covers around us and dim the light. "Sleep my love. I will not leave your side again."

As I drift off to sleep, I open my mind connection to check in with Martha. I feel Shanbri's cock as its girth fills her pussy, and her gasp of passion. It is a strange thing to be able to experience all of my mate's physical sensations. It is almost as if I'm the one being fucked by Shanbri. He holds her hands up above her head and thrusts hard, deep into her cunt, over and over again. I have never felt this level of passion from Shanbri when we have fucked. I feel his large cock massage the pleasure receptors deep inside her tight channel. Ah, that feels good. My cock rises in reaction. I tune in for a little longer, but then I end the connection. My mate is fine, and I shall not disturb her. Rearranging myself so my cock nestles comfortably in Prilor's fine ass, I settle down to sleep, my head and his on the same pillow.

CHAPTER 28

Krantorven

Next morning, I'm woken early by an incoming call from father on my communicator.

"Good morning father," I yawn.

"Krantor, I am sorry to hear about Prilor's injury, but I see he is being well cared for. There have been some new developments for which I have called a council meeting. I would like you there, and your mate. I am sure you can leave Prilor in Fionbal's capable hands for a short while."

I sigh in disappointment, but I know my duty. "Yes of course father, I will be there shortly." He ends the connection and I tune in to Martha. She is fast asleep, so I call Shanbri on my communicator. When he answers sleepily, I say, "Wake her, please." I end the call and tune in to Martha again. I sense instantly the moment she wakens and transmit the latest developments to her. She responds sleepily, *"I'm on my way."*

Moments later, a naked Martha walks into my chamber, followed by Dovtar bearing fresh garments for us to wear. She disappears into the bathroom for a quick wash under the rainmaker—or shower as it's called in her language. I follow her in and wash with her, soaping my hands to clean her intimate parts, which are wet and sticky from her lovemaking with Shanbri. It amazes me how natural it feels to do this with her. She is so much a part of me now, that it is almost as if I am washing my own body. She assists me too, as I turn and present my back to her, scrubbing my skin with her soapy hands all the way down to my ass crack, which she gives a vigorous rub. We rinse off the soap, then dry ourselves.

In the bedroom, Prilor watches us drowsily as we hurriedly pull on our clothes. "What has happened?" he asks.

"I am not sure. Father wants us for a council meeting." He makes to rise, but I push him down gently on the bed. "You, my love, are not going anywhere. I will send Fionbal to make sure you follow the medic's instructions to the letter."

At this, as if summoned, Fionbal enters, catching the last of my words. "Do not worry yourself, my kran. Prilor will be well cared for."

I smile gratefully and give him a gentle kiss on the lips as I exit the room. I hold out my hand for Martha, and together, we walk towards the council room. We arrive shortly after and enter, finding everyone already gathered there. "Welcome Krantor and Marthajar, come and sit yourselves down," says my father on seeing us.

We settle next to each other at the table. "I will let Rivtas fill you in on what is going on."

Rivtas inclines her head and turns towards us. "As you know, we have been examining the boral crystals to try to understand what the Saraxians could want with them. Unfortunately, our investigations have been inconclusive. The crystals have a mild soporific effect on the body, but other than that, we have not discovered anything that could explain the Saraxians' interest in them. The decision was taken to return them to Krovatia. They were dispatched two rotations ago in one of our freighter ships. Unfortunately, we have just received word that our ship was attacked before reaching Krovatia and the boral crystals stolen once again. Our ship has turned back and is on its way home now. Thankfully, none of our people were harmed, but the ship will require some repair when it gets here, as well as an upgrade to its security systems."

My father interjects, "Our need to understand the importance of these crystals has become more urgent than ever. Why do the Saraxians want them so much?"

"You say the crystals have a mild soporific effect," says Martha. "Have you established by what mechanism the crystals induce this effect?"

Rivtas looks puzzled. "I do not know. How is this significant?"

My mind has jumped to where Martha is heading. I'm not sure yet if it's because I can read what she is thinking right now or whether it's because of the sharpened observation skills I've developed since merging our DNAs. I answer for her. "A mild soporific effect could be magnified with a greater concentration of crystals say, or with the crystals reacting with another substance. We would need to know the mechanism by which the crystals induce the effect in order to determine the level of risk they pose to us."

Martha's mind has already jumped to the next possibility. My mate is incredibly quick thinking. "Let us think back to where the crystals were originally discovered," she says. "They were seized in the Utar belt, from Klixians who were supposed to hand them over to the Saraxians but were thrown off course by a sensor failure on their ship. We have been racking our brains wondering why of all places, the meet-up was arranged in the Utar belt. What if there is a connection between the crystals and something else that we have in large supply over there?"

"The dorenium!" father says, beginning to piece together the puzzle.

"Exactly," I say. "Dorenium is a powerful energy source. Could it super-charge the crystals to magnify whatever effect they have on us? We could be going from a mild soporific effect to possibly causing unconsciousness on an individual, or even worse, on a general population."

There is silence as everyone considers the grave implications of what I have just said. Then father springs to action. "Dranlar," he says, turning to his somar, "find the scientist who analyzed the crystals and get him to us."

Dranlar reaches for his communicator and types a quick message. A short while later, an incoming buzz signals the scientist is on the connection. Dranlar projects his face on to the large screen for us all to see, and speaks to him. "Welcome Hontar, we have some questions for you about the boral crystals."

Hontar nods shyly and mumbles, "I am happy to answer any questions you may have."

"Did you establish by what mechanism the crystals were able to induce a mild soporific effect on an individual?"

Hontar looks surprised. "Yes of course, it was in my report." At this, father glowers in annoyance. Somebody did not read the report thoroughly enough.

"Please could you explain it now."

Hontar thinks for a moment. "Well, to put it in simple terms, the crystals act as inhibitors to our neural transmitters."

"Are these the same neural transmitters that enable us to communicate telepathically?" Martha asks.

"Yes, exactly so."

"So, if the effect of the crystals was magnified to double their strength, would that stop Venorians from communicating telepathically?"

"Almost undoubtedly so."

"And what kind of magnification would be required to induce unconsciousness?"

Hontar frowns. "I cannot be sure, but possibly not much more. Our telepathy is such an ingrained part of our brains that having it blocked would cause us some side effects, such as dizziness or nausea. It would not need much higher a dose to then cause unconsciousness."

"Thank you Hontar for this information," I say. "You may go." He nods and ends the connection.

We sit in shocked silence, processing this new data, then father looks straight at us. "It is imperative that the Saraxians do not get their hands on our dorenium. We cannot be sure that it is dorenium which causes a magnified reaction, but the probability is high. Dranlar, open a channel with Rivvol and patch my mate in on this meeting."

A few seconds later, Rivvol and my mother appear on separate screens. Mother is currently on the Onar, patrolling the Utar belt. Father quickly explains the situation to them. "We urgently need to review and upgrade our security on the dorenium colony. I will send Krantor on the Phtar as soon as this meeting is over, and also recall our freighter ship from Krov—"

He's interrupted by the sound of an explosion, and then Rivvol disappears from the screen.

"What the hell happened?" shouts father.

Mother coolly runs some scans from her ship. "There has been an attack on the colony. My sensors are picking up four ships in sector 3. They have blasted and disabled Rivvol's ship. I'm heading there now, but I need urgent back up."

"Understood."

Mother ends the connection as I jump to my feet and head out to get on the Phtar with my somars. I send a message in my head to Martha. *"Please stay with Prilor."*

She responds in my head, running alongside me, *"Of course. I'm going to contact my fellow humans on the exchange program. They are the only people immune to a possible boral crystal attack. We need them in key places."*

I respond, *"Good thinking."*

We reach my quarters and I call out to my somars. They converge on the living area, Prilor hopping on his crutches. I explain the situation as quickly as I can, and they all rush to prepare. I turn to Prilor. "Not you, my love. Stay here with Martha."

"But—"

"No! You are injured Prilor. That is the end of it." I stride towards him and grab him for a fierce kiss. "I love you more than life. Stay here." And then, with Dovtar, Shanbri and Fionbal at my side, I turn to go board my ship.

CHAPTER 29

Martha

I take out my communicator and contact my four fellow humans in a group message.

Me: Drop everything and come to the palace straight away. There is an emergency situation, and we need your help. Will explain when you get here.

Then, I call Dranlar on my communicator. He answers straight away, looking stressed. "Marthajar, what is it?"

"Please send me Hontar's contact details. I want to discuss possible antidotes to the boral crystals."

"Good thinking. I will do that right away."

"Also, I have summoned my fellow humans on the exchange program. As non-telepaths, they will be immune to a boral crystal attack and may be of use to us. Have a think about what key positions you might want to place them in."

"Understood." He ends the connection and promptly sends Hontar's contact information. I call him straight away.

"Good afternoon, Your Highness," he says, looking puzzled to see me again.

"Hontar, we have a possible emergency and I need your help. If an enemy were to find a way to magnify the effect of boral crystals by combining them with an energy source such as dorenium, is there anything we could do to inhibit the effect? An antidote perhaps."

He ponders the question. "Well, we could administer a drug that does the opposite of inhibiting our neural transmitters."

"Is there any such drug out there?"

"Well yes. There is a chemical called frekium which stimulates the neural transmitters. We use it for patients who experience telepathic blockages. It is possible that a dose of frekium could counteract the effects of boral crystals."

"Excellent. Any side effects I should know about?"

"Yes indeed. As well as stimulating neural transmitters, frekium is also known to stimulate fertility in both males and females. I should advise you that there is a risk of unplanned pregnancies."

"In the grand scheme of things," I say dryly, "we'll take that risk. How soon can you get us a supply of frekium?"

"My colleagues in the outpatient clinic should have a ready supply. I will mobilize it immediately and send it on to you. One vial per person should be sufficient to stimulate the neural transmitters and provide protection for at least one rotation."

"Perfect. Please do that now, and thank you for your help."

Next, I open a channel with Dranlar. "Good news Dranlar. Hontar is sending us a supply of frekium which stimulates neural transmitters and can act as an antidote. I'll make sure Prilor and I take some and then send the rest to you. Please ensure all key personnel are given a dose."

"Excellent Marthajar. Thank you!" He closes the connection.

I look up to see Prilor watching me with a strange expression on his face. I probe his mind, then blush. "Thank you," I say. "It's kind of you to say so."

He laughs. "I did not say it; I just thought it. But I will say it now. You make an extremely fine mate for my kran."

"Thanks." I go to sit by him. "Your foot is paining you. Take some medication."

He shakes his head. "It is too much of a risk. I want my wits about me, and the medication will dull them."

I sigh. "You're right."

I sit back on the couch and close my eyes, opening a mind connection with Krantor. *"Hey Martha, I'm fine. Shanbri too."*

I smile *"You read my mind."*

He transmits his amusement. *"It's what I do."* I quickly emit the latest information. *"Good work Martha. Listen, we will be approaching sector 3 shortly, so I better go."*

I sigh, hating to end our connection. *"Ok my love. Keep safe."*

He sends back a virtual hug. *"Will do."*

I open my eyes to find Prilor watching me intently. "They're fine," I say. "About to reach their destination."

He nods, but continues to focus his gaze on me. I feel the weight of expectation of my newfound role as Krantor's mate. I'm expected to lead and take action. Instead, I ask, "So, what do we do now?"

"We wait and we think. If the Saraxians were to attack our planet, what would they target?"

"The vlor? It's our most valuable tradeable asset."

"Yes, that is a possibility. What else would they target?"

I shake my head. "Nothing else comes to mind."

He stares at me, and I read his thoughts. "Ah. I hadn't thought of that."

"You are a target, Martha. If they eliminate you, Krantor not only loses his mate but all the abilities he gained when he mated you. Even worse, the sudden wrench of the mating bond from his body could have disastrous effects on him, even kill him. It has happened to a few krans in the past. Think of this from the Saraxians' viewpoint. With you and Krantor gone, the Tor line would end, leaving Ven without a leader in the near future and vulnerable to attack. Martha, you are at great risk."

"Well, put like that…" I shiver with a sense of dread. Heroics are not really my thing. I force myself to think calmly. "I'm safe here though, in the palace."

Prilor frowns. "I will see about increasing the number of guards outside." He picks up his communicator and starts sending out messages. After a while, he looks up. "Your human friends are here. The guards are letting them in."

I rise and go to the entrance to our quarters. There's a knock at the door and I open it to see my fellow humans standing outside. I smile in relief. "Hey everyone, come in!"

They follow me inside, looking around curiously. "So, what's the emergency?" Troy asks. "Your message was rather cryptic."

"Go on, take a seat. By the way, this is Prilor, one of my somars. Prilor, meet Troy, Dimitri, Gabriel and Shay."

Prilor nods gruffly.

"Would any of you like some *joh* to drink?"

Gabriel shudders. "No thanks, that stuff is way too sweet!"

Shay smiles broadly. "I'll have some! I've developed a taste for that sweet stuff."

"Me too," adds Troy.

I pick up a jug of hot *joh* and pour it into four mugs, one for myself, Prilor, Troy and Shay. We take a few sips, then Troy asks again, "So what's up Martha?"

As quickly as I can, I explain about the boral crystals and how these could be used to incapacitate our people in an attack. Dimitri frowns as he joins the dots quickly in his mind. "You do know Martha, that you now have a target on your head."

I sigh. "Yes, don't remind me."

"Well actually I must, because that's where our efforts need to focus."

Troy glances at Prilor. "If the Saraxians wanted to get to Martha, what would they have to do?"

Prilor responds. "There are several levels of defense they would have to get through. Firstly, our planet is protected by a force field that is only lowered when a ship is allowed in or wants to leave. The Saraxians would have to find a way to lower that force field."

"Any ideas how they would do that?"

Prilor frowns in concentration. "They could capture one of our ships and send a signal from it with a Venorian signature, asking to be let in."

At this, my ears perk up. "There is a ship on its way home now—the freighter ship that was transporting the crystals to Krovatia. The Saraxians attacked it once before, so they could do it again."

Troy nods. "And this time more easily, if they have gotten their hands on some dorenium. If, as we suspect, it magnifies the effect of the crystals, the Saraxians could project a beam with the enhanced crystals onto the ship and immediately render everyone there unconscious."

We're interrupted by an incoming call on my communicator. It's from the head of palace security. "Your Highness, there is a person called Hontar who is here for you. Shall I let him in?"

"Yes, thank you. Please make haste in escorting him here."

"Understood."

I look at Prilor. "We need to take our dose and have the frekium distributed immediately. There's no time to lose. In the meantime, can you check for the whereabouts of our freighter ship?"

Prilor nods and starts tapping on his communicator. Just then, there is a knock on the door, and Hontar enters, looking flustered. I smile at him reassuringly. "Hontar, it's good you're here. We need to dose up on the frekium as a matter of urgency. Have you taken some yourself?"

"Yes, Your Highness, I took the liberty to do so."

"Good. Bring it here."

Prilor puts down his communicator and looks at me in alarm. *Oh shit.* "The freighter ship docked some moments ago," he says. Then he pounds his fist and roars with rage, "Dammit!"

At this, Hontar startles and drops the container he's been holding, scattering vials of frekium all over the floor. "I am so sorry!" he mumbles, bending down to pick them up.

Shay comes over and lays a calming hand on him. "I'll help you," she says, and gets down on the floor with him.

I pick up a vial that has rolled to my feet and hand it to Prilor. "Here, drink this." He takes it from me and puts it to his lips. I bend down to look for more vials, shoving them into my pocket as I go. A sudden searing pain has me clutching my head. I feel myself fall to the ground as blackness descends on me.

CHAPTER 30

Shanbri

We have engaged in a brutal firefight with the Saraxians. Using the powerful cloaking technology on the Phtar, we were able to sneak close to the first ship and blast it to smithereens. However, in the debris that flew back at us, our cloak was revealed and the Saraxian ships began to fire at us in earnest.

Dodging the blasts has been no easy feat, but the Phtar is an agile ship, and Krantor's ability to navigate has been greatly enhanced since his mating with Martha. Together with the Onar, led by Krantor's mother, we were eventually able to disable two further Saraxian ships. Of the fourth, we have seen no sign. I fear it has already plundered our dorenium and gone, under cover of our firefight. It could be heading straight for Ven. Straight for Martha.

My suspicion is confirmed when Krantor's mother hails him on his communicator. "The remaining Saraxian ship has escaped with the dorenium. I can manage here now. You must hurry and give chase to that ship."

"Understood."

Krantor turns to Fionbal. "Scan for Saraxian signatures. We need to know where that ship went." The look on his face tells me he fears what I fear.

A short while later, Fionbal responds. "It looks like the Saraxian ship has headed towards Ven."

Krantor is already setting a course for home. I send a prayer to almighty Lir. *Please keep Martha safe.* But once again, Lir does not seem to be listening.

I sense Krantor trying to open a mind connection with Martha, without success. "I can't get through to Martha," he growls. "Fionbal, open a channel with father."

Fionbal does as instructed, but we get no response. "None of your father's somars are responding either," he says.

I pull out my communicator and call Martha. Again, no response. "Try Prilor," suggests Dovtar. I connect with Prilor. Only it is not his face that appears on the screen, but that of a human—one of the men on the exchange program.

"Where is Martha?" I snap.

Looking pale, he responds. "She's been taken by the Saraxians. They attacked the palace and took her." *Hell and damnation!*

Krantor snatches the communicator from my hands. "What of Prilor?" he cries.

The human visibly shakes. "He tried to protect Martha, but he was outnumbered. They shot him in the chest. Gabriel is working on him now."

"No!" roars Krantor.

"We're doing our best to keep him alive, but he's in a critical condition. It's only us here and one scientist called Hontar. Everyone else is unconscious."

"Do whatever it takes to save him. We're on our way." He closes the connection and shouts to Fionbal. "Can we go any faster?"

Fionbal shakes his head. "We're at maximum speed."

My heart is pounding violently in my chest. They have taken Martha. They have my heart. Barely able to grate out the words, I say to Krantor, "We must go after their ship and find Martha."

He looks at me with crazed eyes. "Prilor needs me!"

I shout back, not caring if I am showing disrespect. "So does Martha!"

Dovtar has been tapping on the monitor and speaks up now. "Our scans have picked up the Saraxian ship. They are headed for Sarax. I can change course now."

"Do not!" thunders Krantor. "We are going to Ven and to Prilor. Stay on course!"

I thunder back, enraged. "We cannot desert Martha. She is your mate!"

His eyes are agonized. "Don't you think I fucking know that? But Prilor needs me now. Only I can save him!"

Dimly, I am aware of the truth of his statement. A transfusion of Krantor's blood could be the difference between Prilor living or dying. But all I can focus on is Martha. My heart.

I make my decision and stand. "Then I will go. I will take the shuttle."

Krantor hesitates, then nods his assent. I rush to the armory and begin pulling on a protective space suit. Dovtar joins me, holding out a pack of food rations and an emergency medical kit. "Just in case," he says.

"Thank you." I open the shuttle pod door.

Dovtar calls out after me. "I have programmed your route on the shuttle. They are only a quarter rotation away, so you should be able to catch up with them. Stay well cloaked."

I nod.

He gives me a quick kiss on the lips. "Good luck my friend." Then I'm boarding the shuttle and starting the throttle on the engine. *I am coming for you Martha. I will go to the end of the universe to find you.*

CHAPTER 31

Krantorven

Dovtar and Fionbal are silent beside me. I can read their minds, so I know they are conflicted by my decision. In the short time they have known her, they have fallen in love with my mate. It pains them that I have decided not to save her. It pains me too. It's ripping my heart in two. She is a part of me, but I cannot abandon Prilor. I know, if only I can get there in time, that I can save him.

It may be the most foolish decision I ever make. I know more than anyone that my life depends on Martha. If she dies, then perhaps so do I. Certainly I would lose my powers and my ability to become the next kran. Even so, I know I have made the right choice. There may still be time to save Martha, but Prilor is hanging on a knife edge.

I've always known I loved him. I have spent the last decade in his constant embrace, loving him with my body and soul. When it came to making a split-second choice—save Martha or save Prilor—there was only one choice I could make. Him.

I hope in time Martha will forgive me—if Shanbri gets to her in time. I can't even contemplate the thought if he doesn't. Martha knows intimately what goes on in my thoughts and heart. If anyone can understand my agonizing decision, it's her. She will forgive me, but I can't dwell on this now. I must get to Prilor.

As we make our final approach towards our home planet, my communicator buzzes with an incoming from Hontar. My heart starts to beat double time. *Please let it be good news.* I pick up. "Tell me," I growl.

"He's lost a lot of blood and sustained serious damage to his liver and kidneys. We have managed to stabilize him, but the situation remains critical."

"Is everyone else still in a state of unconsciousness?"

"Yes, my kran. The boral crystals, powered by the dorenium, are still being beamed on our planet, I do not know from where. This brings me to the real reason for my call. You will need a dose of frekium before you enter our atmosphere, or else you will be affected too. Have you any frekium on your ship?"

I turn to look at my somars and they shake their heads.

"I see," Hontar says. "I have supplies here, so the only sensible course is for me to take a shuttle up to your ship and administer the dose."

"Please do so, and be quick."

"Understood."

A short time later, Hontar's shuttle docks on our ship and he emerges on to the bridge. "My kran, it is good to see you," he says with a smile.

I don't smile back. I am too tense for that. "Please, Hontar, the frekium."

"Of course." He takes the vials out of a small container he is holding and hands one out to each of us.

I drink it quickly. "Now let us be on our way without delay. Hontar, stay aboard with your shuttle."

He inclines his head, and Fionbal begins to manoeuver our ship through the open force field—for which we will need to improve our security protocols in future. We cannot let this happen again.

A short while later, we dock our ship on Ven and jump out to catch a transport to the clinic where Hontar and Gabriel have taken Prilor. I run up the steps and enter the building, then realize I don't know where Prilor has been taken. I turn to face Hontar, giving his mind a quick read. Ah. The recovery room outside the operating theater. I set to running again, passing by the eerie spectacle of countless Venorians passed out on the floor.

Finally, I push open the door of the recovery room and see him. Prilor's massive form is prone on the bed, tubes attached to him. I approach the bed and touch his pale face with hands that tremble. "Prilor mine," I whisper. For a long moment, I stare at his dear face, then I gather myself and look up at Gabriel.

"I will give him blood and donate parts of my liver and kidneys," I say firmly.

"Is that possible? You may not be a genetic match."

"My Tor genetics make it possible. My blood and tissues can adapt to any environment. They will heal him."

"I see."

"Let us begin right away."

Gabriel hesitates. "I am a geneticist," he says softly, "not a transplant surgeon."

"The computer will perform the surgery. Hontar can program it to do the task."

Hontar, who has finally caught up with me, nods his head in agreement. "Yes indeed, it is entirely feasible to go ahead, now that we have a donor. My kran, there is something perhaps you have not considered though. Once Prilor has your blood and organs, he will acquire your memories and abilities, in the same way as your mate did. Your mind will become one with his. Are you sure it is something you want to do?"

I laugh. "Oh yes Hontar, more sure than ever. Hook me up and let us get started."

I turn to Dovtar and Fionbal, who are standing motionless behind me. "Fionbal, while I am incapacitated, you are to assume command until such time as either I am awake or my father resumes consciousness. Your priority is to locate the beam that is projecting the boral crystals and disable it. Please also see if you can track Shanbri's shuttle and find out how he and my mate are getting on. Provide them with whatever assistance you can. Keep my mother apprised of your progress."

"Understood my kran."

I kiss both of my somars lovingly. "And say a prayer for the both of us."

"Yes of course, my kran."

I stroke Prilor's cheek one last time. "Soon, my love," I breathe. Then I start to undress, in readiness for the transplant operation.

CHAPTER 32

Martha

I come awake slowly and sit up, taking stock of my surroundings. I'm in a small room, more like a cubicle, with metallic walls and a bolted door. My head is pounding a little. I use my meditation practice to do an inventory of my body—no major damage and my neural transmitters are working fine. That must mean I'm out of range of the boral crystals that were used to attack us. But where am I? A Saraxian ship? That would make sense.

I close my eyes and focus my mind. *Krantor!* I try again. *Krantor.* There is no answer. I hesitate to think what that could mean. For now, I'm alone and helpless.

What are they going to do with me? I suppose it must be a good sign that they haven't killed me yet. Perhaps they want to hold me hostage for ransom. I get up and walk around my cell, feeling the walls and door for any possible route of escape. Nothing.

I look up at the ceiling. There's an air vent that I could fit through. I stretch up on my tiptoes, but it's out of my reach. Just great. Anyway, even if I could get out through the vent, where would I go? I'm most likely on a ship in the middle of space.

I crumple down to the floor and put my head on my knees, despondent. *Think positive thoughts Martha.* My mind goes to Shanbri. What is he doing now? Is he thinking of me? Yes, of course he is. I don't know why I'm so sure of this. I just am.

Thinking of him lifts my spirits, just a little bit. I sit back and rest my head on the cold hard wall. Maybe I should just dream of Shanbri, and try to remember everything I can about him. I close my eyes and picture him in front of me. His tall, muscular body brushed with fine gold hair. The dark eyes that can sizzle with heat and twinkle with amusement from one moment to the next. The blond tresses that are constantly fighting their way out of his bun. The wondrous cakes and pastries he creates just for me. I slide my hand down my pants and touch the tattoo, his tattoo. Last time we were together, he kissed it reverently before burying his head in my pussy and licking me to a glorious climax. I smile. Such wonderful memories. I think of his long thick beautiful cock that gives me so much pleasure, and of that first time when he fucked me against the bathroom door. Oh yes. If I'm going down in flames, I want my last thoughts to be of his magnificent member.

A strange tapping sound interrupts my pleasant recollections. I open my eyes and tune my senses. It's coming from above. I stand abruptly, looking up. Slowly, the grille of the air vent is pushed to one side, and then I see his face. Shanbri!

He calls out to me softly. "Martha, are you hurt?"

"I'm fine."

"Move aside. I will jump down."

I make room for him and after a little more shifting on his stomach, he's able to swing his legs down through the hatch and jump gracefully down. A moment later, I'm in his arms. He holds me tight. I feel his emotions. *Relief, love, concern.* I telegraph my love and relief back and, *"I'm fine, I'm fine, I'm fine."* Eventually, he pulls away just enough to look into my eyes. "I need to get you out of here. Can you climb on my shoulders to reach the hatch?"

"I'll try. Where do we go from there? No hang on, I'll read it in your thoughts." I pause and focus my mind on his. "Ok, I get it."

He kneels on the floor, and I climb on to his shoulders. Slowly, with immense strength, he rises to his full height and goes to stand under the hatch. I use all my newfound agility from my daily Drekon practice with Flidar to push myself up on my arms and come to standing on his shoulders. Trying not to lose my balance, I carefully reach for the hatch. *Got it.* With all the strength I can muster, I pull myself up. My muscles screaming, I finally pull up high enough to swing my legs up and into the tunnel. As quickly as I can, I move aside to make room for Shanbri. With superhuman strength, he jumps up and catches hold of the hatch, nimbly pulling himself up to crouching beside me.

He touches foreheads with me, to check on my wellbeing. I put his mind at rest. *"All good."*

He sighs in relief. *"I'm glad. Follow me."*

Ever so slowly, we crawl along the small tunnel. I know, from having read his mind, that it leads to another hatch which opens onto a small storage room. From there, we will have to tread carefully to avoid detection. His shuttle is docked by the ship's secondary airlock door. It is cloaked and has not yet been noticed by the Saraxians. Our hope is to be able to make our escape without revealing its position. First though, we will have to make our way to the armory and steal an extra space suit for me to wear, as we will have to spacewalk our way from the airlock door to the shuttle.

We reach the hatch and Shanbri carefully moves the grille, checking that no one is there. With the grace of a cat, he jumps down, then straightens up and looks at me. He wants me to jump into his arms. I hesitate. I'm not a small woman. *"Do it."* With a deep breath, I take the leap. Large, strong arms envelop me, breaking my fall. *"Got you."*

Gently, he lowers me to my feet. A quick touch to my forehead to make sure I'm alright, then he finds the door. We stand for a while, listening. He cocks his head at me. My enhanced abilities can detect the presence of others more clearly than he can. I nod. It's all clear. Carefully, he opens the door and steps out, silently asking me to stay back until he's sure it's safe. There's no one there. His mind calls me, and I follow.

Stopping and starting every so often to check for Saraxians, we finally get to the armory. Methodically, he goes through the space suits until he finds one my size, and hands it to me. Quickly, we pull them on—his suit having been stowed away safely when he arrived on the ship earlier. Fully kitted, we pull our helmets on and check to ensure our oxygen supply is functioning. All good.

I know from having read his thoughts that we have to follow a narrow corridor and turn right before reaching the airlock door. He turns to me. *"Ready?"* I nod. We stand for a while, listening for voices. We don't hear anyone, so we start moving stealthily down the corridor. And that's when my senses suddenly tell me we're no longer alone. I tune in and sense the footsteps before I hear them. Someone is coming our way from behind. I touch Shanbri's shoulder in warning. He looks behind me and then in rapid fire succession, sends me his silent instructions. *"I'll cover. You run to the airlock and get it open. Find your way to the shuttle. I'll follow when I can. If I'm not with you in five minutes, go without me. Don't argue. Just do it!"* I cast him one last look, then run.

I hear the sound of a struggle behind me but try to ignore it and get to the airlock. Our best chance is if I get the shuttle engine started and have it ready to go the moment Shanbri joins me. I won't leave without him, but he doesn't need to know that. With shaking hands, I manage to open the first set of airlock doors, then the second. Using the clamps on my space suit, I carefully crawl towards the shuttle, which is invisible to the naked eye, but which I can detect with my enhanced senses.

With a little effort, I open the shuttle door and step inside. I squeeze through the narrow space and make my way to the controls. It's then that panic sets in. What the heck am I doing? I've never flown a shuttle before! All I have are Krantor's memories. I take a deep breath and focus, looking at all the controls before me. Then I know what to do. I press a few buttons and hear the soft thrum of the engine. I take off my helmet and breathe a little easier, then, using the shuttle's camera feed, I keep watch for Shanbri.

The minutes crawl past, with no sign of him. *Where the fuck are you Shanbri?* Then I see him, crawling towards me, unsure where the shuttle is. I decide to risk it and lower the cloak long enough for him to see where to go. With the shuttle visible, he makes his way towards me with surer movements. Only when I'm sure he knows where to go do I bring the cloak back on.

Shanbri is very nearly at the shuttle door, when I hear shots being fired. *Oh shit. Hurry my love.* I hear the shuttle door open, and the moment it closes, I press the accelerator and propel us up and away from the Saraxian ship. A few moments later, Shanbri joins me, placing a reassuring hand on my shoulder. *"I'm fine. You're doing great."*

I concentrate on the controls, intent on getting us as far away from the Saraxians as possible. Shanbri removes his helmet and comes to sit beside me. He touches a few controls to program our route back to Ven. I check the monitor. We're about a half rotation's journey from home. Yeah, I've started to think in the Venorian language.

After a while, I begin to relax a little. I turn to Shanbri and grip his hand. "You're hurt!"

"I think it's only a scratch."

"Let me see."

I help undo his space suit enough to free his right arm, from which a large gash is oozing blood. His mind transmits, *"There is an emergency medical kit in the large green sack behind you."* I turn around and find it, rummaging through the contents to find bandages. Quickly, I clean and wrap the wound, all the while feeling Shanbri's eyes on me.

I look back at him and smile. "You came for me."

"Of course I did. I will always come for you, my heart."

My face goes serious. "What about Krantor? Why isn't he here with you?"

He doesn't say anything, but transmits his thoughts. I take a moment to read him. My heart aches with pain and betrayal. Krantor, my mate, chose Prilor over me. I take a deep breath. I suppose I shouldn't be surprised. I know the depth of Krantor's feelings for him. It hurts though, more than I thought it possible. I gave up so much to become his mate, and this is how he repays me—by turning his back on me when I needed his help.

Shanbri's arm comes around me as he senses my distress. He sends me thoughts of comfort. *"I'm sorry my heart. It is the way it is. You will always come first with me."*

And all of a sudden, all the stress of the last couple of days catches up with me and I burst into tears. I bury my face against Shanbri's chest and sob away my pain. He strokes my hair, sending me love and reassurance. *"Oh Shanbri. You are worth a dozen Krantors!"*

Eventually, I calm down enough to sit up. Shanbri passes me a cloth to wipe my face. "Are you hungry?" he asks.

I nod mutely.

He hunts about in the sack until he finds a pack of dried food rations. He eyes them ruefully. "It is not the most appetizing meal, but it will fill you up."

I take it from him and bite into a chewy bar. I'm too hungry to care. He passes me a bottle of water, which I gulp down in thirst. Once I'm replete, Shanbri puts everything away and pulls me into his arms. "Rest my sweet. I can take over from here."

I snuggle up into his familiar warm chest and close my eyes, allowing myself to drift off.

I'm woken by the sound of an incoming call on Shanbri's communicator. I sit up with a yawn and see Fionbal on the screen. He notices me and grins. "Martha! I cannot tell you how glad I am to see you alive and well."

"Thanks Fionbal. Tell me, how are things your end?"

"I have good news. Prilor and Krantor have emerged from surgery and are recovering well, though they have yet to awaken."

Krantor in surgery? I scan Fionbal's mind to understand. Ah, so Krantor has donated parts of his liver and a kidney to Prilor, which means our giant friend is now going to share our mind connection and be privy to my most private thoughts. I feel a moment of irritation, then force it away. I'll deal with it when I have to. For now, I should just be glad the Prilor is going to be alright.

"That is good news," I say. "I'm glad."

Shanbri looks puzzled. "Why was Krantor in surgery?"

"He donated organs to save Prilor," I explain quickly.

"Ah, I see. Well this is all good news Fionbal."

Fionbal nods, then says, "Now, for the bad news. I am afraid that we have still been unable to locate and disable the boral crystal beam. You will not be able to enter our atmosphere safely without a dose of frekium. For this reason, it might be best to divert your course and head for our colony on the Utar belt."

Shanbri looks at the fuel gauge on the shuttle. "That will not be possible Fionbal. We have very little fuel left. I am not even sure we have enough to make it all the way to Torbreg."

I have a sudden recollection and feel in my pocket. Yes, there are several vials of the stuff there from when I was picking it up off the floor.

"That's not a problem," I say quickly. "I have some in my pocket."

"Oh good. Well then, safe travels."

Shanbri speaks before Fionbal ends the connection. "Fionbal, I am sure we will not be making it to Torbreg. Can you lower the force field, and we will try for an emergency landing at the nearest location. I will send you our coordinates once we land and we will await your rescue in due course."

"Of course. You have sufficient food rations?"

"Yes, enough for at least three rotations."

"I am sure we will get to you before then, but that is good to know."

He ends the connection, and I pull out the vials of frekium. "Here Shanbri, take one of these." He drinks one of the doses and I take another. I check how many I have in my pocket. Another four doses. "I have enough doses for another two rotations. Hopefully by then they will have either disabled the beam or rescued us."

"It will be fine, Martha."

I smile. "I know Shanbri. With you here with me, everything is fine."

He takes my hand in his and squeezes. "Hold on tight my love, we are about to make a bumpy landing."

Bumpy is the understatement of the century. Up until now, I haven't had any space sickness in the modern, slick cabins of the Venorian ships I've been on. However, I'm reminded now why I don't like space travel. The next forty minutes are about the longest of my life as our little shuttle crosses the force field and enters Ven's atmosphere, burning up a little on contact. I close my eyes and chant a prayer during the last few nauseating instants before we finally come to a standstill.

I put my head on my knees and focus on my breathing, in and out, in and out. I'm safe. I'm on terra firma. God knows where, but no longer in space. I'll take that.

Warm arms wrap around me. I hear his voice in my head, *"It's alright my love. It's alright."*

Slowly, I feel my breathing return to normal. I look up and gaze into the eyes of the most precious man in the universe. "I love you Shanbri," I breathe.

"And I love you, heart of mine."

Suddenly, all I want is to feel his touch, his skin on mine, his taste. I pull his head towards me and plant my lips on his. They part, letting my hungry tongue plunge in to savor his delicious flavor. He kisses me back, sucking my lower lip hungrily into his mouth. In a mad rush, we're snatching at our clothes, haphazardly pulling off our space suits, trying to discard every stitch as quickly as we can.

Oh the relief when I feel his naked skin on mine. *"I need."*

He bites my neck. *"I know. I need too."* His mouth roves downwards, nipping its way to the peaks of my breasts, taking them into his mouth to suckle, then coming back up to take my mouth in another ruthless kiss. *"Mount me, Martha."*

Sitting back on the shuttle seat, he allows me to straddle him and slowly lower myself on to his throbbing shaft. I gasp as I feel him fill me. *"You're mine."*

I echo his thought, *"I'm yours."* Then all thoughts leave our heads as we rut desperately in a rhythm as old as time. He thrusts into me ferociously, and I welcome every hard intrusion. *"Oh Shanbri, I'm coming."* He thrusts even harder, and together we cry out our release. My walls pulse around him as he empties his essence into me. And finally sated, I collapse against him, my head tucked into the comfort of his neck.

After a while, he shifts a little and I slowly lift my pussy off his softening cock. As I do, I feel his cum dripping down my legs. I look down at myself. "I think I'm going to need a clean."

He kisses me softly and releases me. "Let us take a look outside. This area is known for its streams and waterfalls. We should be able to find some water source to clean ourselves. Let me first send our coordinates to Fionbal." He picks up his communicator and gives it a few taps. Once done, he finds my shoes and the remnants of my clothes, and hands them to me. I slip on the minimum to cover my modesty—though I'm not expecting to come across anyone—and follow him out of the shuttle cabin.

Outside, it's tropically warm and sunny. Our shuttle seems to have landed in a small clearing next to some kind of forest. I hesitate. "What about wild animals?" I ask nervously.

Shanbri pats his weapon belt. "You are with me, my heart. I will protect you never fear."

Slightly reassured, I walk alongside him as he looks around, sniffing and listening carefully for a water source. Finally, he smiles and points in the direction we need to go. We walk together for a few minutes, until I hear the wonderful sound of water gushing. A few more strides, and we find ourselves beside a stream of crystal clear water. Shanbri bends down and cups the water in his hands, examining it. "It is clean enough to drink," he finally decides, bending down to slurp some into his thirsty mouth. I follow suit, drinking my fill.

Then Shanbri removes a cloth from his pack and wets it in the water, coming over to me and gently cleaning my intimate parts. He dips the cloth in the water several times, running it over every part of my body, before he cleans himself off as well. Once we're both as fresh as we're going to get, we pull on our clothes and head back towards the shuttle. Inside the cabin, Shanbri pulls the leavers on the seats to recline them and fetches some blankets from his pack. We have a second meal of dried rations, then settle down together on our makeshift bed. He draws me into the warm comfort of his arms. *"Sleep now my heart. I will not leave you."* With my head nestled on his chest, feeling the rise and fall of his chest as he breathes, I fall into a restful slumber.

I come awake slowly the next morning, with a warm feeling of contentment. Then I remember. Shanbri came for me. My heart beats a rapid rhythm of delight. He came for me.

"Good morning, beautiful," his voice rumbles against my face still pressed to his chest.

"Good morning handsome god." He barks out a laugh at that, and I sit up, stretching sleepily.

"I have good news. Dovtar is on his way in his transport to take us back home. He should be here very soon."

"I'm glad. Not that I haven't enjoyed this little interlude, but it would be nice to return to the comforts of home."

He smiles. "I agree." He fishes out some more rations from his pack. "I am getting a little tired of eating this food." He hands me an energy bar and takes one for himself.

We chew in comfortable silence, then a sudden thought occurs to me. "Shanbri."

"Yes, my heart?"

"There is something I forgot to tell you, about the frekium."

"What about it? Do we need to take our next dose?"

"We probably should, but that's not what I need to say."

"What then."

"Well, when I spoke to Hontar, he said that frekium has a side effect. In addition to stimulating our neural transmitters, it also, erm, stimulates our fertility."

Shanbri studies me for a long moment, then his face breaks into a wicked smile. "Well in that case, my beauty, we had better have a quick fuck before Dovtar turns up."

I grin back, relieved. "I think that would be a very, very good idea."

CHAPTER 33

Martha

It took another day to finally locate the boral crystal beam and disable it. The retrieved crystals have now been stored in a secure location, until a suitable convoy of ships can return them to Krovatia.

Since returning to the palace, I've slept in Shanbri's bed, Dovtar having tactfully removed himself to spend his nights in Fionbal's chamber. Prilor and Krantor are still in the clinic, recovering from their operation.

Krantor has regained consciousness, but I haven't been to see him yet. This morning, I sensed him in my mind. I also sensed a second person—Prilor. It was impossible for me to hide my feelings of hurt and betrayal. Both men heard me loud and clear.

"*I am so sorry Martha,*" this thought from Prilor.

"*I'm sorry too, but I couldn't have made any other choice,*" now Krantor.

"*I know, but it hurts. I don't feel like I can be your mate anymore.*"

Prilor, whose big heart has never been in doubt, sends me waves of sorrow and understanding. "*You will always be my mate, Martha.*"

"*You are my mate,*" Krantor replies bullishly.

"*Really? Because a mate is the person you treasure above all else. Your life partner. The yin to your yang. Not the person that comes second best.*"

"*It was the hardest decision I've ever had to make Martha. I love you and no matter what you think, you are my mate. We still have this unbreakable connection.*"

"That's not a good enough reason for me to spend my nights in your bed, or to spend my life with you."

"So what are you going to do? I hate to break it to you, but divorce doesn't exist on Ven."

"Gee thanks for that nugget of information."

"That's enough you two," this from Prilor. *"It might be best to keep some distance until we can work through the feelings of hurt. We will work out an acceptable solution in time."*

"Ok. There's something else," I say to them in my head.

"Yes, I know you fucked Shanbri even though the frekium made you fertile. Has it resulted in a conception?" this thought from the ever charming Krantor.

"I don't know yet."

"You know you're supposed to give me an heir before you have children with my somars."

"Well, tough. You'll have to get in line and wait your turn like everyone else."

"That's fine," Prilor again, soothing the waves. *"We can wait. I look forward to a new baby in the family, whether it's Krantor's or Shanbri's."*

I end the neural connection as I feel Shanbri stir next to me. I stroke the soft hair on his chest and kiss him gently. "Good morning."

He yawns. "Good morning my love."

"I just spoke to Krantor and Prilor. We've agreed a little time apart is needed until we can repair our relationship."

Shanbri's gaze is sad. "I love Krantor. I do not like to see this distance between us. What he did hurt you, but I can forgive him because all he did was follow his heart. Please can you find it in yours to forgive him?"

232

I sigh. "I'll try, but it will take time. Even if I do, I don't think I can go back to him. I want to be with you from now on."

He strokes his hand down my arm. "I would like that too, but there is still the mating bond. Will that not exert a pull on you?"

"I'm not sure. We'll have to see. I suppose I can always go to him when it does, and then return to you. And I have told him he'll have to wait his turn to have a child with me. My first child is going to be yours."

He pulls me on top of him and kisses me. "Well in that case, let us get started on this important task."

I laugh and kiss him back. "Gladly."

One week later

We are sitting in the Kran's office. By we, I mean myself, Krantor and his four somars. Krantor's mother is also present. It feels like we have been summoned to the principal's office. The Kran is not pleased.

We're silent, waiting respectfully for him to speak. He observes us sternly for a long, fraught minute, then launches into his tirade. "A kran who refuses to save his mate when she is in danger!" he booms. "Two mates not speaking to or bedding each other! What in the world do you think you are doing? Have you lost all sense of your duty?"

I squirm and look down at my hands.

"Tell me Krantor. What in Lir's name were you thinking? And don't say you had to save Prilor at all costs, because much as we love him, he is *not* your mate!"

My righteous feeling of injured pride is punctured by the Kran's next blistering attack, this time on me.

"And you, Martha. Turning your back on your mate and showing yourself unwilling to forgive! And what is this I hear of you having a child with Shanbri? Have you forgotten how vital it is to the wellbeing of this planet that Krantor bears an heir?"

Shanbri steps into the breach. "I am sorry my kran. I am at fault too. Do not place the blame entirely on Martha."

The Kran's expression softens. "Shanbri, I have not yet properly thanked you for your courage and service in rescuing Martha. We are all eternally in your debt."

"I would do anything for her."

"Yes, I see this." He sighs and looks at me. "Have you sensed a new life in your body?"

I shake my head. Krantor's mother stands and comes towards me. She places both hands on my belly and listens. Then she smiles and I read her thoughts. *"Congratulations Martha, you are to have twins."*

"Twins?" splutters Krantor.

"Twins?" squeaks Shanbri.

"Yes twins," confirms the Kran's mate.

I'm in a daze. *"Oh my God. Not one but two."*

"Double the joy," Prilor sends the happy thought my way.

Shanbri wraps his arm around me, and I lean into him. I feel his bemusement, mixed with pride and joy.

"Well Martha and Shanbri," says the Kran. "It seems congratulations are in order. I am delighted for you of course, but I must impress on all of you the importance of using the next few months to renegotiate the terms of your relationship with each other. We are all going to be working closely together to ensure the safety of this planet and that an attack such as this never happens again. I need you all to be on good terms again and working in a positive, collaborative manner."

He focuses his laser gaze on me. "And Martha. Your next child must be Krantor's heir. There can be no more delay."

"I understand."

"Good. Now go all of you, and get started on sorting out your relationships. Krantor, I expect you to put in the effort to make this happen."

"Yes father."

We troop out of the Kran's office one by one. Krantor comes forward and touches my arm. "Martha." The word holds a wealth of meaning. I look into his eyes and read his jumbled thoughts. *"I love you. So happy about the news. I miss you. Forgive me."* I walk into his arms and let him hold me. Krantor runs his hands through my hair tenderly just as Prilor comes up from behind to embrace me. He transmits his thoughts. *"We love you, Martha."*

Shanbri is there too, stroking Krantor and raining kisses on the back of his head. I read his mind. *"We all love each other."*

Prilor concurs, *"He's right."*

Out loud I say, "We have to sort this out."

Next morning, I wake to the feel of gentle hands stroking the hair from my face. My lashes flutter open, expecting to see Shanbri, but it's Krantor sitting at my bedside. I cast a quick glance to my right. Shanbri is nowhere in sight. Krantor continues to stroke my hair as he telegraphs this information. *"I sent him out so we can be alone. I need to talk to you, Martha."*

"You talk to me all the time in my head."

"I know, but I think we need to spend some time alone together if we're ever to mend our relationship. Have a quick wash and come out with me. Our transport is waiting."

I sigh, accepting the truth of his statement. We do need time alone to sort things out. I get up and head quickly to the ablution room for a shower. A few minutes later, I'm dressed and ready. I come out of my room to find Krantor waiting for me in the living area, reclining on the circular couch, with Shanbri at his side. Shanbri smiles reassuringly as he stands and comes to enfold me in his arms. "Good morning my love."

I kiss him softly on the lips. "Good morning, my darling."

"I've got some pastries packed in a box for you to eat on your journey." He strokes my face lovingly. "Spend all the time you need and do whatever it takes to mend things with Krantor. Do not worry yourself about me."

"I love you."

He beams. "I love you too. Now go."

He hands me the box of baked goodies, which I take from him with a smile. Krantor comes to me and places a gentle hand on my arm. *"Let's go, Martha mine."*

I grumble, *"I'm not yours anymore."*

"Let's not argue the point. Come on."

With a firm hand, he leads me out of the room. I cast a final glance goodbye at Shanbri and follow him to the transport. Fionbal and Dovtar trail us discreetly at a distance. We all climb into the drone and buckle up.

"Where are you taking me?"

"To your family's estate initially. We're going to take a ride on Saila."

"Oh."

We're silent during the ride to the Jar estate. I can't help a sense of excitement at the prospect of riding Saila again. We land by the griv enclosure and descend from the drone. My great uncle and cousins are nowhere in sight. *"I called them earlier to let them know we're coming. You'll see them after our ride."*

Dovtar brings out Saila, and Fionbal helps him to saddle her up. I go to stroke her soft, brown coat. "Hello girl," I whisper. She sniffles in pleasure, then kneels on the ground to allow me to climb aboard. A moment later, Krantor settles himself behind me. With one hand, he secures me to him and with the other, he takes hold of the reins. Saila slowly comes to standing in readiness for us to go. With a gentle click of his tongue, Krantor instructs her to start moving. We take off at a gentle trot, gradually increasing our speed.

"Where to now?" I ask him in my head.

"You'll see."

He clicks his tongue again, and this time Saila unfurls her wings, flapping them with a great whoosh to lift us off the ground. I feel that same thrill I did before as we rise high in the sky and fly. Nothing beats this feeling.

Krantor echoes my thought. *"I know."*

For long moments, we just enjoy the ride and the heart-pumping excitement of the wind brushing our faces as we zoom through the sky. All too soon, we start our descent. We seem to be approaching a wooded part of the estate. It reminds me a little of our land back in Colorado. As we near the ground, I spy a pool of water and a waterfall. My heart squeezes in my chest. We land in a small clearing, and Saila kneels to allow us to dismount. With trembling steps, I walk to the edge of the pool. As I stare at the crystal clear water and listen to the drumming sounds of the waterfall, I feel tears burn my eyes. *"This is just like it."*

Krantor wraps his arms around me. *"I know."* He kisses the top of my hair. *"I'm told this was your great grandfather's favorite place. He came here often."* He chuckles inwardly. *"Apparently, this was also where he first lost his virginity."*

"Woah, way too much info there! How do you know all this?"

"Poljar. He and your great grandfather shared a bedroom growing up, and they could read each other's thoughts at night. When I spoke to Poljar yesterday, he suggested I bring you here, though I don't think even he realizes the importance of this place for you."

"It's just like the rock pool we have on my family's ranch on Earth."

"I know darling. Your memories are mine too, remember? I wonder what your great grandfather must have thought the first time he saw it on Earth—maybe a little of what you're feeling now. I'm hoping having a place like this to go to will help ease the pain of missing your home on Earth."

"Yes, I think it will." I turn to face him. *"Thanks, Krantor."*

He kisses me gently. *"Martha, I love you and I'm so sorry. I had an impossible choice to make, and I had to do it in a split second. I never wanted to desert you. Please, please forgive me."*

I kiss him back, stroking my tongue with his, tasting his delicious flavor and feeling the tingle of the mating bond. *"I'm getting there Krantor. Give me time. We still have lots of issues to resolve."*

"We'll do it. But for now, how about a skinny dip in the pool?"

I laugh. *"Good idea."*

He starts pulling off his clothes hurriedly. With a smirk, he says out loud, "Last one in the pool goes down on the other." Then we're both hastily getting naked, neither one of us quite sure whether we want to win the bet or not. Krantor makes it into the water a few seconds before me. We splash around like happy kids, enjoying the fresh coolness of the water on our naked skin. Eventually, Krantor lifts me out and deposits me on a smooth rock warmed by the sun. *"Time to pay up, Martha mine."*

He kneels above me and lowers his cock to my waiting mouth. I part my lips, letting him in. With one hand, he supports my head, protecting it from the hardness of the rock under me as he begins to thrust. I taste him on my lips—that sweet flavor that belongs only to him. I drown in his gaze that burns with desire, as he fucks my mouth. My core throbs in answering passion. There's no denying this. I want him. I love him. He's part of me.

"Yes, Martha. I feel it too."

Then he's stretching his other hand behind him and finding my wet pussy. With unerring accuracy, he traces circles on my clit, never stopping his thrusts into my mouth. He groans as his climax approaches, and his cock swells. *"Come for me!"* he commands. So, I do. My eyes roll into the back of my head as I shatter into a million pieces of pulsating pleasure.

Krantor calls out in my mind, *"I love you!"* and spurts his precious cum. I suck it greedily, letting it work its magic, as it prolongs and deepens my own orgasm. Finally, I still, going slack as I fall into a light doze. In my hazy state, I feel Krantor withdraw his cock from my mouth and sit up to cradle me in his arms. I rest against him, tired but content. He strokes my head soothingly, all the while transmitting the same thought over and over. *"I love you, I love you."*

"I know."

Eventually, we sit up and open Shanbri's box of baked goods, eating them hungrily. With each bite, I'm reminded of how much Shanbri loves me too, and I'm overwhelmed with joy. You can't have too much love in this life.

Krantor laughs in my head. *"I agree!"*

Soon, it's time to pack up, get dressed and leave, but I know I'll be returning someday soon to this magical place. Perhaps next time, it will be with Shanbri. I'm already missing him and wanting to be back in his arms. I sense Krantor's eagerness to be reunited with Prilor too.

As we ride back home in the drone, basking in the afterglow of today's happiness, I think about the future and what it holds. We still have so many issues to resolve about how we move forwards.

And that is why, a few days later, we all find ourselves gathered in Dimitri's living room, talking through our issues with him. Excellent therapist that he is, he lets us each have our say—his one request being that we respect his lack of telepathy and voice our thoughts rather than just think them. It takes time, and several sessions more, for us to untangle the mess of emotions, hurt and conflicting needs. Both Fionbal and Dovtar are here too, for I know their needs are far too often overlooked. Krantor may have a position of leadership outside our home, but within our household, we all deserve to live on an equal footing. With Dimitri's wise and rational guidance, we discuss, negotiate and compromise. Eventually, we come to an arrangement.

CHAPTER 34

Martha

"There, all done." Lulu gives the gauzy material of my dress a gentle tug from her kneeling position on the floor. She pushes herself up to standing and examines me. "You look fantastic," she smiles.

"Thanks Lulu."

"So, you ready to walk down the aisle?"

"Oh yes, more than ready," I say.

"Well then, let me go fetch your grandpa."

Poljar is here today, but only as a spectator, as Gramps will be doing father of the bride duties. Grandma is here too, sitting next to her uncle and awaiting my grand entrance. Her reunion with Poljar a few weeks ago was poignant and emotional. Never in a million years did she think she would ever be able to visit her home planet and meet her long lost family. I'm so thankful that she's been given this chance to be here.

I take one final look at myself in the mirror. My white dress is cut empire-style just below the cleavage, to allow for my burgeoning abdomen. At four months pregnant with twins, I'm already showing a small, but obvious bump. I press my hands there and close my eyes, using my senses to detect the double sets of heartbeats. All well. I pick up the bouquet of flowers lying on the table just as Grandpa knocks on the door.

"Come in."

He walks in and grunts. "Well my dear, let's get you married." He holds out his arm and I place mine in his. We make our way out to the large set of doors that open from the farmhouse to the gardens, where a small congregation of family and friends await. At the signal, music begins to play.

To the strains of the Wedding March, we begin to walk slowly down the red carpeted aisle towards the small pulpit where Dimitri is standing. He will officiate today's ceremony, having requested and received a special license from my home state to do so. This marriage today will be legal—on Earth. Here on Ven, it will not be recognized, but that's okay with me. This is a small, private and unofficial ceremony as the Kran thought it unwise to publicize to the general Venorian population the unorthodox nature of my mating.

By the pulpit stands my groom, and behind him, his best man Dovtar. They watch me as I walk towards them, my face beaming with happiness. I come to a stop before him, and he takes my hands in his. He looks incredibly handsome in black pants that do little to hide his strong, powerful thighs, and a gray silk tunic—the color of my eyes—hugging his large, muscular torso. His beautiful blond hair is gathered in a topknot, framing his lovely, dear face. His thumb rubs comforting circles around my palm as he gazes into my eyes, his full of love.

Dimitri begins. "Dearly beloved," he intones in his calm, clear voice. "We are gathered here today to join this man and this woman in matrimony." He addresses my groom. "Shanbri son of Molbri, do you take Martha Jane Reynolds to be your wife?"

Shanbri has his communicator translating Dimitri's words into his ear, but he responds in English.

"I do."

Dimitri now addresses me. "Martha Jane Reynolds, do you take Shanbri son of Molbri to be your husband?"

Without hesitation, I respond, "I do."

Now Shanbri begins to speak slowly in English the vows he has practised over and over. "I Shanbri, son of Molbri, take you, Martha Jane Reynolds, for my lawful wife, to have and to hold

242

from this day forward, for better, for worse, for richer, for poorer, in sickness and in health, until death do us part. I will love and honor you all the days of my life."

On cue, Dovtar passes him the ring, a plain gold band, which he slips on to my finger with gentle, trembling hands. Then, it's my turn to repeat the vows and put a ring on his finger. We both agreed beforehand that we wanted to exchange rings as a visible symbol of our love and commitment to each other.

Dimitri concludes the ceremony with a simple statement. "I now pronounce that you are husband and wife. Shanbri, you may kiss your bride."

At this, Shanbri pulls me to him and kisses me reverently. We put our foreheads together and exchange our thoughts. He sends forth, *"You're mine now, and I will love you forever."*

I respond, *"I'm yours forever and always."*

And of course, like clockwork, my official mate Krantor has to interrupt this intimate moment with his own thoughts. I hear him say in my head, *"Well technically, you're mine, Martha, but I appreciate the sentiment."*

"Krantor!" I shout internally. *"Just for once, get out of my head!"*

Another voice intrudes gently. It's Prilor. *"Krantor, leave them in peace."* Then to me, *"Martha, I wish you much joy with Shanbri as your husband."*

"Thanks." Then I turn my focus back to my husband. He can't hear the internal conversations I have with Krantor and Prilor, but he's aware of the interference to our own private thought exchange. I roll my eyes and he quirks his lips in understanding. He kisses me again, claiming me as his.

Then, we're accepting congratulations from those around us. As well as Lulu and my relatives, my other human friends from the exchange program are all here. This is their last day on Ven. Tomorrow, they will return to Earth on the freighter ship that brought Lulu and my grandparents here together with the Venorians who had been on Earth the past six months. Treylor—Prilor's sister—is here with her constant protector Pravol, grinning happily at me.

Lulu and my grandparents' presence today was a thoughtful wedding gift from Krantor. As part of our "arrangement" hammered out in our therapy sessions with Dimitri, it was decided that while Krantor, Prilor and I are irrevocably joined through the mating bond that pulls us together and allows us to meld our minds, Shanbri and I needed a way to mark the special nature of our own relationship. I suggested marriage—of the human variety—and Krantor granted me that wish. As a way of showing me how much he cares, he set about trying to make my wedding day as special as possible. He was the one that spoke to Poljar, asking if we could hold the ceremony at my ancestral home. And he was the one who got in touch with my family on Earth and arranged for them and Lulu to be here with me on my big day.

We've come a long way, Krantor and I, since that horrible day when I was abducted by the Saraxians. It took me a long time to fully forgive him and to get over the hurt of his desertion, but I got there in the end. Having a mind connection with him, I feel his pain at the decision he was forced to take, and I also feel the strength of his love for me. I know I matter to him. It's just that he also loves Prilor passionately. I hope we never again face a situation where a dreadful choice like that has to be made.

Despite all the pain, I'm glad things happened this way. It forced us into making a decision on how we're to live our lives as mates who also have other loves. That fateful choice Krantor made to save Prilor was a declaration that Prilor was his primary partner. Shanbri's decision to come after me was his own declaration to me. That day, he didn't follow his kran—he followed his heart.

And I, stuck in the middle of it all, had my own choice to make—return to being Krantor's mate with Shanbri only as my occasional lover, or recognizing that Shanbri was my primary partner. I recalled Flidar's wise words to me that first day I met Shanbri. *Attraction may be something out of your control, but who you choose to give your heart to is up to you.* So, I chose him.

Being paired up with the person we've given our heart to hasn't resolved the issue of the mating bond and the strong pull it still exerts on us. There are days when Krantor craves me on an elemental level beyond his control. There are days when I crave him just as much. When that pull happens, we come together, but with a difference. Shanbri and Prilor are always there with us, sharing in the lovemaking.

The first time all four of us made love together was the day we finally hammered out our arrangement with Dimitri. We left his therapist's office together and went back to the palace. On the journey home, I felt Krantor's thoughts. *"Martha, I need you."*

My pussy pulsed in response. It was impossible to hide it from him. *"I need you too."*

When we reached the palace, Krantor grabbed my hand and dragged me to his bedroom, with Shanbri and Prilor trailing us. Dovtar and Fionbal tactfully made themselves scarce. Once there, we all began to strip, Krantor tearing at my clothes in his rush to have me naked against him. With us finally unclothed, he lifted me in his powerful arms and dropped me on the edge of the bed, parting my legs to reveal my wet core. With a growl of hunger, he dived in, frantically licking at my arousal. On either side of me, Shanbri and Prilor took one of my breasts in their mouth, sucking me hard and maximizing my pleasure. In no time at all, I came, my orgasm deep and intense.

245

Krantor raised his dripping face and telegraphed his thoughts. *"I need to fuck you."* Taking hold of his hard cock, he pressed it to my slit, entering me in one sharp thrust. I gasped. "Ahh." Then he was fucking me mercilessly, ramming himself in and out, desperately chasing his release. Through our melded minds I could feel both the sensation of him inside me and his intense pleasure as my tight pussy clamped around him. On and on we fucked, feeling this feedback loop of sensation.

"I'm coming," I sent through our mind connection.

"Do it!" he commanded me in my head.

At this, Prilor and Shanbri simultaneously bit my nipples as Krantor gave one final mighty thrust. We came together, shouting out our release. My core tightened and spasmed around his pulsing cock, which flooded me with his hot, potent cum, triggering more aftershocks in me.

Eventually, we stilled and got our breaths back. That's when I heard another voice in my head, aching with need. Prilor. *"Martha, I need to fuck you. Please, please let me."*

Then Krantor's voice interjected, this time aloud so Shanbri could hear. "It's time Martha. Prilor has need of you. For the love of God, let him fuck you."

I sat up and eyed Prilor's massive erection, already wet with precum. In that moment, I wanted him inside me more than anything, but I turned to Shanbri. He nodded his assent, his eyes hot with desire. Seeing the exchange, Krantor bit out, "And you Shanbri, will suck my cock while our two loves fuck each other."

Grabbing his silky blond strands, he pulled Shanbri towards him for a hard, passionate kiss. When their lips finally disengaged, Krantor grunted, "I've fucking missed you, Shanbri mine."

Shanbri replied hoarsely. "I've missed you too, my kran."

"Suck me!"

"Yes," he breathed, and fell to his knees. In one hungry move, he took Krantor's length into his mouth, sucking him hard. Krantor groaned, "Ahh," then fixed his burning gaze on Prilor and me.

"Fuck her."

Prilor took his monster cock in his hand and guided it to my slit, which dripped with Krantor's cum. As gently as he could, he eased himself into me. It was an impossibly tight fit. Inch by inch he filled me until at last all his shaft was buried inside me. I had never felt so full in my life.

On the edge of his control, Prilor spoke to me in my head. *"Are you ready for me? I need. Oh God I need."*

"Yes," I transmitted back.

He pulled back and thrust. I cried, on the edge of pain, but with pleasure also tingling in all my nerve endings. Prilor's control vanished. He started to fuck me hard and desperately. I felt each thrust deep in my core, as well as Prilor's pleasure as my pussy clenched around him. And on top of it all, I also felt Krantor's rapture as he fucked Shanbri's mouth, the three of us in a feedback loop of intense sensation. Overwhelmed, I screamed my climax, releasing in wave after wave of intense pleasure—so intense that I blacked out for a short time.

I came back to consciousness to find myself lying in Shanbri's embrace, with Krantor spooning me from behind and Prilor's large arm wrapped around his chest. Shanbri kissed me softly, and I tasted Krantor's cum on his mouth. He looked dazed, feeling the effects of that powerful cum, but still able to focus on me and my needs. "Are you alright?" he whispered.

"Yes," I breathed.

He pulled me close, and we all closed our eyes to sleep.

I'm brought back from my recollections by Krantor's arms coming around me. As he kisses me, he talks to me in my head. *"I'm so happy for you Martha. And yes, that first time all four of us fucked was mind blowing. I can't wait to do it again."*

"You'll have to wait until we're back from the honeymoon."

He chuckles. *"I'll wait. They say patience is a virtue."*

Prilor comes up to me next and wraps me in his trademark bear hug. *"I look forward to it too. You are amazing, Martha, and I'm so happy for you."*

"Thanks guys."

Prilor has one more thing to transmit. *"And Martha, I promise both Krantor and I will stay out of your head during your honeymoon. This will be your private time with Shanbri."*

I have my doubts. *"Can he manage to resist snooping on me?"*

Prilor is firm. *"I'll make sure he does. I have my methods to distract him."*

Krantor growls. *"Stop talking about me as if I'm not here. And yes, I can resist snooping on you. Go and enjoy yourselves. Just know I expect us to fuck on your return."*

I give him a smart salute then turn to my husband, looping my arm in his. We make our way back to the house where a lavish feast awaits us.

Some hours later, the festivities are over and it's time for us to go. Everyone walks us outside. We hug and kiss tearful goodbyes. The human contingent, including my grandparents, will be returning to Earth tomorrow. I don't know if or when I will see them all again.

Then Shanbri is leading me down the steps towards our transport—not a drone, but my favorite griv, Saila. She's saddled and laden with our bags, waiting for us to mount her. Shanbri lifts me in his arms and deposits me on her back, coming to sit behind me. His arms wrap around me protectively. "Ready?" he asks.

"Yes, I'm ready."

We give everyone one final wave goodbye, then Senjar makes a clicking sound and the griv comes to stand. Moments later, we're cantering away, gathering speed until her great wings unfurl, flapping to lift us off the ground. With a whoosh we soar higher and higher until the house and people below are little dots on the ground.

With flaps of her massive wings, Saila flies us away and on to our destination, which Shanbri has somehow managed to keep a secret from me. I feel his thoughts as he presses his face to the back of my head. "*Happy?*"

"*So, so happy.*"

We fly on for an hour or two more until I feel Saila's gradual descent. Below me is an endless expanse of turquoise sea, but as we get closer and closer, I notice a small island with a white sandy beach. We touch the sandy ground at a gallop, slowly reducing our speed until we're travelling at a light canter. Ahead of us is a house, right by the beach.

Finally, we come to a stop and Saila kneels to the ground to let us off. Shanbri jumps down first, then reaches for me. "What is this place?" I ask.

"This island was gifted to my family by the present Kran's father. I have not been here for many sun rotations, but I thought you might like it for our honeymoon. There is no one else here; it is totally private. I had the house stocked with everything we will need for our stay, and Saila will come back for us when we are ready to return. For now, I will feed her and let her rest overnight, before she flies home."

He leads the gentle griv to a small outbuilding where there is already a pile of straw and a water trough for Saila to feed on.

Once she's settled, he takes our belongings and leads me by the hand to the main house.

The interior is warm and cosy, with myriads of photos framing the walls of Shanbri and his family over the years. I stop before a photo of him sporting an enormous gap-toothed grin, looking to be about four years old—and incredibly cute. He follows my gaze and smiles reminiscently. "This was taken here, on our last vacation before the war with the Saraxians broke out." He pauses. "I have not liked to come back here. There are so many memories of the family I lost. But perhaps now, we can make new memories."

I turn to kiss him. "Yes, my love, we will. Maybe we can bring the twins here for vacations when they're older."

He touches his brow to mine and speaks with his thoughts. *"I would like that very much."* He pulls away slightly to smile wickedly. "But now, I would very much like to fuck my wife."

I sigh happily. "I would very much like that too."

EPILOGUE

Martha

Six years later

I'm lying on my side in bed, my body curled around a long, sturdy pillow. It's about the only comfortable position I can find to sleep these days, with my swollen belly. Shanbri's warm body is at my back, one leg tucked supportively behind my knee and a hand placed below my belly bump.

I'm in that hazy zone between sleep and wakefulness. There's a trickle of sensation in my head before I hear a voice. *"You up yet? Junior is lying on top of us demanding some of uncle Shanbri's pancakes."*

Another voice, Prilor's. *"The twins are about to take apart Dovtar's communicator again."*

I stretch tiredly and respond, *"Can't Fionbal or Dovtar do something about it?"*

Amusement ripples my way. *"Dovtar's running after that dervish of a daughter of his and Fionbal's still dead to the world."*

It takes some effort to shift to a sitting position. *"Ok, I'm coming. Someone wake the sleeping beauty."*

Behind me, Shanbri is stretching his massive frame and getting out of bed. "Good morning, wife of mine," he murmurs sleepily.

I smile as I always do when I hear him say that. "Good morning husband mine," I reply.

Slowly I come to a standing position and turn to Shanbri. "The twins are up to their usual fun and games."

He grins. "Dovtar's communicator?"

"The one and only."

He heads out the door. "I'll get them."

I walk to the bathroom and quickly relieve my bursting bladder, then make my way to the bathing room for our daily communal bath. The bathing room is large, designed to accommodate a kran, his mate and his somars—and now also our children. Bathing together every day is one of our rituals, though Fionbal no longer has the job of washing each of us. We're all capable of running a washcloth over our own bodies, thank you very much. *"Yes, but it was nice having Fionbal doing it."* Krantor again, invading my mind, as he does countless times a day.

Our eyes meet as he enters the bathing room with Prilor at his heels holding Junior by the hand. Our son and heir is named Krantor, just like his father, so we call him Junior to distinguish between the two. Krantor's eyes twinkle appreciatively as they take in my nude body, rounded with Prilor's son in my belly. I do believe Krantor is the more excited of the two about this baby. *"I'm over the moon!"* he laughs silently.

I step into the welcoming and fragrant warm water of our bath—more like a pool—and submerge my body, feeling a welcome relief to my aches and pains. As my head bobs back to the surface, I see Dovtar wade into the water, our one-and-a-half year old daughter, Rivtar, tucked securely in his arms.

As promised, both Dovtar and Fionbal waited without pressure until I was ready to make love to them. In the case of Dovtar, it happened one day about two months into my marriage to Shanbri. We were all in the bathing room, as we are today, and my eyes followed Dovtar's backside appreciatively as he climbed out of the bath. Shanbri caught that look and came up to nuzzle me. "I am thinking, wife, that you might be ready for some intimacy with Dovtar. Shall I invite him to our bed tonight?"

I turned to kiss my husband, thinking his offer through. Over the last few months, my feelings for Dovtar had deepened and I had been noticing his beautifully lithe body more and more lately. Perhaps it was time to take that next step. With my lips still on Shanbri's, I transmitted my response. *"Yes."*

What followed was one of the sweetest bouts of lovemaking, as together Shanbri and Dovtar worshipped my body, while I got the chance to sink my teeth into the gentle somar's sexy ass. We made love repeatedly through the night, then fell asleep, the three of us entangled in each other's arms. Since then, we've made love regularly, developing a deep and lasting connection. A few years after I gave birth to Krantor's son and heir, Dovtar shyly approached me about having a child with him. I didn't hesitate to say yes. The result—this bundle of endless energy.

I hold out my arms to her, and she swims like a mermaid towards me, gurgling happily. I hold her to me and kiss her soft cheek. "How's my little girl this morning?"

She smiles and burbles, "Ma, ma." She has Dovtar's beautiful almond shaped, caramel eyes. And beneath her angelic smile is a little demon who keeps her father, mother and uncles on their toes all day. I lower her back into the water and watch her swim over to her older brother, Junior. They splash about merrily while Prilor tries to run a washcloth over the both of them.

Dovtar pulls me to him for a good morning kiss. He touches his forehead to mine, probing my mind and emotions. Reassured that all is well with me, he steps back with a smile. "Good morning my love."

"Good morning Dovtar mine."

We look up as Shanbri shepherds our five-year-old twins, Molbri and Sonbri, into the bathing room. "I was trying to fix it for uncle Dovtar," I hear Molbri say plaintively.

"We have talked about this before," his father tells him sternly. "We must not touch things that do not belong to us."

Sonbri jumps in to defend her brother. "We were only trying to make it better. The light was flashing blue, and it should be pink just like on ma's comcator."

They all step into the bathing pool and swim towards me. I kiss them both good morning, then take hold of Sonbri. "Come let me wash your hair, then you can play," I say. I press the nearby pump for some shampoo and quickly massage my fingers through her soft blond hair, while Shanbri does the same for Molbri's hair. Once the shampoo is rinsed off, I hold my sweet, gentle daughter to me and say, "I know you were trying to help your uncle Dovtar, but next time, promise me you will ask before you touch his belongings."

She looks at me shamefaced. "Yes ma."

"Ok, now go play while I finish washing. We need to hurry, or we'll be late for school."

Twenty minutes later, we're all dressed and sitting at the large kitchen table, tucking hungrily into the delicious pancakes Shanbri has just made. Shanbri discovered the wonders of pancakes on our first visit back to Earth. On his return to Ven, he worked strenuously on perfecting a recipe that would replicate the fluffy, tender disks with the Venorian ingredients to hand. The result—pancakes even better than anything I've ever eaten back on my home planet. They are in hot demand in our family, and Shanbri is always happy to oblige.

Breakfast over, we each make our way to our various destinations for the day. Myself, the twins and Junior go to the school that I set up a few years ago with my best friend Lulu. She enjoyed her first visit to Ven so much that she decided to return for a more permanent stay. Our school is bicultural, teaching Venorian and Earth languages. We have both Venorian and human students, from the small but growing human expatriate population here on Ven. We try to foster greater understanding and cooperation between our people through the simple act of educating our children together. Not for me the traditional life of a kran's mate, leading expeditions into space. I am after all a teacher by training. So, while I attend the weekly council meetings and provide my advice when needed, my main job is to teach and lead my school, of which I'm very proud.

Little Rivtar stays home with her father Dovtar, who elected to be the stay-at-home dad in our household. He enjoys it far better than galivanting into space on the Phtar, something Krantor hadn't been aware of until he developed his power to read minds. So these days, it's only Krantor and Prilor who go and do the day job of being a kran, with Fionbal's assistance. Through the melding of their minds, they're able to multi-task very effectively. Every few weeks they take the Phtar on various missions to the Utar belt and other planets in our vicinity. They have worked very hard on upgrading the security of our planet, and thanks to them, we have been blessedly free of attacks from the Saraxians. *"Oh good, it's nice to be appreciated,"* Krantor chimes into my head.

"Oh, do go away for half a minute."

As for Shanbri... he has been free to follow his real love. I don't think Krantor had realized, until he could read our minds, just what ambitions Shanbri had given up to become his somar. In an unprecedented gesture of generosity, Krantor agreed to release Shanbri from his duties as somar in order to pursue his real love, on the caveat that, should there be an emergency, Shanbri would drop everything and return to his military duties.

After enrolling in culinary school, my husband graduated and set up his own bakery—Shanbribakes—which has become a massive success thanks to his talent and hard work. He comes to me now, and folds me into his arms, his forehead to mine, checking in that all is fine with me before we go out for the day. I'm still several weeks away from my due date, but this child is big—well of course it's Prilor's—and we all suspect he will make his appearance sooner than expected.

Shanbri smiles and kisses me softly. "See you soon, my heart. I hope you have a fruitful day."

"Save me some of your best cakes," I say, kissing him back.

"Always."

Just then, Fionbal rushes into the room, buttoning up his tunic. Krantor raises a brow at him. "You're late, Fionbal mine."

He goes to his kran and kisses him, then grabs a pancake left for him by the ever thoughtful Shanbri. "Sorry. It is my night with Martha tonight. I needed to stock up on my sleep!"

Yeah, that's another part of our arrangement. Once I had become intimate with both Fionbal and Dovtar, we had a discussion, all of us together, about the most equitable way for me to be with them, whilst still maintaining Shanbri as my primary partner. We agreed that there would be one night of every week which I would share with either Dovtar or Fionbal, along with Shanbri of course, as he is always with me no matter what.

No such rota is to be had for my other two lovers—my mates Krantor and Prilor. With them, it's more a matter of when the mating bond urges us to get together. We can go for weeks without being together, and then at other times, we need our sexual fix every day. There have been several occasions where I've been summoned in the middle of the day, having to leave a substitute teacher to cover for me while I rushed back to the palace for some loving with Krantor and Prilor. On such occasions, I have always called Shanbri on my way there, to make sure he came along too.

All this is not exactly the exclusive relationship I once craved, but it's as good a compromise as any. As the Kran once put it to Shanbri, *sometimes we cannot have what we want in its entirety, but we can have enough to make us content.* If I'm being honest, having multiple partners adds welcome spice to my life. Making love with my other mates is always a fun, wild, sexy ride—all the more so because at the end of it all, I get to return to the comforting embrace of Shanbri, my husband.

Never in a million years did I expect my life to turn out the way it did, on that day I enrolled for the Venorian exchange program. I'm so glad now that I did. *"So am I,"* echoes Krantor.

"Me too," adds Prilor. *"I couldn't imagine life without you, Martha my love."*

I go to kiss the both of them goodbye. *"Yeah. It can be a pain in the neck having you in my head sometimes, but I couldn't imagine life without you either."*

Prilor strokes my large belly, then kneels to kiss it softly. "Take care little one," he says softly. "Be kind to your mother."

"Hurry up, ma, or we'll be late!" calls out Molbri.

I smile at my mates. "Time for me to go." With another quick kiss, I pick up my purse and rush out the door, stopping only to give Fionbal a quick peck on the cheek. "See you tonight, my love." Then I'm gone like a whirlwind, herding my brood of kids into the transport drone, and off to start another day.

FAMILY TREE OF THE MAIN CHARACTERS

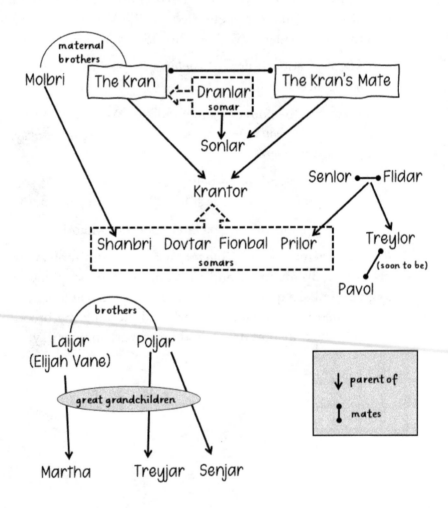

GLOSSARY OF VENORIAN TERMS

Ablutenizer

An automated system for brushing teeth located in the ablution room of Venorian households. A person places their lips around the spout and presses a button to start the process. Warm liquid enters the mouth followed by a set of automated brushes that cleanse teeth guided by a sensor.

Blint

Attractive looking Venorian fruit that is extremely spicy.

Boral Crystals

Crystals that inhibit the neural transmitters of the Venorian people and can induce a mild soporific effect on them when used alone. Combined with dorenium, boral crystals can cause unconsciousness in Venorians.

Dorenium

A mineral used as an energy source to power Venorian spaceships. It is mined on a colony in sector 3 of the Utar belt.

Drekon

A spiritual/physical form of exercise similar to yoga which requires practitioners to hold different poses in order to achieve strength and flexibility.

Dria berry

A sweet red berry, similar to a raspberry.

Driskians

A friendly race of people with whom the Venorians trade.

Frekium

A chemical that stimulates the neural transmitters in Venorians, used to treat telepathic blockages. It can also be used as an antidote to boral crystals. A side effect of using frekium is that it stimulates fertility in Venorian males and females.

Gan

A Venorian musical instrument, similar to a piano.

Griv

A large four-legged animal that is a cross between a horse and a dragon. Venorians can ride grivs and also fly on them, as they have a set of powerful wings. Grivs pass on their memories from mother to child.

Joh

A hot and spicy beverage drunk by Venorians, similar to a Chai Latte.

Kalso

A tree with wonderfully aromatic purple and pink blossoms.

Kran – also known as the Holy Father of Ven

Both a spiritual and military leader in charge of defending the planet Ven. The Kran is gifted with special telepathic skills upon bonding with his fated mate. Once mated, he is able to mind meld with his mate as well as read the minds of people around him. His blood and saliva have special healing powers.

Kroot

A delicious, leavened bread with a savory filling reminiscent of cheese.

Krovatians

A friendly race of people with whom the Venorians trade. Boral crystals are mined on their planet and used for spiritual worship.

Klixians

A slimy race of people known for their deception and treachery. Venorians and their allies do not engage in trade with them.

Lir

The god worshipped by Venorians.

Litor

Venorian currency, named after the Kran's family, the Tors.

Moon rotation

The time it takes for one of Ven's two moons to orbit the planet—the equivalent of an Earth month.

Onar

Venorian spaceship jointly commanded by the Kran and his mate.

Phtar

Venorian spaceship commanded by Krantor. It is agile and has superior cloaking technology.

Pilat

A chewy meat with a sour tang.

Ploh

A refreshing lemonade-like drink

Preon

A type of Venorian fruit similar to a pear.

Prot

A type of Venorian meat that is mostly eaten roasted.

Rotation

Venorian word for a day.

Saraxians

A neighboring alien race who have a history of conflict with the Venorians.

Somar

A male Venorian who has pledged his life to a kran. Each kran has four somars. They act as both his protectors and sexual companions. A somar is not allowed to have his own mate but must mate with the kran's fated mate. He is allowed to procreate with her once she has begotten an heir for the kran.

Sun rotation

The time it takes for the planet Ven to orbit its sun–the equivalent of an Earth year.

Tor

The Kran's family name.

Torbreg

The capital city of Ven, named after the Tor family.

Utar belt

A neutral zone separating the planet Ven from Sarax, a planet whose people have been in conflict with the Venorians. A peace treaty was signed with the Saraxians six years ago which states that Saraxians should not enter this neutral zone.

Venorian names

Full Venorian names are composed of three syllables. First syllable is the person's given name, the second syllable is their family name, and the third syllable is Ven, to show they are from the planet Ven. For example, Martha's great grandfather is called Laijarven—Lai is his given name, Jar is his family name, and Ven is the name of his planet.

Vlor

A precious stone mined on the planet Ven that comes in shades of pink and purple. The purple vlor stone is known for its healing properties. It has a powerful regenerative effect on the body and can cut healing time for wounds by being placed on the affected area. It is also used to combat the effects of aging.

AFTERWORD

Dear reader,

I hope you enjoyed reading Krantor's Mate. To find out how Martha's ancestor, Laijar, came to be on Earth, please see the link below to download a free copy of the prequel, Laijar's Temptation.

Download link: https://BookHip.com/PLVZSAZ

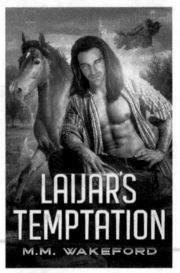

May I ask you for a small favor?

Reviews are the life blood of independent authors. Please could you help spread the word about this book by submitting a review on Amazon and/or on Goodreads. Thank you! For latest news and freebies, please subscribe to my newsletter on my website, mw-author.com.

M.M. Wakeford

ABOUT THE AUTHOR

M.M. Wakeford

M.M. Wakeford loves writing romances that capture that heady feeling of falling in love. If you're looking for escapism, HEAs and plenty of steam, you've come to the right place.

BOOKS BY THIS AUTHOR

Love Against the Odds Series

Liberation (Book 1)

Two people meet one day in a coffee shop and bond over their love of cinnamon rolls. On paper, they're nothing alike. Different backgrounds, different lifestyles, different life experiences. Yet they click...

The odds are stacked against them. Can they overcome them to be together?

What people say about Liberation:

"The mindset around sensuality and sexuality was just next level. I absolutely loved this... I rated it 5 stars." Tiffany, Tiff Talk Pages channel on YouTube

"This book blew my mind. It had so many levels of sexuality and the spicy scenes had flames and steam coming off of them. Everyone loves a happy ending but I can't wait to see where this series goes!" Reviewer on Goodreads

Duplication (Book 2)

What are the odds that two people, from two separate universes should meet and fall in love?

Will they overcome the odds to be together?

This is a romance like you've never read before, partly set in a fictional universe with a very different moral code to ours. As always with works by M.M. Wakeford, there is a guaranteed HEA and plenty of steam!

What people say about Duplication:

"This is a fantastic, sometimes weird and very very spicy read!" 5 star Amazon Review

"I was shook and in awe of the unique premise. I devoured this opposites attract romance, set in a dimension that is a mirror to ours, but culturally hedonistic." 5 star Goodreads review

Determination (Book 3)

Two people, living miles away from each other, from very different walks of life.

Audrey

Growing up in foster homes was tough, but with determination, I've managed to build a secure life for myself. By day, I'm a registered nurse. By night, I'm "Emily Steel", fantasy fiction author.

Jacob

I'm the successful CEO of a major digital media company based in LA. Life is good. Business is booming. I have a beautiful and sexy girlfriend. What more could I want?

Circumstances bring Audrey and Jacob briefly together. Sparks fly, but the odds are stacked against them. Can they overcome them to be together?

What people say about Determination:

"The build up and plot of this book kept the pages turning quickly and the spicy scenes were surprisingly extra steamy and amazing!" Reviewer on Amazon/Goodreads

Infatuation (Book 4)

A friends-to-lovers multicultural romance

Two people meet on a plane and begin a close friendship. They're from very different backgrounds – Kamal a devout Muslim and Liv, a chef whose friendship with her two male best friends includes "benefits". Can Kamal and Liv overcome the odds and become more than just friends?

Author's note:

This is a sizzling romance with a guaranteed HEA and no cheating. For maximum enjoyment, it is advisable to read the novels in this series in the correct order. However, it is not absolutely necessary, as this story can be read as a standalone romance.

What people are saying about Infatuation:

"So good! With some hot scenes thrown in there as well as a whole lot of sexy. Definitely a good read. Highly recommend." 5 star Amazon Review

"Great Book. I've read several books written by M.M. Wakeford; she is becoming one of my favorite authors." 5 star Amazon Review

CPSIA information can be obtained
at www.ICGtesting.com
Printed in the USA
BVHW051940200423
662743BV00012B/228